Sabine Baring-Gould, Henry Fleetwood Sheppard

Songs and Ballads of the West

A Collection made from the Mouths of the People

Sabine Baring-Gould, Henry Fleetwood Sheppard

Songs and Ballads of the West
A Collection made from the Mouths of the People

ISBN/EAN: 9783744780674

Printed in Europe, USA, Canada, Australia, Japan

Cover: Foto ©Andreas Hilbeck / pixelio.de

More available books at **www.hansebooks.com**

Songs & Ballads of The West

A·Collection·made·from·the·Mouths·of·the·People

by the
Rev. S. BARING GOULD, M.A.
and
Rev. H. FLEETWOOD SHEPPARD, M.A.

Harmonised and Arranged for
VOICE AND PIANOFORTE
By the Rev. H. FLEETWOOD SHEPPARD, M.A.

• • • • • • •

London
Methuen & Co., 36, Essex Street, W.C.

DEDICATED TO

D. RADFORD, Esq., J.P.,

Of Mount Tavy,

Tavistock,

AT WHOSE HOSPITABLE TABLE THE IDEA OF
MAKING THIS COLLECTION WAS
FIRST MOOTED.

CONTENTS.

I. By Chance It Was.
II. The Hunting of Arscott of Tetcott.
III. Upon a Sunday Morning.
IV. The Trees they are So High.
V. Parson Hogg.
VI. Cold Blows the Wind.
VII. My Garden Grew Plenty of Thyme.
VIII. Roving Jack, the Journeyman.
IX. Brixham Town.
X. Green Broom.
XI. As Johnny Walked Out. (*For Four Voices.*)
XII. The Miller and His Sons.
XIII. Ormond the Brave.
XIV. Fathom the Bowl.
XV. Sweet Nightingale.
XVI. Widdecombe Fair.
XVII. The Imprisoned Lady. (*For Four Voices.*)
XVIII. The Silly Old Man.
XIX. The Seasons.
XX. The Chimney Sweep.
XXI. The Saucy Sailor.
XXII. Blue Muslin.
XXIII. The Squire and the Fair Maid.
XXIV. Hal-an-Tow, the Helston Furry Dance.
XXV. Blow Away, ye Morning Breezes.
XXVI. A Hearty Good Fellow.
XXVII. The Bonny Bunch of Roses.
XXVIII. The Last of the Singers.
XXIX. The Tythe Pig.
XXX. My Lady's Coach.
XXXI. Jan's Courtship.
XXXII. The Drowned Lover.
XXXIII. Childe, the Hunter.
XXXIV. The Cottage Thatch'd with Straw.
XXXV. Cicely Sweet. (*Duet.*)
XXXVI. A Sweet Pretty Maiden.
XXXVII. The Green Cockade.
XXXVIII. The Sailor's Farewell.
„ Ditto. (*As Duet and Chorus.*)
XXXIX. A Maiden Sat a Weeping.
XL. The Bonny Blue Kerchief.
XLI. An Evening so Clear.
XLII. The Warson Hunt.
XLIII. The Green Bushes.
XLIV. The Broken Token.
XLV. The Rout is Out.
XLVI. Why Should we be Dullards Sad?
XLVII. May Day Carol.
XLVIII. Nancy.
XLIX. Lullabye.
„ (*With Violin Accompaniment.*)
L. The Gipsy Countess, in Two Parts.
LI. The Grey Mare.
LII. The Wreck off Scilly.

CONTENTS.
(Continued.)

- LIII. Henry Martin.
- LIV. Plymouth Sound.
- LV. Farewell to Kingsbridge.
- LVI. Furze Bloom.
- LVII. The Oxen Ploughing.
- LVIII. Something Lacking.
- LIX. The Simple Ploughboy.
- LX. The Wrestling Match.
- LXI. The Painful Plough.
- LXII. Broadbury Gibbet.
- LXIII. The Orchestra.
- LXIV. The Golden Vanity.
- LXV. The Bold Dragoon.
- LXVI. Trinity Sunday.
- LXVII. The Blue Flame.
- LXVIII. Strawberry Fair.
- LXIX. The Country Farmer's Son.
- LXX. The Hostess' Daughter.
- LXXI. The Jolly Gosshawk.
- LXXII. Fair Girl, Mind This.
- LXXIII. On a May Morning so Early.
- LXXIV. The Spotted Cow.
- LXXV. Cupid the Ploughboy.
- LXXVI. Come, my Lads, Let us be Jolly.
- LXXVII. Poor Old Horse.
- LXXVIII. The Dilly Song. (For Three Voices.)
- LXXIX. The Mallard. (Duet and Chorus.)
- LXXX. Constant Johnny. (Duet.)
- LXXXI. The Duke's Hunt.
- LXXXII. The Bell Ringing.
- LXXXIII. A Nutting We Will Go.
- LXXXIV. Down by a River Side.
- LXXXV. The Barley Rakings.
- LXXXVI. Deep in Love.
- LXXXVII. The Rambling Sailor.
- LXXXVIII. A Single and a Married Life.
- LXXXIX. Midsummer Carol. (For Four Voices.)
- XC. The Blackbird.
- XCI. The Green Bed.
- XCII. The Loyal Lover.
- XCIII. The Streams of Nantsian.
- XCIV. The Drunken Maidens.
- XCV. Tobacco is an Indian Weed. (Canon.)
- XCVI. Fair Susan Slumbered.
- XCVII. The False Lover.
- XCVIII. Barley Straw.
- XCIX. Death and the Lady. (Solo, or Quartette.)
- C. Adam and Eve.
- CI. I Rode my Little Horse.
- CII. The Saucy Ploughboy.
- CIII. I'll Build Myself a Gallant Ship. (For Four Voices.)
- CIV. The Everlasting Circle.
- CV. All in a Garden.
- CVI. Hunting the Hare.
- CVII. Dead Maid's Land.
- CVIII. Shower and Sunshine.
- CIX. Haymaking Song.
- CX. Bibberly Town.

PREFACE.

WHEREVER Celtic blood flows, there it carries with it a love of music and musical creativeness. Scotland, Wales, Ireland, Brittany, have their national melodies. It seemed to me incredible that the West of England—the old Kingdom of Damnonia—Devon and Cornwall, where the Celtic element is so strong, should be void of Folk-Music. When I was a boy I was wont to ride round and on Dartmoor, and put up at little village taverns. There—should I be on a pay-day—I was sure to hear one or two men sing, and sing on hour after hour, one song following another with little intermission. But then I paid no particular attention to these songs.

In 1888 it occurred to me that it would be well to make a collection—at all events to examine into the literary and musical value of these songs, and their melodies. I could not find that any one had taken the pains to gather in this field. The only Cornish songs generally known were the "Helston Furry Dance," which is claimed by Cornishmen as an ancient British melody, but which is a hornpipe in common measure, not older than the middle of last century; and "Trelawny," which is a ballad reconstructed by the late Rev. R. Hawker, Vicar of Morwenstowe, the tune of which is merely "Le Petit Tambour," and therefore not Cornish at all. Through local papers I appealed to the public in the West for traditional songs and airs. I received in return a score of versions of *one*, "The Widdecombe Fair." However, I heard from the late C. Spence Bate, Esq., of The Rock, South Brent, that there were two notable old men singers in that place; and I also knew of one in my own neighbourhood. The latter, James Parsons, a day labourer, well known in public-houses as a "song-man," was the son of a still more famous song-man, now dead, who went by the nick-name of "The Singing-Machine." I sent for him, a man of about 74 years, and, after a little urging, persuaded him to sing. From him I procured about five-and-twenty ballads and songs, some of a very early and archaic character, certainly not later than the reign of Henry VII., which he had acquired from his father.

Accompanied by F. W. Bussell, Esq., Fellow of Brazenose College, Oxford, an accomplished musician, I then visited South Brent, and we enjoyed the hospitality of Mr. Spence Bate. Then, on that occasion, we obtained some more songs. A second visit to South Brent, with the Rev. H. Fleetwood Sheppard, resulted in almost exhausting that neighbourhood, from which we derived about fifty. The chief singers there were an old miller and a crippled labourer, who broke stones on the road.

At Belstone, as I learned from J. D. Prickman, Esq., of Okehampton, lived an old yeoman, with stalwart sons, all notable singers. Mr. Sheppard and I met this old man. Belstone is a small village under the rocks of Belstone Tor, on the edge of Dartmoor, a wild and lonesome spot. From this yeoman we acquired more songs.

The Rev. H. Fleetwood Sheppard and I next penetrated to the very heart of Dartmoor, and saw Jonas Coaker, an old blind man, of 89 years, very infirm, and only able to leave his bed for a few hours in the day. He is, however, endowed with a remarkable memory. From him, and helped by Mr. J. Webb, captain of a tin mine, hard by, who could recall and very sweetly sing the old melodies, we gleaned several important and interesting songs, with their traditional airs.

Further stores were yielded by a singing blacksmith, John Woodrich, at Wollacott Moor, in the parish of Thrushleton; also by Roger Luxton, of Halwell, N. Devon, aged 76; James Oliver, tanner, Launceston, aged 71, a native of St. Kewe, Cornwall; William Rice, labourer, Lamerton, aged 75; John Rickards, of Lamerton; John Masters, of Bradstone, aged 83; William Friend, labourer, Lydford, aged 62; Edmund Fry thatcher, a native of Lezant, Cornwall; Will and Roger Huggins, Lydford; John Woolrich, labourer, Broadwoodwidger; Matthew Baker, a poor cripple, aged 72, Lew Down; some songs taken down from moor-men on Dartmoor in or about 1868 were sent me by W. Crossing, Esq., of South Brent; others from Chagford, Menheniot, and Liskeard, and more recently from Mawgan in Pyder, and Padstow.

I find that in addition to one large common store of songs and ballads, each place visited and explored yields up two or three which are, so to speak, particular to each village, or musical centre. I have no hesitation in saying that several hundreds of ballads and songs, with their melodies, may by this means be collected, of which perhaps a third are very good, a third good, and the remainder indifferent.

The singers are nearly all old, illiterate,—their lives not worth five years' purchase, and when they die the traditions will be lost, for the present generation will have nothing to say to these songs,—especially such as are in minor keys, and supplant them with the vulgarest Music Hall performances. The melodies are in many instances more precious than the words. Ballads that were printed in London, Bristol, Exeter, Plymouth, became common property throughout England, but then, here in the West, these ballads imported from elsewhere, were set to tunes already traditional. The words were less frequently of home growth than the airs. For instance, the 17th century song, "I sowed the seeds of Love," I found was known by James Parsons, but not to the tune to which wedded elsewhere, and to which the verses are said to have been written. "The Outlandish Knight," again, is sung to an entirely indepenent tune. On the other hand, "Cuper's Garden," a song of the beginning of last century, was sung to me to the same tune, slightly varied only, as that given by Chappell. In a good number of cases I have found that the illiterate men sing a less corrupt form of a ballad that such as appears on broadsides. The younger men always sing from the broadside copies.

The minstrels were put down by Act of Parliament in 1597, and most, if not all early ballad tunes belong to a period still earlier. There was a recandescence—excuse the word—of ballad music in the reign of Charles II., but the character of the tunes of that period is distinct. We have been able to recover several early ballad tunes, some in their most archaic form, which consisted of four lines in C.M. only, but others altered and extended, for in process of time singers added four more lines, which are a slight variation of the theme. We have preserved these additions, as they do not interfere with the original melody.

In the reign of Charles II. appeared Tom D'Urfey, a native of Exeter, who compiled six volumes of songs, with their airs; to two of the volumes all the words are his own, but the tunes he took whence he could, and unquestionably he utilized for his purpose melodies he had heard in his native county, and which, through the press, he gave to become the common property of all Englishmen. Nay, further, some of them crossed the border and were appropriated as Scotch songs. A fashion had set in for Scotch songs, and several demonstrably English airs were set by D'Urfey and his imitators to quasi Scotch words. Then came Allan Ramsay and Burns, who discarded the ridiculous imitation Scotch dialect of these English composers, and set these same tunes to real Scottish words, and so these melodies came to be claimed as belonging to the land beyond the Tweed. One instance of the manner in which English tunes were appropriated may be given. James Johnson, of Edinburgh, published his collection of what he considered to be native songs of Scotland at the end of last century, yet, within the first twenty-four songs of his first volume were compositions by Purcell, Arne, Hook, Berg, and Battishill. Scottish compilers had the notion that all Scotch songs were without certain intervals, and they did not at all scruple to adapt English tunes and give them a Scotch flavour by altering such notes as contravened this imaginary canon. When we come to consider the dates of the melodies collected, we find that they vary very considerably, and the affixing of a date can only be tentative. Tunes may be roughly classed by the instruments by which they were intended to be accompanied, or on which they were to be played. The earliest melodies were composed to the harp, the lute, and the bagpipe. Then came the fiddle, and finally the hornpipe. All C.M. hornpipe tunes belong to the 18th century. The triple time tunes are somewhat earlier. Chaucer speaks of the hornpipe as a Cornish instrument. A good many of the words in the old songs have lost their meaning to the singers, and a correct version is only to be obtained by comparing several obtained in different quarters. I was much puzzled when I took down "Cuper's Garden" by the lines—

"The third she was the virgin,
And she was lorrioware;"

but when I looked at the printed song, I found that the original stood thus:—

"The third she was a virgin,
And she the laurel wore."

One must not be surprised to find "Tragedy" turned into "dragotee," "galore" into "glorore," and "The Outlandish Knight" converted into "The Outlandish Cat," and "The Bay of Biscay" into "The Bag of Biscuits." We have endeavoured to trace the tunes in the six volumes of D'Urfey, in "The Musical Miscellany" (1731), in six volumes, "Apollo's Cabinet" (1757), and in several of the editions as "The Complete Dancing Master." There were eighteen of these between 1650 and 1728. We searched also such ballad-operas as we could obtain, but without much success. Chappell's "Popular Music of the Olden Time" has also been of great assistance. Some of the airs are later, and these, it is possible, may have been printed; if so, it is without our knowledge. Our object is, as far as possible, with only a rare exception or two, to confine ourselves to printing such as we believed to be unpublished, and all we give, with such exceptions as shall be notified, are taken down from oral recitation.

In some instances the ballads reveal a rudeness of manner and morals that make it impossible for me to publish the words exactly. We have endeavoured to obtain three or four versions of the same ballads and tunes, and are by this means enabled to arrive at what we believe to be the most correct form of both. But as to the antiquary everything is important exactly as obtained, uncleansed from rust and unpolished, it is the intention of Mr. Sheppard and myself to deposit a couple of copies of the songs and ballads, with their music *exactly as taken down*, one in the library of the Exeter, the other in that of the Plymouth Institution, for reference.

As already said, in five years' time all will be gone; and this is the supreme moment at which such a collection can be made. Our traditional music lies in superimposed beds. Among the yeomen and farmer class, a few, chiefly hunting songs remain, such as "Arscott of Tetcott," and such as "The Widdecombe Fair." They know nothing of those in the social bed below, which is the most auriferous, and the old song-men who sang for their "entertainment" in taverns do not know the songs sung at the firesides of the yeomen.

It has been asked by not a few—How is it that these songs are so unprovincial? For one reason: Because they are an heirloom of the past, from a class of musicians far higher in station and culture than those who now possess the treasure. In many cases, probably, our West of England song-men are lineal descendants of the old minstrels or gleemen put down by Act of Parliament in 1597, and forbidden to go about from place to place. In the next place, all such broad dialect songs as have come to us, prove to be modern compositions by educated writers, who have amused themselves in writing dialect songs, as Lord Tennyson wrote his "Northern Farmer," and as many Scottish poets have written provincial dialect songs. The songs and ballads were, of course, recited and sung to me in broad Devonshire or Cornish, but this was not of the essence of the songs, and I have not thought it necessary to reproduce the dialect. It can always be added, by anyone familiar with it.

When the minstrels were forbidden to journey from place to place, by the Act of 1597, they settled down in country places, married, took to some trade, or became workers on the land, and supplemented their wages from what they could pick up at Whitsunales, May-games, Sheep-shearings, Harvest Homes, Christmas Feasts, Wakes, and Weddings. They handed on their stock-in-trade of old ballads and songs to their sons, and thus it came about that certain families were professional village musicians from generation to generation. In process of time they dropped out of their collection some of the ruder melodies and ballads, and adopted such as had come into fashion; thus there was a continuous accretion on one side, and loss on the other. Nevertheless, a considerable residuum of early music has remained. We have given samples of all kinds. In some cases—but not many—the melodies *may* have been composed by the song-men themselves, or, what is more likely, they have taken known melodies and altered them according to their own provincial musical ideas. An example or two of these will be given.

I have said that I think that some of the melodies *may* have been composed by the song-men themselves, but, I contend, only some, an infinitesimally small number, and such are musically worthless, and I doubt if one of these is included in this collection. It must be borne in mind that folk-music is nowhere spontaneous and autochthonous. It is always a reminiscence, a heritage from a cultured past. The yokel is as incapable of creating a beautiful melody as he is of producing a piece of beautiful sculpture, or of composing a genuine poem.

M. Loquin, in a series of articles on the Folk-music of France, in "Melusine," 1888-9, points out that nearly *all* Gallic folk-melodies are derived from the early masters of music in France, Lully, Lambert, Campra, Gilliers, &c. They have not all been traced, but they are almost all traceable. In England the opera never influenced folk-music as it did in France; the reverse took place, the folk-music drove out at one time the Italian opera, and Ballad operas were all the vogue, the old folk-melodies being united to new words. But it does not follow that these folk melodies were the spontaneous productions of the people. On the contrary, they were heirlooms preserved by the people, the creation of skilled musicians in the past. I have stated that the minstrels were put down by Act of Parliament in 1597. Still more severe Acts were passed against them in the Third Parliament of Oliver Cromwell. The result was that the minstrels settled down in the country and followed trades, supplementing their earnings from their trade by what they made at village festivals. So also the cultured musicians attached to cathedrals and theatres were dispersed by the Puritans at the time of the Commonwealth, and they also settled down in the country places, where they taught village choirs, or else went abroad. Thus we have music of Henry VII. and Henry VIII.'s reigns, and we have music of the time of James I. and Charles I., sung by our villagers,—none of it their own production, all inherited from the minstrels and the Caroline musicians. In the Hanoverian period there were musical men understanding counterpoint throughout the land, a school of them in Cornwall and Devon. Their old, somewhat elaborate church music remains in MS. in many an old church chest, and Mr. Heath, of Redruth, has recently published some of their carols.

Now, our folk-music, and not ours only but that of Scotland and Ireland, of France and Germany, and Italy as well, is a veritable morraine of rolled and ground fragments from musical strata far away. It contains melodies of all centuries down to the present, all thrown together into one confused heap.

Of French folk-music M. Loquin says: "To the question, Have all popular melodies an artistic origin? I would not answer with an unqualified Yes; that would be going a little too far, but I do say that we have no reason to assert that a melody is original because we have so far failed to track it. Some day or other it is almost certain to turn up in some unengraved ballet music, or—such as the *malice des choses*—in a collection every one has in hand, one turned over by every writer on music, and yet for some reason or other it has not been recognised there. What I do assert is that *nearly all* the popular melodies have a perfectly well established musical urban origin. That I can affirm with confidence, for I have the evidence in both hands. But that is not all. Of such tunes as have been composed by village singers, very few they are,—what are they, in fact? Naught but a jumble of phrases caught from pre-existing songs, reminiscences badly fused together of songs sung in the towns at one time and then forgotten. So true is it that everything here below has its origin, which origin is not always easy to find."

Now, if this be so—and that it may be so is quite possible—it may be asked, what is the good of collecting folk-melodies? and secondly, what right have you to claim those you have collected as belonging to the Celtic parts of Devon and of Cornwall? I will answer both questions at once.

Directly the Exe is crossed we come into a different musical deposit. I do not say different in *kind*, for music was the same everywhere in certain epochs, and where certain instruments were in use. For instance, a harp tune was of the same character in Ireland, in Wales, in Cornwall, in Scotland, and in France; and a bagpipe tune or a hornpipe tune had the same character everywhere. But what I find is that songs and ballads sung to their traditional melodies in Somersetshire, in Sussex, in Yorkshire, and Northumberland, are sung to quite independent airs on Dartmoor and in Cornwall. How is this? Because the same process went on in the West as in Scotland.

The Celtic tongue retrograded and finally expired in Cornwall. Then English ballads and songs found their way into Cornwall, as they found their way into Scotland and Ireland, and were set to already familiar melodies thenceforth dissociated from their no longer understood words. Take an instance. There is in Welsh a song on the pleasures of the bottle, "Glân meddwdod mwyn." Now precisely the same melody was sung in Cornwall, almost certainly to words of a like nature. When the Cornish tongue ceased to be spoken, then this melody was applied to a broadside drinking song, "Fathom the Bowl." But "Fathom the Bowl" has, everywhere else, its own traditional air.

Another well-known song is "Tobacco is an Indian weed," another is "Joan's Ale is New," both wedded one would have supposed indissolubly to their traditional airs known everywhere else in England. But not so in Cornwall and on Dartmoor; there these words are set to quite independent melodies—melodies that probably had accompanied words in the old Cornish tongue in former times. To descend later. Broadside ballads, and songs in "Warblers," and "Apollo's Cabinets," &c., got down into the West, unassociated with music. Then, again, the local composers went to work and set them to tunes of their own creation. Thus, "Sweet Nightingale" was a song by Bickerstaff, to which Dr. Arne wrote music in 1761, and it was sung in an opera in London. The words got into a song-book, "The Syren," which found its way into Cornwall. Some village musician—no bumpkin at the plough tail—set it, and it was sung by the miners in their adits and the labourers in the fields to the locally produced air, not to that by Dr. Arne.

Consequently, I am able to answer both questions at once. I hold that these melodies are of West of England origin in a majority of cases, and that they are worth collecting, because they are the remains of a school of cultured musicians that has passed away unheard of out of their own counties.

Now for another point.

Were any of the melodies sung in the West borrowed, as were many of the words? Certainly they were. All people borrow. The Irish have borrowed. The Scotch have "lifted" English folk-tunes by the scores. The Flemmings, the Germans, the French have all borrowed of the English. Horace Walpole heard "Buttered Pease," and "Cold and Raw," and other country dances played at the palace of the Grand Duke of Tuscany in 1740. Quite recently (1890) a volume of English music in MS. has turned up in the library of Trent. The song, "Shall Trelawney die?" is sung to "Le petit Tambour," a French melody. I have heard an old ballad sung in Devon to the Scotch "Auld lang syne." The Irish sing "The wearing of the Green" to an old English melody. They, on one side, and the Scotch on the other, have appropriated the ancient English melody of "Paul's Steeple," found in Playford's "Dancing Master," in 1650, and have converted it in the one case into "Cruiskeen Lawn," in the other into "John Anderson, my Jo." There has been give and take on all sides: with regard to old English airs mostly take. How many of the melodies we have collected in the West can be determined as borrowed we are unable to say. Mr. Sheppard has not had the time, nor have I the ability to follow the track of melodies through the vast collections of past days. All we pretend to do is to give up what we have gathered.

One word further as to our *method*.

We have taken down all the variants of the same air we have come across, and have given that form of the air which seemed to us most genuine. In some cases where we could obtain no variants, we have printed what we received, as received from the only singer we found who knew that air. The necessity for having several variants arises from this fact. When a party of singers are together, or when one man sings a succession of ballads, the memory becomes troubled; the first two or three melodies are given correctly, but after that, the airs become deflected and influenced by the airs last sung. At Two Bridges one old singer, G. Kerswell, after giving us "The Bell-ringer," sang us half-a-dozen other ballads, but the melody of the bells went through them all and vitiated them all so as to render them worthless. On another occasion, we took down four or five airs all beginning alike, because one singer impressed this beginning on the minds of the others. At another time, when this impression was worn off, they would sing truly enough, and then the beginnings would be different. To obtain the music we have gathered is not so easy a matter as might be supposed; and I venture to think that only a native of the West, one thoroughly understanding the people, their ways, their prejudices, the turns and twists of their minds, could do it. The aged men from whom the collection has been made have been laughed down, and silenced for thirty or forty years. The generation that has grown up since those singing days heartily despise this old world music. One day Mr. Bussell and I had been sitting in a little thatched cottage listening to two aged song-men, one nearly blind, the other childish with age, and had reverently and lovingly noted down their ballads and melodies. Then we went into a farm-house, and there asked our direction across the moors; we told the farmer and his wife what we had been doing. They laughed till the tears ran down their cheeks at the bare idea of anything worth having being obtained from old Gerard and Stoneman. "Ah!" said the farmer's son, "Come in. I'll sing you a song, a first-rate one. 'What a shocking bad hat.' That is something worth your having." We have driven and walked in storms of rain and wind over Dartmoor, and have sat with hands that shivered with cold on a moorstone taking down ballads from some old shepherd or an aged crone. But we have also gathered the hearty moor-men about a great fire, and after a good supper have spent with them very merry evenings. I venture to believe that the warm shake of the hand and the cheery smile that welcome us wherever we go, are evidence that we have reached the hearts of these old and failing men—and have kindled in them again a spark of pride in their old world loved music that has been disparaged, jeered at, by the board-school bred new generation, and so have enabled them proudly to raise their old grey heads again, in the thought that they have been the means of transmitting to the new age a whole body of precious melody, that but for them would have been absolutely and irretrievably lost. I am glad also to be able to say that I have been able, through profits realised by concerts of this West of England music, to help some of these poor old fellows when suffering from accidents and the infirmities of extreme old age. In conclusion, I must express my thanks to Mr. F. W. Bussell for his unflagging good humour and readiness to go with me anywhere and in any weather after a song-man. I am unable myself to note a melody if I have not an instrument, and most of these airs must be gleaned in the cottages, often miles away from any piano.

Mr. W. Crossing, of South Brent, and Mr. T. S. Cayzer have given us melodies collected on the moor twenty and thirty years ago. Those noted down by Mr. Sheppard are so described in the text. Our budget must not be supposed to be exhausted; something like 300 airs have been collected. What we have done is to give samples of the various sorts, with not too large a preponderance of the earliest and most ancient melodies, which, though to us of the highest interest, would not perhaps meet with general appreciation. We have found it more difficult to decide what to omit, than what to include.

I. **"By Chance it was."** Music and words dictated by James Parsons, hedger, Lew Down. Learned from his father, "The Singing Machine," a very famous song-man, who, when turned on could go on and never stop—so it was reported. His son says that his father certainly knew 200 ballads and songs. Some of the best and earliest melodies have been derived by us from Parsons.

This song is to be found (as far as the words go) in a collection of early ballad books in the British Museum, entitled "The Court of Apollo." It consists of six verses, the first three of which are almost word for word the same. The others vary somewhat. In "The Songster's Favourite," another and later collection, the same song occurs. It is in three verses only and in a very corrupt form.

A second version of the melody was obtained from Bruce Tyndall, Esq., of Exmouth, who learned it from a Devonshire cook in 1839 or 1840. The melody was slightly modernised.

II. "**The Hunting of Arscott of Tetcott.**" This song, once vastly popular in North Devon, and at all hunting dinners, is now nearly forgotten. The words have been published in " John Arscott of Tetcott," Luke, Plymouth. A great many variations of the words are found. An early copy was supplied me by R. Kelly, Esq., of Kelly. Another by a gentleman, now dead, in his grandmother's handwriting, with explanatory notes. In the first edition I stated that as it was impossible to reconcile the date, 1752, with any John Arscott, I thought the date must be 1652, and the song refer to the then squire of Tetcott, John Arscott, buried in 1708. But in one of the versions I have received the date is not 52, but 72, and that will answer for John Arscott, who died in 1788, the last of his race.

The "Sons of the Blue," it is supposed, were Sir John Molesworth, William Morshead, of Blisland, and Bradden Clode, of Skisdom,—so the annotations to the printed version by Luke, of Plymouth. But neither Sir J. Molesworth nor Mr. Morshead were, as it happens, naval men, so that the identification is not satisfactory. Now, if the date be 1652, it is right as far as Sir J. Molesworth of that time is concerned, for he was Vice-Admiral of Cornwall, and Pencarrow is the Molesworth place. John Arscott is still believed to hunt the country, and there are men alive who declare they have heard his horn, and seen him and his hounds go by in the park at Tetcott.

The author of the song is said to have been one Dogget, who used to run after Arscott's fox hounds on foot. If so, then he probably followed the habit of all rural bards of using for his purpose an earlier ballad, and spoiling and vulgarising it; such poets are incapable of originating anything. I think this because along with much wretched stuff there are traces of something better, and smacking of an earlier period. As Dogget's doggerel has been printed, and I have taken down from ten to twelve versions all widely differing, I have not considered it worth preserving except only where there are pre-Doggetian verses, incorporated by him into his copy; and I have ventured to recast the conclusion. The tune was obtained through the assistance of Mr. J. Richards, schoolmaster at Tetcott. The same tune is found in Wales to the words "Difurwch gwyr Dyfi" (E. Jones' Musical Relicks of the Welsh Bards, 1794, I., p. 129).

It—or rather half of the tune—was introduced by D'Urfey into his "Pills to purge Malancholy," to the words "Dear Catholic Brother" (Ed. 1719-20, Vol. VI., p. 277). From D'Urfey it passed into the "Musical Miscellany" (1731, Vol. VI., p. 171), to the words "Come, take up your Burden, ye Dogs, and away." D'Urfey was a Devonshire Man, and he probably picked up the tune when a boy in the West, and used as much of it as he wanted to set to his song. The air is much older than the age of D'Urfey; it probably belongs to an early stock common to the Celts of Wales and Cornwall. A very fine variant from J. Benney, Menheniot.

And sing Fol-de-rol,

III. "**Upon a Sunday Morning.**" The melody taken down from old Robert Hard, a crippled stone-breaker, at South Brent. He sang to the air the words of Charles Swan,

' 'Twas on a Sunday morning, before the bells did peal,
A note came through the window, with Cupid on the seal," &c.

These words were set to music by Francis Mori, in 1853. The character of Mori's melody is distinct from that of old Hard, the opening strains alone being alike in both. In the first edition we printed Swan's words, not knowing whose they were. Hard obtained them indirectly from a broadside by Catnach, of Seven Dials. Having since discovered their origin, I have written fresh words to Hard's melody.

IV. "**The Trees they are so high.**" Words and air taken in 1888 from James Parsons and Matthew Baker, a cripple on Lew Down. The same ballad to the same melody obtained in 1891 from Richard Broad, aged 71, at Herodsfoot, near S. Keyne, Cornwall. Some verses completing the ballad we have, since the publication of the first edition, obtained from Roger Hanaford, of Lower Widdicombe, but his melody was not the same; it was less archaic. There are several versions of this ballad; some very fragmentary, by Catnach and other broadside printers—a very fairly complete one printed in Aberdeen at the end of last century or beginning of this.

Johnson, in his "Museum" professed to give a Scottish version:

"O Lady Mary Ann looks owre the Castle wa'
She saw three bonny boys playing at the ba'
The youngest he was the flower among them a';
My bonny laddie's young, but he's growing yet."

But of this version, only three of the verses are genuine, and they are inverted; the rest are a modern composition.

A much more genuine Scottish form is in Maidment's "North Country Garland" (Edinburgh, 1824); but it is an adaptation to the story of a young Lair of Craigstoun. It begins:

"Father, said she, you have done me wrong,
For ye have married me on a childe young man,
And my bonny love is long
Agrowing, growing, deary,
Growing, growing, said the bonny maid."

But by far the truest form is that in an Aberdeen broadside; it will be found in the British Museum, under Ballads (1750—1840), Scottish, (Press mark, 1871 f.). The Scottish version has verses not in the English, and the English has a verse or two that are not in the Scottish.

I have also received an Irish version as sung in Co. Clare by a old lady some years ago; it is in six verses, but that about the "Trees so High" is lacking. The rhyme is more correct than any of the other printed versions; the lines are in triplets that rhyme. One verse runs:

"O Father dear Father, I'll tell you what we'll do,
We'll send him off to College for another year or two
And we'll tie round his college cap a ribbon of the blue.
To let the maidens know he is married."

In one of the versions I have taken down (Hannaford's), there were traces of the triplet, very distinct, and the tune is akin to the Irish melody sent me from Clare.

Again, another version of this ballad I obtained from William Aggett, a paralysed labourer of 70 years, at Chagford, to an entirely different melody. Apparently, there exist two distinct variants of this ballad, each to its peculiar melody.

For broadside version, see Ballads collected by Crampton, B.M. (1162, h.), Vol. VII.; it is No. 63 of Such's Broadsides.

In most versions, the age of the boy when married is 13, and he is a father at 14. I advanced his age a little, in deference to the opinion of those who like to sing the song in a drawing-room or at a public concert.

The Scotch have two airs, one in Johnson's Museum, the other in "The British Minstrel," Glasgow, 1844, Vol. II., p. 36, entirely distinct from ours.

V. "**Parson Hogg.**" This was sung by my great uncle, Thomas Snow, Esq., of Franklyn House, near Exeter, when I was a child. It was given me by my cousin, Edmund Snow; it was also a song sung in old days by the Winchester boys. Another version I obtained from Mr. H. Whitfeld, Brushmaker, Market xv.

Alley, Plymouth. The words are to be found, not quite the same, but substantially so, in "The New Cabinet of Love," a collection of songs sung at Vauxhall, Ranelagh, &c., n.d., but about 1810, as "Doctor Mack." Broadside versions exist by Catnach, of Seven Dials, and Bachelor, of Hackney Road, also as "Doctor Mack." Also in "The Universal Songster," n.d. II., p. 348. In Oliver's "Comic Songs," circ. 1815, it is "Parson Ogg, the Cornish Vicar."

VI. "Cold blows the Wind." The words originally reached us as taken down by Mrs. Gibbons, daughter of the late Sir W. L. Trelawney, Bart., from an old woman, Elizabeth Doidge, who was, sixty years ago, in the service of her father. The Doidge family belongs to the neighbourhood of Brentnor. She sang it to the air given subsequently, No. 33, to "Childe the Hunter." Another person who sang this song was J. Woodrich, blacksmith, Wollacot Moor, Thrustleton, to the melody here given. We obtained the same melody from Mr. H. Westaway, a yeoman at Belstone. At Huckaby Bridge, on Dartmoor, we got the same melody from Mary Satcherly, an old woman, who sang it to the ballad of "Lord Thomas and the Fair Eleanor," to which, according to Chappell, it properly belongs ("Pop. Music of the Olden Times," I., p. 145). It is the air "Who list to lead a Soldier's Life." In Peele's *Edward I.*, 1593, is the direction "Enter a harper, and sing to the tune of 'Who list to lead a soldier's life,'" &c. In Delaney's "Strange Histories," 1607, is a song on the life and death of Richard III., to be sung to this melody. Ophelia's song. "Good Morrow, 'tis St. Valentine's Day," is only a different version of the same.

I ventured to *add* the last verse, as the original tune taken down from Westaway by Mr. Sheppard was in the major, and it was thought advisable to have two verses in that key. For much information relative to this ballad, I must refer the reader to Professor Child's "British Ballads," now in process of publication in America, where it is treated of exhaustively.

Also, to complete the story of the ballad, I have added verses 6, 8, and 10 from a West of England folk-tale, which probably is this ballad turned into prose.

VII. "In my Garden grew plenty of Thyme." Taken down from James Parsons. After the second verse he broke away to "I sowed the seeds of love," a well-known folk song composed about 1670 by Mrs. Fleetwood Habergam to the air of "Come, open the door, Sweet Betty," and to that melody it is usually sung. Parsons's tune was distinct.

Three verses, a fragment, as sung anciently in Scotland, in "Albyn's Anthology," 1816, I., p. 40. Mr. Kidson, "Traditional Tunes," 1891, p. 69, gives five stanzas. From Joseph Dyer, an old labourer at S. Mawgan-in-Pyder, I took down six. None of these versions agree except in the initial verse, which is the second in Mr. Kidson's Yorkshire version, and the last verse of Dyer's agrees with the last of Mr. Kidson's. But Dyer had a stanza found in no other:—

> "O! and I was a damsel so fair,
> But fairer I wished to appear,
> So I washed me in milk, and I dressed me in silk,
> And put the sweet Thyme in my hair."

He, like Parsons, imported portions of "The Seeds of Love" into this song. Dyer's melody was practically the same as that of Parsons, but the third line was different, and he sang in common time. So doubtful am I what were the original words of this song, that I have thought it advisable to add fresh verses after the first two taken from Parsons. For the Scottish air see "Albyn's Anthology;" for the Yorkshire air, Mr. Kidson's "Traditional Tunes;" for the Northumbrian, see "Northumbrian Minstrelsy," 1882, p. 90. All these airs differ from ours.

In the "Westminster Drolleries," 1671, is a song:—

> "*Heartseas*, an herb that somehow hath bin seen
> In my love's garden plot to flourish green,
> Is dead, and withered with a kind of woe,
> And bitter *Rue* in place thereof did grow."

Then follows a similar play on *Thyme*. My impression is that Mrs. Habergam's was a re-writing of an earlier ballad.

VIII. "**Roving Jack.**" Taken, words and melody, from James Parsons; again to the same air from Wm. Aggett, an old crippled labourer at Chagford. An inferior version of the words on Catnach's broadsides. Aggett followed the broadside. In Catnach the town is Carlow. Ballads, B.M. (1162, h.) Vol. VII. Another, printed in Edinburgh. Ballads (1750—1840) B.M. (1871. f.).

IX. "**Brixham Town.**" Words taken down from Jonas Coaker, of Post Bridge, on Dartmoor, aged 85, and blind. The melody was sung to us by Mr. John Webb, captain of a tin mine hard by, and was noted by Mr. Sheppard. Another version, to the same melody, was obtained where the town was North Tawton. Again, another version of the words was given me by the Hon. and Rev. A. F. Northcote, who took it down in 1877 from an itinerant pedlar of 90 years at Buckingham.

There is an additional verse in the latter edition.

> "Now there be creatures three,
> As you may plainly see,
> With music can't agree,
> Upon this earth.
> The swine, the fool, the ass,
> And so we let it pass.
> And sing, O Lord, thy praise,
> Whilst we have breath."

The words and tune alike belong to the 17th century. The words were clearly composed at the time of the Puritan *régime*, 1640—1661.

X. "**Green Broom.**" Words and melody taken down from John Woodrich, blacksmith; he learned both from his grandmother when he was a child. The Hon. and Rev. J. S. Northcote sent me another version taken down from an old woman at Upton Pyne. Another again from Mr. James Ellis, of Chaddlehanger, near Tavistock, another from Bruce Tyndall, Esq., of Exmouth, as taken from a Devonshire cook, in 1839 or 1840. This, the same melody as that from Upton Pyne. Woodrich's tune is the brightest, but the other the oldest. D'Urfey, in his "Pills to Purge Melancholy," Ed. 1720, Vol. VI., p. 100, gives this ballad in 14 verses, with a different conclusion. All the versions except Woodrich's begin "There was an old man who lived in the West." Broadside versions by Disley and Such (No. 66); see also "The Broom-man's Garland," in LXXXII. old ballads collected by J. Bell, B.M. (11621, c. 2). Bell was librarian to the Society of Antiquaries, Newcastle-on-Tyne, 1810-20. See also "Northumbrian Minstrelsy,' where the air is different, and words also.

XI. "**As Johnny walked out.**" Words and melody from James Parsons. The original words in six verses; these I have compressed for the convenience of modern singers. The words with verbal differences are found in a good many early collections, set about 1750, to an air by "Mr. Dunn." It was first published to Dunn's tune in "Six English Songs and Dialogues as they are performed at the Public Gardens," n.d., but circ. 1750. Then in "The London Magazine" for September, 1754; in " Apollo's Cabinet," Liverpool, 1757, p. 250; in " Clio and Enterpe," Lond., 1758, vol. I., p. 34. But our melody, of which we have taken down some four or five versions, and one was taken down by Mr. T. S. Cayzer, at Post Bridge, in 1849, is quite different from Dunn's air.

XII. **The Miller and his Sons.** Taken down, words and music, from Helmore, miller, South Brent. The words occur in the " Roxburgh Collection," III., p. 681. It is included in Bell's " Songs of the English Peasantry," p. 194, and in the " Northumbrian Minstrelsy," Newcastle, 1882. In the North of England it is sung to the melody of "The Oxfordshire Tragedy," Chappell, p. 191. Our air bears no resemblance to this.

XIII. **Ormond the Brave.** This very interesting ballad was taken down, words by myself and melody by Mr. Sheppard, from J. Peake, Tanner, Liskeard; it was a song sung by his father, about 60 years ago. It refers to Ormond's landing in Devon in 1714. Ormond fled to France in the first days of July, " a duke without a duchy," as Lord Oxford termed him, when it was manifest that the country was resolved on having the Hanoverian Elector as King, and unwilling to summon the Chevalier of S.

George to the throne. In the end of October the Duke of Ormond landed in Devon at the head of a few men, hoping that the West would rise in the Jacobite cause, but as not a single adherent joined his standard, he returned to France. This song is particularly curious as it is a Jacobite ballad proclamation, in which Ormond, who was a poor creature, is glorified as though a hero. From the same singer we derived another ballad relative to Ormond, recounting his exploits at Vigo in 1703. The melody is certainly not later than the words, and is probably older considerably. In our first editions we gave here a composition by Mr. Sheppard and myself. This we have withdrawn now for a genuine West country ballad.

XIV. **Fathom the Bowl.** Taken down, words and air, by the Rev. H. Fleetwood Sheppard, from Robert Hard, of South Brent. Another version from H. Whitfeld, Plymouth, who said it had been sung by his grandfather. In "Notes and Queries," 3rd s., XII., p. 245, inquiry was made relative to this song, but elicited no reply. Broadside editions exist by Catnach, Pitts, and Such. This melody is also found in Wales, sung to "Glan Meddwdod Mwyn," and it has the character of a harp air. Jones, "Bardic Relicks," 1794, I., p. 149. In other parts of England this song is sung to an entirely different melody. Broadwood and Lucas, " Sussex Songs," 1890, No. 20.

XV. **Sweet Nightingale.** In " Ancient Poems, Ballads and Songs of the Peasantry of England, by Robert Bell." London, 1857, the author says, " This curious ditty, which may be confidently assigned to the 17th century . . . . we first heard in Germany, at Marienberg on the Moselle. The singers were four Cornish miners, who were at that time, 1854, employed at some lead mines near the town of Zell. The leader, or Captain, John Stocker, said that the song was an established favourite with the miners of Cornwall and Devonshire, and was always sung on the pay-days and at the wakes; and that his grandfather, who died thirty years before, at the age of a hundred years, used to sing the song, and say that it was very old. The tune is plaintive and original." Unfortunately, Mr. Bell does not give the tune. The melody was first sent me by E. F. Stevens, Esq., of Terrace, St. Ives, who wrote that the melody "had run in his head any time these eight and thirty years." I have since had it from a good many old men in Cornwall, always to the same air. They say it is a duet, and has therefore been so set. Mr. Bell has taken liberties with the words; the original I did not recover till the first edition was out. I have traced the song to Bickerstaff's " Thomas and Sally," 1760, a ballad opera, the music by Dr. Arne. The Cornish melody is, however, quite distinct from that by Arne. The melody is not later than the middle of last century.

XVI. **Widdecombe Fair.** At present the best known and most popular of Devonshire songs. The original Uncle " Tom Cobleigh " lived in a house near Yeoford Junction. The names in the chorus all belonged to Sticklepath. The tune and words first came to me from W. F. Collier, Esq., of Woodtown, Horrabridge. Other versions, slightly varying, then poured in. A slight variant has been published by Mr. W. Davies, of Kingsbridge. There is one more verse in the original, which I have been forced to omit from lack of room. I obtained on Dartmoor the same song to a different air, an old dance tune.

XVII. **The Imprisoned Lady.** Words and melody from James Parsons. The fullest broadside version, but very corrupt, is one published at Aberdeen. Ballads, B. M. (1871, f., p. 61), another, shorter, by Williams, of Portsea. In both great confusion has been made by some ignorant poetaster in enlarging and altering, so that in many of the verses the rhymes have been lost. This is how the Aberdeen broadside begins :—

> "You maidens pretty
> In country and city
> With pity hear
> My mournful tale:
> A maid confounded
> In sorrow drowned
> And deeply wounded
> With grief and pain."

In the third line the "pity" has got misplaced, and "sad complain" has been turned into "mournful tale" to the loss of rhyme. Verse four has fared even worse, it runs, literally :—

    "My hardened parents
    Gave special order
    That I should be
      Close confined be, (*sic*.)
    Within my chamber
    Far from all ranger
    Or lest that I
      Should my darling see."

A parody of it was written by Ashley, of Bath, and sung in "Bombastes Furioso," Rhodes' burlesque, in 1810 (performed at the Haymarket, August 7), to the Irish tune of "Paddy O'Carrol." This appears also in "The London Warbler," 3 Vols., n.d., but about 1826, 1., p. 80.

    "My love is so pretty, so gay and so witty,
    All in town, court, and city, to her must give place,
    My Lord of the woolsack, his coachman did pull-back
    To have a look, full smack, at her pretty face," &c.

The metre was a favourite one in former times. Songs in that metre were composed in the reigns of Henry VIII. and Elizabeth. Others are found in Allan Ramsay's "Tea Table Miscellany," 1724; and in D'Urfey, 1719. Indeed Chaucer's "Virelai" lacks but a syllable to be in it. A favourite old English ballad, "Ye Beaux of Pleasure" was in the same metre; the melody was taken into several of the ballad-operas, as "The Lover's Opera," 1729, "The Footman," 1732, "The Jovial Crew," 1731, etc.

Words and melody are probably of the Elizabethan age.

XVIII. **The Silly Old Man.** A ballad that was sung by the late Rev. E. Luscombe, some five and forty years ago. He was then curate of Bickleigh, and by ancestry belonged to a good old Devonshire family, and he was particularly fond of ancient West of England songs, which he sang in the truest Devonshire brogue. I have had it from one of his old pupils, W. Weekes, Esq., of Willestrew, Lamerton. Another version from old Suey Stephens, a char-woman at Stowford. Another, as sung in 1848, by Dr. Reed, of Tiverton. Mrs. Mason, in her "Nursery Rhymes and Country Songs," 1877, gives a slight variant, also from Devonshire.

The ballad is found printed in Dixon's "Songs of the English Peasantry," published for the Percy Society in 1846, and taken down by him from oral recitation in Yorkshire in 1845. It exists in a chap-book under the title "The Crafty Farmer," published in 1796. In Yorkshire the song goes by the name of "Saddle to Rags;" there, and elsewhere in the North of England, it is sung to the tune of "The Rant," or "Give ear to my frolicsome Ditty," an air better known as "How happy could I be with Either." It has been published as a Scottish song in Maidment's "Scottish Ballads and Songs," Edinburgh, 1859. The tune to which this song is sung in Devonshire is quite distinct and independent. The words may also be found in "A Pedlar's Pack of Ballads and Songs," Edinburgh, 1849, p. 126, in 20 stanzas. The West of England version differs somewhat from that current in Yorkshire. The tune is very fresh and spirited. There are broadside editions by Birt, of Seven Dials, &c.

XIX. **The Seasons.** Still a popular song among the labouring class. Three versions of the air and words were taken down, one at South Brent, one at Belstone, and one at Post Bridge. The words slightly vary, and are crude. The air is clearly an old dance tune. The version we preferred was that given by J. Potter, of Post Bridge, taken down by Mr. Sheppard.

XX. **The Chimney Sweep.** Taken down from J. Helmore, South Brent. We have been quite unable to trace this song. It belongs to the end of last century or beginning of this.

XXI. **The Saucy Sailor.** Words and melody taken from James Parsons. A broadside with a different ending was printed by Disley, Pitts, Such, and Hodges, also by Pratt, of Birmingham; the metre also is not quite the same, and the air to which sung in other parts of England, I am informed by Dr. A. W. Barrett, is distinct from ours. This will be found in F. Tozer's "Forty Sailors' Songs," Boosey & Co., No. 33. Parson's air bears a strong likeness to "When in Death I shall Calm Recline" in Moore's "Irish Melodies." He gives the tune as "unknown" as to its origin, and as not having any Irish words fitted to it. It is probably an English air carried to Ireland, or one merely appropriated by Moore, as he did others that took his fancy, viz., "The Girl I Left Behind Me," "My Lodging is on the Cold Ground," "Bobbing Joan," "Alley Croker," "The Black Joke," &c.

XXII. **Blue Muslin.** Taken down, words and melody, from John Woodrich, blacksmith. A quaint song of an individual character. This is thought to require great skill in singing owing to the reversal of the stanzas, and is taken as a test whether a singer is sober or not. When he fails to give the order correctly, he is regarded as having had just one drop too much. Muslin had been introduced into England in 1670, and cork in 1690. Both are spoken of as novelties, and muslin is sung to the old form of the word, mous-el-ine.

Miss F. Crossing sent me another version taken down from an old woman in South Devon, in or about 1850.

   1. "My man John, what can the matter be?"
    "I love a lady, and she won't love me."
    "Peace, sir, peace, and don't despair,
    The lady you love will be your only care:
     And it must be gold to win her."

   2. "Madam, will you accept of this pretty golden ball,
    To walk all in the garden, or in my lady's hall?"
    "Sir, I'll accept of no pretty golden ball
    To walk all in the garden, or in my lady's hall.
    Nor will I walk, nor will I talk with you."
     Chorus: "My man John," &c., as verse 1.

   3. "Madam, will you accept of a petticoat of red,
    With six golden flounces around it out-spread?"
    "Sir I'll accept of no petticoat," &c.

   4. "Madam, will you accept of the keys of my heart,
    That we may join together, and never, never part?"
    "Sir, I'll not accept of the keys," &c.

   5. "Madam, will you accept of the keys of my chest,
    To get at all my money, and to buy what you think best?"
    "Sir, I will accept of the keys of your chest,
    To get at all your money, and to buy what I think best;
    And I'll walk, and I'll talk with you."
    "My man John, here's a bag of gold for you,
    For that which you have told me, has come true,
    And 'twas gold, 'twas gold, that did win her."

Another version comes from Yorkshire. See Halliwell, Nursery Rhymes, (4th Ed., 1846). Another to a different air from Cheshire. Another again in Mason's "Nursery Rhymes and Country Songs." Metzler, 1877, p. 27. Melody quite different.

XXIII. **The Squire and the Fair Maid.** Taken down, words and music, from J. Hoskin, labourer, South Brent, also from James Parsons, John Woodrich, in fragments, very full from John Masters, Bradstone, an old man of 80. Another very full from H. Smith, Post Bridge, Dartmoor. A form of the same, the same theme, in Johnson's Museum, 1787-1803, Vol. IV., p. 410. The same toned down in Lyle's Ballads, 1827, "I am too young." He says, "This ballad in its original dress at one time from my recollection was not only extremely popular, but a great favourite amongst the young peasantry in the West of Scotland. To suit the times, however, we have been necessitated to throw out the intermediate stanzas, as their freedom would not bear transcription; whilst the second and third have been slightly altered from the recited copy."

Allan Cunningham took the song from Johnson's Museum and rewrote it in his second volume.

It has been necessary to somewhat tone down a couple of the stanzas for the same reason as that given by Mr. Lyle.

The Scottish ballad begins:—

> "As I went out one May morning,
> A May morning it happened to be,
> Then I was aware of a weel fa'rd lass,
> Come linking o'er the lea to me.
> She had a voice that was more clear
> Than any damsel's under the sun,
> I ask'd at her if she'd marry me?
> But her answer it was, I am too young," &c.

I have not been able to find it in any collection of broadsides, and the two versions are almost certainly variants of some early English ballad that found its way on one side into Scotland, and on the other into Celtic Cornwall and Devon. The Scottish air is quite different from ours, which is an early ballad tune.

XXIV. **The Helston Furry Dance.** On May 8th, annually, a festival is held at Helston, in Cornwall, to celebrate the incoming of spring. Very early in the morning a party of youths and maidens goes into the country, and returns dancing through the streets to a quaint tune, peculiar to the day, called the "Furry Dance." At eight o'clock the "Hal-an-tow" is sung by a party of from twenty to thirty men and boys who come into the town bearing green branches, with flowers in their hats, preceded by a single drum, on which a boy beats the Furry Dance. They perambulate the town for many hours, stopping at intervals at some of the principal houses.

At one o'clock a large party of ladies and gentlemen, in summer attire,—the ladies decorated with garlands of flowers, the gentlemen with nosegays and flowers in their hats, assemble at the Town Hall, and proceed to dance after the band, playing the traditional air. They first trip in couples, hand in hand, during the first part of the tune, forming a string of from thirty to forty couples, or perhaps more; at the second part of the tune the first gentleman turns with both hands, the lady behind him, and her partner turns in like manner with the first lady; then each gentleman turns his own partner, and then they trip on as before. The other couples, of course, pair and turn in the same way, and at the same time.

The dancing is not confined to the streets, the house doors are thrown open, and the train of dancers enter by the front, dance through the house, and out at the back, through the garden, and back again. It is considered a slight to omit a house. Finally the train enters the Assembly Room and there resolves itself into an ordinary waltz.

As soon as the first party is finished another goes through the same evolutions, and then another, and so on; and it is not till late at night that the town returns to its peaceful propriety.

There is a general holiday in the town on Flora Day, and so strictly was this formerly adhered to, that anyone found working on that day, was compelled to jump across Pengella, a wide stream that discharges its waters into Loo Pool. As this feat was almost impracticable, it involved a sousing. The festival has by no means ceased to be observed, it has rather, of late years, been revived in energetic observance.*

The "Helston Furry Dance" is a relic of part of the Old English May Games. These originally comprised four entirely distinct parts. 1st. The election and procession of the King and Queen of the May, who were called the Summer King and Queen. 2nd. The Morris Dance, performed by men disguised, with swords in their hands. 3rd. The "Hobby Horse." 4th. The "Robin Hood."

---

* See Forfar. The Helstone Furry Day, Helston, 1803.

The first began with the dispersing of the young of both sexes over the country and through the woods collecting flowers. Chaucer, in his "Court of Love," says that early on May Day, "Forth goeth all the court, both most and least, to fetch the flowers afresh." In the reign of Henry VIII. the heads of the Corporation of London went to the high grounds of Kent to gather the may, the King and his Queen, Catherine of Arragon, coming from their palace at Greenwich, to meet them on Shooter's Hill. This was called the Bringing Home the May. Then came the decorating of the houses. Herrick describes this as performed in Devon.

> "——Come, and coming mark,
> How each field turns a street, and each street a park,
> Made green and trimmed with trees; see how
> Devotion gives each house a bough
> Or branch; each porch, each door, ere this
> An ark, a tabernacle is
> Made up of white-thorn neatly interwove."

Then ensued the election and coronation of the King and Queen. This Spenser describes in the Shepherd's Calendar.

> "I saw a skole of shepherds outgo
> With singing, and shouting, and jolly cheer;
> Before them yode a lusty tabrere,
> That to the many a horn-pipe play'd,
> Where to they danced each one with his maid.
> Then to the greenwood they speeden them all,
> To fetchen home May with their musical:
> And home they bring him in a royal throne
> Crowned as king; and his queen attone
> Was lady Flora, on whom did attend
> A fair flock of fairies and a fresh bend
> Of lively nymphs—O that I were there
> To helpen the ladies their May-bush to bear."

The dance to the May-pole and round it then ensued.

2nd. The Morris dance was a masque. With this we need not now concern ourselves. 3rd. The Hobby Horse was a feature also introduced, and almost certainly was a relic of Odin and his horse Sleipnir. 4th. The Robin Hood Games was a play fully described in Strutt's novel "Queen Hoo Hall," it has been mixed up with rapier dancing and the gambols of the Hobby Horse, and is still performed in various places at Christmas.

In the Helston performance we have a fragment only of the original series of pageants; the bringing home of the May and the dance, and the song about Robin Hood. At Padstow, the Hobby-horse still figures. The two earliest extant representations of the Old English May games are found in a Flemish print, given by Douce in his "Illustrations of Shakespeare," and in Tollett's celebrated painted window, described in Johnson and Steven's "Shakespeare." The "Helston Furry Dance" tune was first printed in Davies Gilbert's Christmas Carols, 2nd Ed., 1823. His form is purer than ours, which is as now sung.

XXV. "**Blow away, ye Mountain Breezes.**" Taken down, words and music, from R. Hard; melody noted down by Mr. Sheppard. This very curious song is sung as a duet; that is to say, the first voice taunts the other, and the second replies to the taunt, then both unite in the chorus. We have omitted the retort, which is simply an application of the same words to the first singer. It is certainly a very early composition. One passage in it occurs also in "The Knight and the Shepherd's Daughter," in Percy's Relicks, Child's British Ballads, &c.

> "Would I had drunk the water cleare
> When I had drunk the wine,
> Rather than any shepherd's brat
> Should be a lady of mine,
> Would I had drunke the puddle foule
> When I did drink the ale," &c.

The chorus, or burden, "Blow away, &c.," occurs also in the ballad of "The Baffled Knight," in Percy. Bell gives a Northumbrian version of this ballad of the Baffled Knight. Air in "Northumbrian Minstrelsy." I obtained a very full one of 15 verses,—some in no other copy I have seen, from James Olver. The chorus to each verse was:—

> "O! Blow the winds of the morning, O!
> Blow the winds, heigh-ho!
> And clear away the morning dew,
> Blow the winds, heigh-ho!"

XXVI. **The Hearty Good Fellow.** Taken down, words and music, from Robert Hard, South Brent. Although in the Roxburgh Ballads there is a whole class given up to "Hearty Good Fellows," this ballad does not occur among them. I have, however, a broadside by Pitts, of last century, with it, entitled "Adventures of a Penny." The first verse runs:—

> "Long time I've travelled the north country
> Seeking for good company,
> Good company I always could find,
> But none was pleasing to my mind,
>   Sing whack fal de ral, &c.,
>   I had one penny."

The rest is very much the same as our version.

XXVII. **The Bonny Bunch of Roses.** Of this we have taken down a great number of versions. The melody is everywhere the same, with insignificant variations, and a very fresh and charming air it is. In most of the versions the youth is Napoleon Bonaparte, and wonderful it is to see how the metre is disregarded in order to lug in this name. That history does not agree with what is said in the song matters as little as the discrepancy of the metre. The song is unmistakeably an anti-Jacobite production, adapted at the beginning of this century to Napoleon, when an additional verse was added relative to Moscow. In this later form it issued from Catnach's press, and from him it was copied by Harkness, of Preston; Paul, of Spitalfields; Pitts, of Seven Dials; Williams, of Portsea, &c. In the broadsides of Williams, and of Hodges it is said, "To the tune of The Bunch of Roses, O!" indicating an earlier form of the song. This was a favourite fo'castle song some 40 or 50 years ago.

XXVIII. **The Old Singing Man.** The melody taken down from William Huggins, mason, of Lydford, who died in the Cottage Hospital at Tavistock, in March, 1889. He had been zealously engaged that winter going about among his ancient musical friends collecting old songs for me. The words he gave were— "The little Girl down the Lane," and were of no merit, and much more modern than the air to which he sang them. I have therefore discarded them, and written fresh words, and dedicate them to the memory of poor old Will.

XXIX. **The Tythe Pig.** Words and air taken down from R. Hard, South Brent. It is also well known to the old miller, J. Helmore. The song appears as a broadside, printed by Disley, Jackson, of Birmingham; Harkness, of Preston; Ross, of Newcastle; Catnach, and others. There are 10 verses in the original. I have cut them down to seven. To what air sung elsewhere I do not know.

XXX. **My Ladye's Coach.** This was sung fifty years ago by Anne Bickle, of Bratton Clovelly. The tune, to other words, also by James Parsons. A second melody to it, obtained at South Brent, we give as No. 70, "Broadbury Gibbet." My Ladye is, no doubt, Death personified, the Hela of Norse mythology; but locally supposed to be Lady Howard, daughter and heiress of Sir John Fitz, of Fitzford, Devon, b. 1596, who is supposed to travel nightly from Okehampton Castle to Fitzford Gate, Tavistock, in a coach of bones preceded by a phantom dog. I have added verses 4, 5, and part of 6; there were, however, originally many more, but I have not been able to recover them.

XXXI. **Jan's Courtship.** Words and air from Mr. R. Rowe, Longabrook, Milton Abbott. Another set, words and air, but slightly varied, from W. Crossing, Esq.,

South Brent; another, practically identical, from Mr. Chowen, of Burnville, Brentor; as "Poor Bob," it occurs in "The Universal Songster," n.d., but about 1830. To what tune I have not ascertained. Other tunes to the same words have been sent me. In the Roxburgh Ballads, VI., 216-7, is what is probably the earliest form. "Come hither, my dutiful son, and take good counsel of me." This was sung to the air "Grim King of the Ghosts." Another variant probably is referred to in "Beggars' Opera," Act iii., sc. 8. "Now, Roger, I'll tell thee, because thou'rt my son;" but the melody is not the same as ours. Our air is rugged and early.

XXXII. **The Drowned Lover.** Taken down, words and melody, from James Parsons, air noted down by Rev. H. Fl. Sheppard.

This is a very early song. It first appears as "Captain Digby's Farewell," Roxburgh Ballads, IV., p. 393, printed in 1671. In Playford's "Choice Ayres," 1676, I., p. 10, it was set to music by Mr. Robert Smith. Then it came to be applied to the death of the Earl of Sandwich, after the action in Sole Bay, 1673. A black letter ballad, date circ. 1675, is headed "To the tune of the Earl of Sandwich's Farewell." The original song consisted of three verses only; it became gradually enlarged and somewhat altered, and finally Sam Cowell composed a burlesque song on the same lines, a parody of the original, which has more or less served to corrupt the versions of the old song, since printed on broadsides by Catnach, of Seven Dials, Harkness, of Preston, and others.

The black letter ballad of 1673 begins:—

> "One morning I walked by myself on the shoar
> When the Tempest did cry and the waves they did roar
> Yet the noise of the Winds and the Waters was drownd
> By the pitiful cry, and the sorrowful Sound,
>   Of Ah! Ah! Ah! My Love's dead.
>   There is not a bell,
>   But a Triton's shell,
> To ring, to ring, to ring my Love's Knell."

"Colonel Digby's Lament" begins as follows:—

> "I'll go to my Love, where he lies in the Deep,
> And in my Embrace, my dearest shall sleep,
> When we wake, the kind Dolphins together shall throng,
> And in chariots of shells shall draw us along.
>   Ah! Ah! My love is dead.
>   There was not a bell, But a Triton's shell
>   To ring, to ring out his knell."

The next verse resembles our third. A second version of the melody, but slightly varied from that we give, from old Parsons, was sent me by Mr. H. Whitfeld, of Plymouth, as sung by his father. Our melody is entirely different from that given by Playford, and is probably the older air, which Playford hoped to displace by the more elaborate composition of Mr. R. Smith. What makes this probable is that it is sung to the same air, slightly varied, in Ireland.

XXXIII. **Childe the Hunter.** Words taken from Jonas Coaker, of Post Bridge, aged 82, and blind. He died in the spring of 1890. I am glad to be able to say that through some profits obtained by concerts of these West of England songs, I was able to send the poor old fellow some money, that eased his last days. He had used up the material of this ballad, incorporating it into a "poem" he had composed on Dartmoor, and vastly preferred his own work to what was traditional; but that was natural. The melody given is that to which the Misses Phillips, who were born and reared at Shaw, on Dartmoor, informed me they had heard it sung fifty years ago. It is the air we give an account of as having been received from Mrs. Gibbons to "Cold blows the wind," No. 6. It is unquestionably an early harp tune, not later than the reign of Henry VII. For the story of Childe of Plymstock, see Murray's "Handbook of Devon," Ed. 1887, p. 208; more fully and critically, W. Crossing's "Ancient Crosses of Dartmoor," 1887, p. 51.

XXXIV. **The Cottage Thatched with Straw.** Taken, words and melody, from John Watts, quarryman, Alder, Thrushleton. This is one of the best known, and next to "Widdecombe Fair," most favourite songs of the Devon peasantry. Sung also by one or two old men at Looe, Cornwall. So far we have not been able to trace either words or melody, though neither can be earlier than the beginning of this century.

XXXV. **Cicely Sweet.** Words and air from J. S. Hurrell, Esq., Kingsbridge, who had learned both 50 years ago from Mr. A. Haloran, a Devonshire schoolmaster. It has been published already, as "Sylvia Sweet," in Dale's "Collection," circ. 1790, with two additional verses. Two verses are given by Halliwell as a traditional nursery rhyme, in his Nursery Rhymes, 4th Ed., 1846, p. 223.

XXXVI. **"A Sweet Pretty Maiden."** Melody taken down from James Parsons by Mr. Sheppard. The words of his ballad were very interesting and poetical, the story similar to that of the Scottish ballad "Our young lady's a hunting gone," in Johnson's "Musical Museum," 1787, V., p. 437. Unfortunately, it deals with a topic not advisable to be sung about in the drawing-room. We have, therefore, set to it another song, on the same theme as "Oh for a Husband" in D'Urfey's "Pills to Purge Melancholy," Ed. 1719, p. 56.

XXXVII. **The Green Cockade.** Words and melody from Edmund Fry, thatcher, Lydford, but a native of Lezant, Cornwall. The words of this ballad are sometimes mixed up with those of another that begins "It was one summer morning, as I went o'er the grass," printed as broadside by Keys, of Devonport, and given by Bell in his "Ballads of the English Peasantry," p. 230.

In the "Duke of Gordon's Garland," in a collection of Stray Garlands, B.M. (11621, a. 6) is an Irish form of the ballad. It is there "The Blue Cockade."

"So now my love you've changed
From the Orange to the Blue."

XXXVIII. **The Sailor's Farewell.** Words and music taken from J. Helmore, South Brent. A broadside version by Williams, of Portsea. We have given first the traditional song to its air unaltered, and then an arrangement as a *scena*, as we obtained it from another singer in dialogue form.

This song in full, but in bad metre and rhyme, will be found in a broadside by Wright, of Birmingham, entitled "Lovely Nancy," date circ. 1830.

"Adieu, my lovely Nancy, ten thousand times adieu,
I'm going to cross the ocean to seek for something new
Come, change your ring, my dear, with me,
As that will be a token when I am on the sea.

"When I am on the sea, my love, you know not where I am,
But letters I will write to you all from a foreign land,
With the secrets of my mind, my dear, and the best of my good will,
And let my body be where it may, my heart is with you still," &c., &c.

This is in a collection of Ballads printed in Birmingham B.M. (1876, c., 2).

XXXIX. **The Forsaken Maiden.** Words and melody from James Parsons, noted by Mr. Sheppard. In our opinion, a very delicately beautiful song; tune probably of 16th century. Again heard at Chagford.

XL. **The Blue Kerchief.** Words and air from John Woodrich, blacksmith. The words have appeared with slight variations on broadsides, in ten verses—Catnach, Such, Ross, of Newcastle, &c. Catnach published a parody on it, "The Bonny Blue Jacket." In Dr. Barrett's "English Folk Songs," the air is set to "Paul Jones."

XLI. "An Evening so Clear." Music from poor Will Huggins. His words were:—

> "One evening so clear, in the meadows did pass,
> Her eye full of tear, a beautiful lass.
> The age she did bear, it was scarcely sixteen,
> She around her did wear, a girdle of green.
> Her lips as the rubies, and sparkled her eyes,
> As diamonds precious, or stars in the skies.
> The meadows along, she sang as a dove,
> And all her sad song, was concerning her love."

The ballad was long and uninteresting. Moreover, it is found "As down in the Meadows I chanced to pass, &c.," in the "Musical Miscellany," 1729, I. 62, and Allan Ramsay's "Tea Table Miscellany," 1724, and in "The Merry Musician," II., 129. It goes by the name of "Susan's Complaint," see Chappell, p. 648. Our air is quite distinct, and as "Susan's Complaint" is a melody associated for near two hundred years with these words, I have thought it best to write a fresh copy of verses to go to Will Huggins' tune. "Susan's Complaint" may also be found in a Collection of Garlands in the British Museum, press mark, 11,621, c. 4, Vol. II., No. 74. Curiously enough, Huggins' version was more correct in rhyme; also from J. Peake, Liskeard.

XLII. The Warson Hunt. Words and melody taken down from James Parsons, Edmund Fry, Richard Horne, a miller, and others. A song well-known in the neighbourhood of Lew Trenchard. Of Squire Arthur Kelly, of Kelly, whose hounds were in this memorable run, an epigram was made by a carpenter in Milton Abbott, on the death of the squire in 1823.

> "Here lies my old Tom Cat, I tell'y,
> He died, same day as did Squire Kelly.
> One hunted hares, the t'other rats;
> Squires they must die as well as cats."

XLIII. The Green Bushes. Words and melody taken down from Robert Hard, South Brent. Again to another air from James Parsons. Mr. Crossing sent me the same words to the same air as sung by Parsons, heard by him on Dartmoor, from a labouring man, in 1869.

In Buckstone's play of "The Green Bushes," 1845, Nelly O'Neil sings snatches of this song, one verse "I'll buy you fine petticoats, &c.," in Act I., and that and the following verse in Act III. Nowhere is the complete ballad given. That, however, owing to the popularity of the drama, was published soon after as a "popular Irish ballad sung by Mrs. FitzWilliam, in the drama of 'Green Bushes.'" Later, it was attributed to the husband of that lady, Mr. E. F. FitzWilliam; but it was not published as by him in his lifetime. That Buckstone believed it to be an Irish melody is likely enough, but a good many of the so-called Irish melodies, to English words, are English that have been carried to Ireland by the soldiers quartered there. Thus, the old English "Packington's Pound" has been converted into "The wearing of the Green," and called an Irish air. The words are substantially old, in this form are a softening down of an earlier ballad which has its analogue in Scotland, "My daddie is a cankered carle," each verse of which ends:—

> "For he's low down, he's in the broom
> That's waiting on me."

This is in Grier's Musical Cyclopædia, Glasgow, 1835. The English form is "Whitsun Monday," an early copy of which is to be found in one of the collections in the British Museum, date about 1760. Each verse ends:—

> "And 'tis low down in the broom
> She's waiting there for me."

and the last verse ends:—

> "My dear, said she,
> So farewell to the bonny broom."

This is an undesirable form of the ballad. Broadsides by Such and Disley, the latter different from Buckstone's. In a collection of early ballad books in the British Museum is "The Lady's Evening Book of Pleasure," printed in Cow Lane, n.d., but about 1760. This contains a ballad that begins thus:—

"As I was a walking one morning in May,
I heard a young damsel to sigh and to say,
My love is gone from me, and showed me foul play,
It was down in the meadow, among the green hay."

Again, another—a north country form very distinct—is found in Broadside Ballads.

As I walked through the meads, one morning in May,
Delighted to see the young lambkins at play,
Among the Green Bushes I met a sweet maid,
I saluted (her) kindly, and to her I said,—

I'll give you fine jewels, and I'll give you fine rings
With diamonds so costly, and many fine things
With gowns and silk petticoats flounced to the knee,
"I'll leave father and mother to marry with thee.

"My father's a shepherd, he keeps sheep on yon(der) hill,
And you may go to him and ask his good will;"
In truth I will, lassie, I'll go instantly,
All among those Green Bushes my Jenny meets me.

Good morning, old man, you are tending your flock,
Will you give me a ewe-lamb to breed me a stock?
"Indeed will I, laddie, there up on the lea."
And among the Green Bushes my Jenny meets me.

"O!" says the father, "you have me beguiled,
For little I thought it was my dear child;
But, since it is so, even so let it be."
And among the Green Bushes my Jenny meets me.

To church then they went, without any delay,
Unto her fond lover she would not say Nay,
And he oftentimes sings as she sits on his knee
Among the Green Bushes my Jenny meets (met) me!

This was published by Hodges, of Seven Dials. Ballads, B.M. (1875, b. 19).

Dr. Joyce, in his "Ancient Irish Music," 1873, gives the genuine Irish air to the "Green Bushes," as sung by the peasantry, not the same.

As I do not think the "Green Bushes" can be by Buckstone, nor the melody Irish, I have admitted it into this collection.

XLIV. **The Broken Token.** Words and melody from Robert Hard, South Brent; noted by Rev. H. Fl. Sheppard from his singing. Broadside variant by Such, as "The Brisk Young Sailor," or as "Fair Phœbe," as "The Dark-eyed Sailor," by Wheeler, of Manchester, and as "The Sailor's Return," by Catnach.

Dibdin composed a song on the same theme, and called it "The Broken Gold." The Catnach ballad, to an entirely distinct air, I obtained from Harry Smith at Two Bridges. The broadsides are very rude and corrupt.

The same air was noted down by Mr. S. Reay, about 1830-5, from a ballad singer in the market, at Durham. He has most kindly sent it me. The differences are slight. The air is known throughout Cornwall.

XLV. "**The Rout is Out.**" Words and melody taken down from John Woodrich.

I have a broadside by Bloomer, of Birmingham, circ. 1780, entitled "Lancashire Lads," that is certainly a rude version of the same original. Instead of *his* dressing *her* in "velvet red, and wrangling her hair in blue," *he* "is clothed in scarlet and turned up with blue." The air cannot have been the same. There is no chorus of "Adieu my boys, &c."

XLVI. "**Why should we be dullards sad?**" Words and air from Edmund Fry, Will Huggins, and James Olver, of Launceston, who learned it in 1828, when apprenticed to a tanner at Liskeard, from one George Brooks, the foreman in the tanyard, a native of Grampound, in Cornwall. In 1760, or thereabout, Isaac Bickerstaff wrote a song to this melody for one of his ballad operas. It is found as a copper-plate engraved sheet song, "The Social Powers," about 1765; then in "Calliope," Lond., 1788, p. 278.

XLVII. **May Day Carol.** Melody noted down a good many years ago by J. S. Cayzer, Esq.; was sung, till of late years, in my neighbourhood, where a bunch of flowers at the end of a stick is carried about by children. The history of this carol is curious. It was customary in England, as it is still in Tyrol and in Swabia, for a lover on May morning to take a green bough to the house of the beloved. If she opens the door and takes it in, it is a token of acceptance. At the Puritan epoch, this custom was altered, and the song was converted into a carol with a good deal of pious sentiment added on, and it was given to children to sing. Thus the original significance was completely lost. See "Notes and Queries," 3rd Series, IX., p. 380; also Hone's "Every Day Book," I., p. 567; Chambers' "Book of Days," I., p. 578. Herrick refers to the custom of youths bringing their May bushes to the maids of their choice, when he says:

> "A deale of youth ere this is come
> Back, and with white thorn laden home.
> Some have dispatched their cakes and cream,
> Before that we have left to dream."

In "The Bath Musical Garland," n.d., but about 1745 (B.M. 1162, c. 1., No. 29), is a "Pleasant Dialogue betwixt two lovers, in which the lady presents a bunch of May and some Thyme to her discontented lover." He says:

> "Your riddle I can Read
> . . . .
> This May was took in Time,
> Grant that in *Time* I *May*
> Gain your Love and sweet contentment.'

The melody is a very early one, and is much like that of the carol:

> "The moon shines bright, the stars give light
> A little before the day,"

still sung in Cornwall, and known also in Sussex. Broadwood and Lucas, "Sussex Songs," 1890.

XLVIII. **Nancy.** Taken down from William Friend, of Lydford, James Parsons, and Robert Hard. All had the same melody somewhat varied. As taken from their singing, it had an archaic character:

Mr. Sheppard, who did not take down the tune, considers this form to be due to the way in which the men sang the air, and he has restored it to what he conceives to be the correct form. The words occur in a collection of forty early ballad books in the British Museum, in Book 11., "The Lover's Jubilee," date end of 17th or beginning of the 18th century.

XLIX. **Lullaby.** Noted by me from recollection as sung by a nurse, Anne Bickle, of Bratton Clovelly, about 50 years ago. The tune known also to James Olver, of Launceston. The words I have recomposed to the best of my ability—

partly from recollection. "Hush-a-by baby on the tree top" was also sung to this tune. The air cannot be older than the end of last century. We have treated it in modern fashion.

L. The Gipsy Countess. The melody of the first part from James Parsons, as well as the words, the second melody from John Woodrich. Three more verses in the original I have been unable to admit for lack of room.

The Scottish ballad of "Johnny Faa" first appeared in Allan Ramsay's "Tea Table Miscellany,' 1724, from which it was taken into Herd's and Pinkerton's Collections, Johnson's Museum, and Ritson's Scottish Songs. All these turn on a story —utterly unhistorical—that Lady Jean Hamilton, married to the grim Covenanter, John, Earl of Cassilis, fell in love with, and eloped with, Sir John Faa, of Dunbar, who came to her castle disguised as a gipsy along with some others. She was pursued, and Faa and his companions where hung. I venture to suggest that the Jacobites took an earlier ballad of a gipsy girl married to an Earl, and adapted it to serve as a libel on Lady Cassilis, who was the mother of Bishop Burnet's wife. Such things were done—ballads were utilised for political purposes, and D'Urfey did the same. If this be so, then the existence of the earlier part of the ballad, and the variation in our second part of "Johnny Faa" is explained. Versions also from Peter Cherton, shoemaker, Oakford, near Tiverton; William Setter and George Kerswell, Two Bridges, Dartmoor. But some of these are taken from the broadsides which are reproductions of "Johnny Faa." Mr. Robert Browning composed on this theme his poem "The Flight of the Duchess," having heard a beggar woman sing the ballad. Mrs. Gibbons tells me that as she remembers the ballad as sung by her nurse sixty years ago, it was the story of the girl going back to her brothers. For a very full account of the "Johnny Faa" ballad see Child's "English and Scottish Ballads," No. 200. He is of opinion that the English ballad of the gipsies who carried off the lady is derived from the Scottish. I have no doubt that our broadside versions are so, but in my opinion—whatever it be worth—the Scottish are a re-shaping for political purposes of an earlier ballad, of which our Devonshire Gipsy Countess is a no doubt corrupted version. In Parsons' ballad there was no division into parts. We have separated the parts so as to give both melodies.

LI. The Grey Mare. The melody and a fragment of the song taken down by Mr. Sheppard from J. Hoskin, South Brent. Again from Jas. Olver. Neither knew the song in its complete form, only a verse or a few lines here and there. I have, therefore, had to reconstruct it. A broadside version by Such to a metre that will not fit the air as sung in the West. See Kidson, Trad. Tunes, p. 78.

LII. The Wreck off Scilly. Words and Melody from James Parsons. It properly consists of seven verses. Broadside by Catnach, which ends:—

"'Tis Polly love you must lament
For the loss of your sweetheart,
'Tis the raging seas, the stormy winds,
Caused you and me to part."

But this seems nonsense. The singer does come home, and is not lost. I have ventured to give a different conclusion to the song, having been told by a friend that he heard this ballad sung in Cornwall by a mendicant sailor. The air belongs to the Dibdin era.

LIII. Henry Martyn. Words and melody from Roger Luxton, Halwell. This air noted down by Mr. Sheppard. Again from Matthew Baker, a cripple on Lew Down. Again from J. Masters, Bradstone. Again from a shepherd on Dartmoor. The versions of words somewhat varied, but the melody was always the same. In one the ship had the Lifeguards on board, in another the King's Mariners. In one Henry Martyn received his death wound, in another it is the King's ship which is sunk by the Pirate. Professor Child, editing "The British Ballads," informs me that he has heard a version sung in the U.S.A. by an immigrant, and he called the pirate Andrew Bawbee. The real name was Andrew Barton. In 1476, a Portuguese squadron seized a richly-laden ship commanded by John Barton, in consequence of which letters of reprisal were granted by James IV. to the three sons, Andrew, Robert, and John, and these were renewed in 1506. Hall, in his chronicle under 1511, says that the king (Henry VIII.) being in Leicester, tidings reached him that Andrew Barton so stopped the king's ports, that the merchant vessels could not pass out, and he seized their goods pretending that they were Portuguese. Sir Edward Howard, Lord High Admiral, and Sir Thomas Howard were sent against him. Their two ships were separated, but a fight ensued in which Andrew was wounded, and his vessel, the *Lion*, was taken. He died of his wounds. Buchanan, twenty years later, tells the story also.

There is a long ballad of Sir Andrew Barton, in Percy and elsewhere, quite different. That in Percy is the ballad as recomposed in the reign of James I., when there was a perfect rage for re-writing the old historical ballads. Unhappily, as these new compositions were printed, and the old were not, they have been preserved to the loss of the far finer early ballads. There the Scotch have the advantage of us. What the original form of this ballad was it is hard to say, as it has become sadly altered in process of handing down through three hundred and fifty years. It does not appear in print, that I am aware of, before 1820-30, on a broadside, and that is in a very corrupt form. It is easy to see how Andrew pronounced *Andree* Barton, yet altered into Henry Martyn. The air is probably of Henry VIII.'s reign. See in reference to Sir Andrew Barton, Child's "English and Scottish Ballads." New Ed., No. 167.

LIV. **Plymouth Sound.** Melody taken down from Roger Luxton, to a song of this name. The original words were not only very poor, but somewhat coarse. There are three songs that go by the title of "Plymouth Sound." Broadsides by Keys of Devonport and Such. The air cannot be earlier than the beginning of this century.

LV. **Farewell to Kingsbridge.** Taken down, words and air from Roger Huggins, mason, Lydford, who learned them in 1868, from a man called Kelly, in Tavistock. There are old men in Kingsbridge who can recall when soldiers were stationed there. The song belongs to the year 1778-80. It exists as a broadside by Such, but without naming Kingsbridge, so that probably it was a song of the time adaptable to other places as well. A form of the same ballad, beginning "Honour calls to arms, boys," refers to fighting the French in North America, circ. 1759, published in broadside by Hodges.

LVI. **Furze Bloom.** Taken down from Roger Luxton, of Halwell. The original words of "Gosport Beach" were worthless. Moreover, "Gosport Beach" has its own traditional melody to it elsewhere. I have therefore written fresh words to it, embodying the folk saying in Devon and Cornwall—

"When the Furze is out of bloom,
Then Love is out of tune."

LVII. **The Oxen Ploughing.** This song was well known throughout Devon and Cornwall seventy years ago. It went out of use along with the oxen at the plough. We found every old singing man had heard it in his boyhood, but none could recall more than snatches of the tune and a few of the words. We were for three years on its traces, always disappointed. Those who recalled the strains did not agree as to its metre, and with the metre the strain varied. Then we heard that there was an old man at Liskeard who could sing the song through. Mr. Sheppard and I hastened thither, to find that he had been speechless for three days and that his death was hourly expected. By great good luck, however, we found a labouring man, Joseph Dyer, at S. Mawgan-in-Pyder who could sing the song through. We gladly throw out a joint production of Mr. Sheppard and myself that occupied this place in the first edition, to replace it with this genuine old-folk song.

LVIII. **Something Lacking.** From Thomas Dark, labourer, Holcombe Burnell, age 74. This was most difficult to note, owing to the old fellow changing his key when asked to re-sing it for purpose of notation. I am not satisfied that it is right now.

LIX. **The Simple Ploughboy.** This charming ballad was taken down, words and air, from J. Masters, of Bradstone. Mr. Sheppard noted the melody. The broadside versions that were published by Fortey, Hodges, Taylor of Spitalfields, Ringham of Lincoln, and Pratt of Birmingham, are all very corrupt. The version of old Masters is given exactly as he sung it, and it is but one instance out of several of the superiority of the ballads as handed down traditionally in the country, to those picked up by the ballad-mongers employed in towns by the broadside publishers.

LX. **The Wrestling Match.** Words and air taken down from James Olver of Launceston, Tanner. He said that when he was a boy this was wont to be sung at wrestling matches at Liskeard. Such matches took place every week day evening, from Lady-Day to Michaelmas, in a field, strewn with tan, outside the town.

LXI. **The Painful Plough.** Words and melody from Roger Huggins, mason, Lydford. The air noted down by Mr. Sheppard. It is in reality a much longer song, and consists of 9 or 10 stanzas. Under the title of the "Ploughman's Glory," it runs to 25 verses. Bell gives nine verses in his "Ballads of the English Peasantry." It is found on broadsides. In the original it consists of a contention between the ploughman and the gardener as to which exercises the noblest profession. Our melody, as I am informed by Dr. W. A. Barrett, is not the same as that to which "The Painful Plough" is sung in the Midlands and South-East of England. The earliest copy of the words I know is in a volume of Garlands in the British Museum (1078, p, 16). There it occurs as "The Plowman's Glory" in "The Irish Girl's Garland," Hull, "Printed and sold in the Butchery" and consists of 25 stanzas. Date, I suppose, about 1779. One verse runs:—

> "Three mighty powers in Europe
> Against us do advance,
> Led by the crafty notions of
> That restless Fox of France."

And one concludes with, "Long life to our King, and confusion to his foes by George's sword."

This is, I suspect, a re-writing of "The Farmer's Glory," an earlier song found in "Bonny Jockey's Garland," in a collection made by J. Bell; all printed by J. White, who died 1769, and T. Saint, who died 1788. Here are two verses:—

> "The Parson he doth con his lesson
> And prays for all his congregation.
> But the Devil may take both me and you,
> If he was not upheld by the Plow.

> "So to conclude and end my ditty,
> No tradesman that's in town or city,
> But what will say these lines be true,
> So let us sing to speed the Plow."

As in the same garland is one on Pamela, the date is probably about 1740-5.

LXII. **"Broadbury Gibbet."** This tune was an alternative to that already given (No. 30) for "My Lady's Coach," and was taken down at South Brent by Mr. Sheppard. As the melody was weird and gruesome, and we had no other old ballad that seemed appropriate, I wrote a fresh set of words. The gibbet on Broadbury was standing in 1814, and the beam is still in existence in a barn near the spot. One man was hung on it in chains for at an atrocious murder committed on two sisters. His name was Wellon. He was a stranger passing by the house in which the sisters Rundle lived. He asked for bread and was given it. He returned later to the house, murdered them, and robbed them of £5. He then walked to Ashburton, where over his cups he told of the murder committed at Bratton, before the news had arrived there, and this led to his arrest.

XLIII. **The Orchestra.** The melody taken down from John Woodrich, of Thrushleton. The words began:—

> "I went unto my true love's house
> At eight o'clock at night,
> And little did my true love know,
> I owed her a despite."

It then went on to describe a singularly brutal murder. The words exist in a broadside by Catnach and Such, "The Cruel Miller." The earliest form, however, is in a broadsheet by Pitts, of Seven Dials, "The Berkshire Tragedy, or the Wittam Miller," and this is in 22 verses. It begins:—

> "Young men and maidens give ear
> Unto what I shall relate,
> O mark you well, and you shall hear
> Of my unhappy fate.
> Near famous Oxford town,
> I first did draw my breath, &c."

As the tune clearly did not belong to these words I ventured to write fresh words, and Mr. Bussell has somewhat developed the original melody which was limited to four lines.

LXIV. **The Golden Vanity.** Taken down words and air from James Olver, of Launceston. Melody noted down by Mr. Bussell. This ballad was printed as "Sir Walter Raleigh sailing in the Lowlands, showing how the famous ship called the *Sweet Trinity* was taken by a false galley; and how it was recovered by the craft of a little sea-boy, who sunk the galley," by Coles, Wright, Vere, and Gilbertson (1648—80). In this it is said to be sung "to the tune of the Lowlands of Holland," and in it there is no ingratitude shown to the poor sea-boy. In this version there are fourteen verses. It begins:—

> "Sir Walter Raleigh has built a ship
> In the Netherlands,
> And it is called the Sweet Trinity,
> And was taken by the false Gallaly,
> Sailing in the Lowlands."

It has been reprinted in Ashton: "A century of Ballads," p. 201. Under the form of "The Goulden Vanity," it is given with an air (of no value, and quite unlike ours), in Mrs. Gordon's Memoirs of Christopher North, 1862, ii., p. 317, as sung at a convivial meeting at Lord Robertson's by Mr. P. Fraser, of Edinburgh, before Mr. J. C. Lockhart and Professor Wilson. This begins:—

> "There was a gallant ship,
> And a gallant ship was she,
> Sik iddle dee, and the Lowlands low.
> And she was called the Goulden Vanitie,
> As she sailed to the Lowlands low."

This also is in fourteen verses. The broadside version printed by Such, and Pitts, of Seven Dials, begins:—

> "I have a ship in the North Countrie,
> And she goes by the name of the Golden Vanity;
> I'm afraid she will be taken by some Turkish gallee,
> As she sails on the Lowlands low."

This is in seven verses, and very imperfect. Verse two contains five lines, verse three only three, verses four and six have four lines, verses five and seven have three lines. Consequently it would not be possible to "put a tune to it." Olver's melody is a very fine and striking one. It was adopted with some modernisation that spoiled it by Clifton, in the early part of this century, for his song of "The Oyster Girl." "Sir Walter Raleigh," says Mr. Ebbsworth, in his introduction to this ballad in the Roxburgh Ballads (V., p. 418), "never secured the popularity, the natural affection which was frankly given to Robert Devereux, the Earl of Essex. Raleigh was deemed arrogant, selfish, with the airs of an upstart, insolent to superiors, unconciliating with equals, and heartlessly indifferent to those in a lower position. The subject of the following ballad is fictitious—sheer invention, of course. The selfishness and ingratitude displayed by Raleigh agreed with the current estimate. He certainly had a daughter." The tune to which "The Golden Trinity" was set in the broadsides was "The Sailing in the Lowlands," and must therefore be an older air than the ballad. We obtained the same ballad at Chagford as "The Yellow Golden Tree." Our air is not earlier than the end of last century. To a different tune it was a favourite fo'castle song forty or fifty years ago. We have heard this ballad to the tune we give at Mawgan-in-Pyder.

L.XV. The Bold Dragoon. Words and melody taken down by W. Crossing, Esq., of South Brent, many years ago, from a labouring man on Dartmoor, now dead. The words were very corrupt. I have taken down a fuller version from a man at Huckaby Bridge, Dartmoor, and have discovered an early version, "The Jolly Trooper," in "The Lover's Garland," n.d., but of the beginning or middle of last century. It begins:—

> "There was a Trooper in the *West*
> And with riding he was weary;
> He knocked at, he rapped at,
> And he asked for his kind deary.
>
> . . . . . .
>
> She took the horse by the bridle rein,
> And led him to the stable,
> She gave him corn and hay to eat,
> As much as he was able," &c.

As in the original, in singing, the last two lines were repeated, and the story was very lengthy, I have condensed it, by making each stanza of six lines instead of four. Moreover, as the original was too coarse to be presentable, I have recast it. There is naught about a chimpanzee in the old ballad. The press mark in the British Museum is 11,621, c. 5.

LXVI. Trinity Sunday. Melody noted down by T. S. Cayzer, Esq., in 1849, at Post Bridge, from a moor man; the original words were unsuitable, a broadside ballad of a murder.

This is certainly a fine old dance tune.

To convert it into a three-stanza song instead of six stanzas, a slight liberty has been taken with the tune; the music has been expanded after line four, by the addition of five and six; the original air ends at "all the year."

In connection with this charmingly fresh air, I will give Mr. Cayzer's account of taking it down in 1849, which he has kindly extracted for me from his diary:— "This air, together with 'As Johnny walked out' (No. 11), I got from Dartmoor; nor shall I soon forget the occasion. The scene was a lonely one (I think Two Bridges, but it may have been Post Bridge). It had been raining all day. There was not a book in the house, nor musical instrument of any kind, except two hungry pigs and a baby that was being weaned. Towards nightfall there dropped in several miners and shepherds, and I well remember how the appearance of these Gentiles cheered us. We soon got up a glorious fire—such a fire as peat only can make, and drew the benches and settles round. By the friendly aid of sundry quarts of cyder I, before long, gained the confidence of the whole circle, and got a song from each in turn; and noted down two that were quite new to me: no easy matter, considering that they were performed in a strange mixture of double bass and falsetto. The action with which they accompanied the singing was extremely appropriate. They always sing standing."

Many a similar evening have Mr. Sheppard, Mr. Bussell, and I spent in like manner over the peat fire with the burly, red-faced moor men and shepherds, standing to sing their quaint old songs, and very happy evenings they have been.

LXVII. The Blue Flame. Melody taken down by Mr. W. Crossing, from an old moor man, to "Rosemary Lane." Roger Luxton and James Parsons also sang "Rosemary Lane" to the same air. The words are objectionable. Moreover, in other parts of England, this broadside song is always sung to one particular air. We therefore thought it well to put to our melody entirely fresh words.

It is, or was, a common belief in the West of England, that a soul after death appears as a blue flame; and that a flame comes from the churchyard to the house of one doomed to die, and hovers on the doorstep till the death-doomed expires, when the soul of the deceased is seen returning with the other flame, also as a flame, to the churchyard.

LXVIII. **Strawberry Fair.** Melody taken down from Jas. Masters, of Bradstone, by Mr. Sheppard. The ballad is a recast of "Kytt hath lost her key," given by Dr. Rimbault in his "Little Book of Songs and Ballads gathered from Ancient Music Books," 1851, p. 49; but this was a parody in 1561 of "Kit hath lost her keye (cow)." The song was certainly early, but unsuitable; and I have been constrained to re-write it. The old air was used, in or about 1835, by Beuler, a comic song writer, for his "The Devil and the Hackney Coachman."

"Ben was a Hackney Coachman rare,
Jarvey! Jarvey!—Here I am, your honour."

Beuler composed the words of a good number of songs, and set nearly all to old airs. Thus he wrote "The Steam Coach" to "Bonnets of Blue," "Don Giovanni" to the air of "Billy Taylor," "the Sentimental Costermonger" to "Fly from the World," "Honesty is the best Policy" to the old melody of "The Good Days of Adam and Eve," "Ireland's the nation of Civilization" to the tune of "Paddy O'Carrol," and "The Nervous Family" to "We're a Nodding."

The same thing was done by Hudson, and a score of comic song writers. They took good old tunes and set them to vulgar words, which were, in some cases, no doubt an improvement, for vulgar words are better than those which are obscene. That "Strawberry Fair" is a genuine old melody I have no doubt. The ballad is sung everywhere in Cornwall and Devon to the same melody. The words are certainly not later than the age of Charles II., and are probably older. They turn on a *double entendre* which is quite lost—and fortunately so—to half the old fellows who sing the song. It seems to me impossible to believe that the air should have become dissociated from Beuler's words and attached to very early words of the peculiar metre required. I have never found a singer who had any knowledge of "The Devil and the Hackney Coachman," but all have heard "Strawberry Fair," and some men of 70-80 say they learned it of their fathers. The earliest date of Jacob Beuler's song is 1834, and if what the old singers tell me is true, then certainly Beuler adopted a tune taken from a folk ballad, and did not contribute a tune to folk melody.

LXIX. **The Country Farmer's Son.** Taken down by Rev. H. Fleetwood Sheppard from John Woolrich (not Woodrich), labourer, Broadwood Widger. The original ballad, "The Constant Farmer's Son," is found in a broadside by Ross, of Newcastle. It is a good, robust tune of the end of last century.

LXX. **The Hostess' Daughter.** Taken down by Mr. Sheppard from J. Masters, of Bradstone. The frankness and rudeness of the original words demanded modification before the song was fitted for the drawing room.

LXXI. **The Jolly Goss-hawk.** Melody taken down by Mr. Sheppard from H. Westaway, yeoman, of Belstone. The tune is set to a nonsense counting-song for children, and is then called "The Nawden Song." This begins:—

"I went to my ladye the first of May
A Jolly goss hawk and his wings were grey.
Come let us see who'll win this fair ladye—you or me."

To the 2nd of May is a "two-twitty bird," then "a dushy cock," a "four-legged pig," "five steers," "six boars," "seven cows calving," "eight bulls roaring," "nine cocks crowing," "ten carpenters yawing," "eleven shepherds sawing," "twelve old women scolding." A Scottish version in Chambers' "Popular Rhymes of Scotland," 1842, as "The Yule Days." A Northumbrian version, "The XII. days of Christmas," with air, not like ours, in "Northumbrian Minstrelsy."

A version of this is the "Gousper ou ar Ranad" (the Frogs' Vespers) sung by the peasants of Brittany. "Chansons Populaires de la Basse Bretagne," par Luzel, 1890, p. 94. The West of England song has got mixed up with the "Goss Hawk," another song. The same melody did for both, but one was a nursery song and the other was not. A rather corrupt form of the "Goss Hawk" is to be found in "The Fond Mother's Garland," in a collection of early Garlands in the B. Museum (11,621, c. 5).

LXXII. **"Fair Girl Mind This!"** Taken, words and melody, from James Parsons. He learned this from his father 70 years ago. His father once sang it at a tavern in Plymouth, whither he had driven some cattle for the farmer for whom he worked. Next morning the landlady came to him and said, "Zing me thicky (that) zong again, now do'y, and you shall pay naught for your bed and board." So old Parsons sang the song. "Zing it me again," said the landlady. When he had so done she said, "There now, take what you can carry away in eaten' and drinken,' and welcome, and mind this, never you come to Plymouth again without coming here, and never you come here wi'out zinging thicky zong to me—as long as I be alive."

I have discovered this song in "The Contented Wife's Garland," date about 1730. It is in a collection of early garlands that belonged to Mr. Halliwell, and was acquired in 1832 by the British Museum. It is there as sung by the wife, not the man, and instead of coffee she gets him chocolate. The order of the verses is different, but the number is the same. It begins with our second verse, and the moral which in Parson's version comes first, is thrown in the Garland to the end. The melody is probably the original; it fits the words admirably.

LXXIII. **On a May Morning so Early.** This melody belongs to the song or ballad "I'm Seventeen on Sunday," which is known elsewhere than in Devon and Cornwall. The air was taken down by Mr. Sheppard, from Roger Huggins, at Lydford. Taken down again by Mr. Bussell, from William Bickle, of Bridestowe. Bickle sang it to the broadside ballad, "Seventeen on Sunday," but Huggins' words, as far as they went, were earlier and better. The original ballad was altered by Burns to the "Wakeriffe Mammy," which he re-wrote for Johnson's Museum, IV., p. 410; and Allan Cunningham arranged a song on this topic, as the original was objectionable. Lyle gives it in his "Ballads," 1827, saying: "This ballad, in its original dress at one time, from my recollection, was not only extremely popular, but a great favourite among the young peasantry of the West of Scotland. To suit the times, however, we have been necessitated to throw out the intermediate stanzas, as their freedom would not bear transcription, whilst the 2nd and 3rd have been slightly altered from the recited copy." An Irish version (re-written) to the Irish air, in Joyce: "Ancient Irish Music," 1873, No. 17. He says: "I cannot tell when I learned the air and words of this song, for I have known them as long as my memory can reach back. For several reasons [the original words] could not be presented to the reader." It was not possible for us either to give the ballad in its original form. Mr. Sheppard re-wrote it.

LXXIV. **The Spotted Cow.** Words and air from James Parsons, J. Helmore, H. Smith, and from John Woodrich, Thrushleton, noted down by Mr. Sheppard. The earliest version of the words is found in a Garland of last century, printed by Angus, of Newcastle. Brit. Mus. Garlands (11,621, c. 4), Vol. II., No. 53. There are several later broadside versions by Disley, Such, Dodds, of Newcastle, Keys, of Devonport, &c. As sung, it consists of four lines, and the two last are repeated. To avoid monotony, and to curtail the ballad, I have made each stanza to consist of six lines. The air to which sung everywhere in Devon is different. Dr. W. A. Barrett informs me, from that to which sung elsewhere. About 1760, Dr. Berg set the same song to a recast in Scotch form of the words, so as to transform it into a Scottish song: "As Jamie gang'd blithe his way, along the Banks of Tweed," &c., and so it was sung at Ranelagh. "The Bulfinch," n.d., p. 159.

LXXV. **Cupid, the Plough Boy.** Words and music taken down from J. Watts, Alder quarry, Thrushleton. He sang of "Cubick, the Plough-boy," and made Cubick marry the damsel in the end. Broadside versions, very corrupt, by Catnach, Fortey, &c. The earliest copy is "Cupid, the Pretty Plough-boy," a new song;" no date or place, but about the latter half of last century in the B.M. (1875, b. 19). This ballad is, I believe, a mere recomposition of "Cupid's Triumph," a black letter ballad, circ. 1670, Roxburgh Ballads, IV., p. 13; but this is a sequel to another piece, "Cupid's Courtesy." The air was a Saraband. Perhaps that given by Chappell, p. 497. Barrett's "English Folk Songs," No. 16.

LXXVI. **"Come my Lads, let us be Jolly."** Words and melody from James Olver, of Launceston, and Edmund Fry, of Lydford. Olver acquired it at Liskeard, in 1828, along with "Why should we be dullards sad?" from G. Brooks, of Grampound. Fry had the melody incomplete. Olver knew the whole of it. Barrett's "English Folk Songs," No. 6, as "Sheep-shcering Song;" we have never so heard it used. We have heard it sung also by a hind, J. Hockin, Menheniot, Cornwall, with no reference to a sheep-shearing. We have taken down a notable variant from Samuel Gilbert, Landlord of the Falcon, aged 81, at Mawgan-in-Pyder In that the chorus runs:—

> "Let union be with all its fun,
> And we will join all hearts in one,
> And we'll go through as we've begun,
> Since it 's our holiday."

In this also no reference to a sheep-shearing. Also the air of this chorus differed from ours, as well as from that given by Dr. Barrett. Mr. Gilbert's ran thus:—

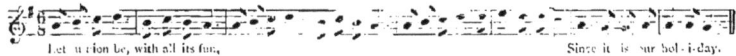

Let union be, with all its fun,   Since it is our hol-i-day.

The verse was the same as our chorus, in common time.

LXXVII. **Poor old Horse.** Words and melody taken from Matthew Baker Lew Down, the melody noted by Mr. Sheppard. This song is given in Bell's "Ballads of the English Peasantry," p. 184, as sung by the mummers in the neighbourhood of Richmond, Yorkshire. He says: "The rustic actor who sings the song is dressed as an old horse, and at the end of every verse the jaws are snapped in chorus. It is a very old composition, and is now (circ. 1864) printed for the first time." This is not so—it exists as a broadside, printed by Hodges, of Seven Dials, and by Such. Our tune, which has not any merit, is not the same as that to which it is sung in the Midlands and Sussex. I differ from Mr. Bell as to the age of the song. I do not fancy it older than the latter half of last century. The Midland air and form of the song in Mason's "Nursery Rhymes and Country Songs," 1877.

LXXVIII. **The Dilly Song.** A great number of versions of this song have been taken down, and a good many were sent to the pages of the *Western Morning News*, in 1888, from various parts of Cornwall and Devon. This is known throughout Cornwall, and is, indeed, still sung in the chapels. When a party of amateurs performed some of these "Songs of the West" in Cornwall, 1890, the Dilly Song always provoked laughter among the good folk at the back of the halls; this puzzled the performers, till they enquired into the reason of the laughter, and learned that folk laughed because it was their familiar chapel hymn. In the text I have given the version of the words with least of the religious element in them. Here are some of the other versions.

2. Is God's own Son, or Christ's natures, but, in a Horrabridge version *two* are the strangers o'er the wide world rangers: another, "the lily white maids" not "babes."

3. The strangers are probably the Three Wise Men. In a Cornish version "Three is all eternity." In another, "Three is the Thrivers."

4. "The Gospel Preachers;" at S. Austell, "The Evangelists."

5. "Five is the Ferryman in the Boat"; at Horrabridge, "The Dillybird;" another, "The Nimble Waiters."

6. "The Cherubim Watchers," "The Crucifix," "The Cherry-bird Waiters." In an American version "The Ploughboys under the Bowl," "The Cheerful Waiters."

7. "The Crown of Heaven," see Rev. i., 16, but more likely the Pleiades, "The Seven Stars in the Sky."

8. "The Great Archangel," "The Archangels;" at Horrabridge, "Eight is the daybreak."

9. "Nine are the Nine Delights," *i.e.*, the Joys of Mary. "The Moonshine, bright and fine," "The Pale Moonshine." "The nine that so bright do shine."

10. "The Commandments." "Begin again."

11. "The Eleven Disciples." "They who go to Heaven."

There are very similar verses in German and Flemish. The Flemish version in Coussemaker: "Chants populaires des Flamands," with three variants of the air, which is a corruption of "Adeste fideles." The Scottish version in Chambers "Popular Rhymes of Scotland," 1842, p. 50. *Dilly*, as applied to the song, the hour, the bird, is probably the Festal Song, &c. (Welsh *dillyn*, pretty, gay, pl. *dillynion*, finerics, jewels.)

Sir Arthur Sullivan has introduced a song of the same character into his "Yeoman of the Guard," but the melody is not quite the same as ours.

The air to which the Dilly Song is sung in Somersetshire is similar to ours, and *is*, in fact, an artistic canon.

This song is very familiar throughout Brittany, as "Gousper ou Kerné," Les Vêpres de Cornouaille.

"Dis moi ce que c'est qu'un ?
Un Dieu, sans plus, qui est au ciel.
Qu'est-ce que c'est que deux ?
Deux testaments.
Les trois Personnes de la Trinité.
Quatre évangélistes," &c.

"Chansons populaires de la Bretagne," par Luzel, 1890, p. 88. Also M. Villemarqué gives two rude melodies (Barz-Breiz, 1846, Nos. I. & VIII.) to which it *is* sung by the Bretons. There was a Mediæval Latin form of the song which began "Unus est Deus." A Hebrew form as one for instructing children in truths, is printed in Mendez: "Service for the First Night of the Passover," London, 1862. It begins: "Who knoweth one? one is God who is over heaven and earth." The numbers go up to thirteen.

"Thirteen divine attributes, twelve tribes, eleven stars, ten commandments, nine months preceding childbirth, eight days preceding circumcision, seven days of the week, six books of the Mischna, five books of the law, four matrons, three patriarchs, two tables of the Covenant, but one is God alone, &c.

A Moravian form in Wenzig: Slawischer Märchenschatz, 1857, p. 295.

LXXIX. The Mallard. A country dance tune, so called because of some silly words that go to it relative to the gobbling up of a Mallard. They begin:—

"Oh what have I ate, and what have I ate?
I have eaten the toe of a Mallard,
Toe and toe, nevins and all,
And I have been to billery allery,
And so good meat was the Mallard."

I have written fresh words to the tune, which is an excellent example of an early dance tune, as the words do not belong properly to the tune. We have had the same sung in Dartmoor, and in Cornwall to entirely different melodies. It was taken from J. Masters, of Bradstone. This also is a song, like the last, and like

The Everlasting Circle (No. 104), and like the Nawden Song (No. 71), common to the Cornish and the peasants of Brittany. The Breton version is "Dispennais ar Voualc'h" (Dépecer le merle), given in "Chants Populaires de la Basse Bretagne," par Luzel, p. 80.

LXXX. **Constant Johnny.** Words and melody taken down from Roger Luxton, of Halwell, the melody noted by Mr. Sheppard. It has been arranged by Mr. Sheppard as perhaps originally set, in duet form, such lovers' duets being a common feature in folk song. Ravenscroft gives one in broad Devonshire in his "Brief Discourse," 1614, entitled "Hodge Trellindle and his Zweethart Malkyn." Our duet seems to be based on "Doubtful Robin or Constant Nanny," printed as a "new ballad," in or about 1680, in black letter; it is given in the 4th Vol. of the Roxburgh Ballads. The tune to that is "Would you be a Man of Fashion," or "The Doubting Virgin."

LXXXI. **The Duke's Hunt.** Words and melody taken down from James Olver, Launceston. I have heard another version at Stoke Gabriel, near Dartmouth; another at S. Mary Tavy, another at Menheniot. This is a mere cento from a long ballad, entitled "The Fox Chase," narrating a hunt by Villiers, Duke of Buckingham, in the reign of James I. Reprinted in Hindley's "Roxburgh Ballads," I., p. 453. It was originally printed by W. Oury, circ. 1650, but probably there was an earlier edition, not now extant. The air, noted down by Mr. Bussell, is very bright and pleasant. None is indicated in the heading of the ballad in 1650, which is merely headed, "To an excellent tune, much in request." It consists of eighteen verses. The dogs in this early and original version are Dido, Spanker, Ruler, Bonny Lass, Caper, Countess, Comely, Famous, Thumper, and Cryer. In it the dog who never looks behind him is Ruler.

The ballad begins:—

"All in a morning fair,
As I rode to take the air,
I heard some to halloo most clearly;
I drew myself near
To listen who they were,
That were going a hunting so early.
I saw there were some gentlemen,
Who belonged to the Duke of Buckingham," &c.

This hunting ballad also occurs in "A Collection of Forty Early Ballad and Song Books," in the British Museum, in the 20th book of that collection. "The Vauxhall Concert," with a print of William and Mary on the title page. Also on a broadside "Dido and Spandigo." Ballads collected by Crampton, B.M. (11,621 h.), Vol. VIII.

LXXXII. **The Bell Ringing.** Words and air from William George Kerswell, a moorland farmer, an old man, near Two Bridges, in the heart of Dartmoor. Broadwood Widger, Ashwater, and North Lew are small villages situated near Broadbury Down, the highest land between Dartmoor and the Atlantic. When sung by the old farmer over a great fire in the kitchen, his clear, robust voice imitating the bells, produced an indescribable charm.

LXXXIII. **A Nutting we will Go.** Taken down from J. Gerrard, aged 68, and nearly blind, a labouring man, illiterate, Cullyton, near Chagford. He knew, however, only the melody of the chorus, the complete tune was taken down by Mr. Sheppard, from Robert Hard, labourer, South Brent, who sang to it a ballad called "Jack of all Trades." The same tune to the "nutting" song at Menhenoit. The same also by James Parsons. Bunting, in his "Irish Melodies," 1840, gives the same tune to a fragment of the same words, and says he took it down in 1792 from Duncan, a harper. Duncan remembered half or a good portion of a tune he had heard, perhaps from English soldiers, and eked it out with some other tune. Then came S. Lover, and he took this air from Bunting, and wrote "The Lowbacked Car" to it. But the original melody is found, not only in Cornwall and Devon, but also in the North, and Mr. Kidson gives it in his "Trad. Tunes" as "With Henry Hunt we'll go," a song sung in Manchester in connection with the arrest of Hunt in 1819. The air was then adapted to this song from "The Battle of Waterloo." When we find the same words to the same air in Ireland and in Cornwall, and in the North of England as well, we may well believe that our tune belonged originally to "A Nutting we will Go." It is probable, therefore, that the air we give is more genuine than "The Low-backed Car" which has become popular, and its inartistic quality and incongruities have been forgiven. There is a broadside version, "The Nut Girl," printed by Fortey, Ryle, &c. See Ballads collected by Crampton, B.M. (11,621, h.), Vol. I., and (1875, b. 19); but these are both without the chorus. The printed broadside has lost somewhat. For instance, Gerrard's

"His voice rang out so clear and stout
It made the horse-bells ring,"

has become

"His voice was so melodious
It made the valleys ring."

But the broadside is longer, it consists of fourteen verses. Neither can be given untoned down, to make the song tolerable for polite ears.

A still earlier broadside version, by Pitts, with chorus.

LXXXIV. **Down by a River-side.** Taken down by Mr. Sheppard from the singing of Jas. Townsend, Holne. It was a song of his grandfather's, who was parish clerk at Holne for fifty years, and died in 1883, over eighty years old.

LXXXV. **The Barley Rakings.** Taken down from Roger Hannaford, of Lower Widdecombe, Dartmoor, by Mr. Sheppard. The words exist in broadside versions, by Such, Bingham, of Lincoln, Robertson, of Wigton, &c. Such's version consist of six verses, the others of four. Hannaford's verses, 2 and 3, were unlike those of Bingham and Robertson, but resembled 3 and 4 of Such. He had not 2 and 6 of Such, and his lines and rhymes were not identical with the London version. Moreover, he had a curious line in verse 2: "They had a mind to *style* and play" (the Anglo-Saxon *styllan*, to leap or dance), not found in the printed copies. As none of these versions would be tolerable in the drawing-room, Mr. Sheppard has modified the words considerably. The melody to which "Barley Rakings" is sung in other parts of England is wholly different, ours is probably an early dance tune.

LXXXVI. **Deep in Love.** This very curious song was obtained by the late Rev. S. M. Walker, of Saint Enoder, Cornwall, from an old man in his parish. Miss Octavia L. Hoare sent it me as preserved by Mr. Walker. We have obtained the same song from Mary Sacherley, aged 75, perfectly illiterate, at Huckaby Bridge, Dartmoor. Mary Sacherley is daughter of an old singing moor man, who was a cripple, on Dartmoor. She possesses the unique distinction of having a house that was built and inhabited in one day. The circumstances are these: Her husband's father had collected granite boulders to erect a cottage on a bit of land that he deemed waste, but a farmer interfered as he began to build. He accordingly had all the stones rolled down hill to a spot by the road side, heaped one on another in rude walls, rough beams thrown across, and covered with turf, and went into the house the same night. In that house his grandchildren are now living.

Two of the stanzas, 3 and 6, are found in the Scotch song, "Wally, Wally, up the bank," "Orpheus Caledonicus," 1733, No. 34; stanzas 4 and 5 in the song in "The Scott's Musical Museum," 1787—1803, VI., p. 582; Herd's "Scottish Songs," 3rd ed., 1791, I., p. 140; part of last stanza is like our conclusion. In "The Wandering Lover's Garland," circ. 1730, are two of the verses worked into an independent ballad, showing that the original is earlier. Again taken down from W. Nichols, of Whitchurch, near Tavistock, it was a song of his grandmother's, who sixty years ago was hostess of the village inn.

LXXXVII. **The Rambling Sailor.** Taken down by Mr. Sheppard from Roger Hannaford, South Widdecombe. A hornpipe tune. There are several broadside versions of this. Originally the song was "The Rambling Soldier," and so appears about the middle or latter end of last century. Then some poetaster of Catnach's re-wrote it as "The Rambling Sailor," destroying all the wit and point of the original; which wit and point, by the way, were characteristic of the age; but as in the West it is set to a hornpipe, we have retained the song as one of a sailor, only modifying the words where objectionable. The "Rambling Soldier," the early copy I have seen, is in the possession of Dr. Barrett; a later copy, circ. 1820, by Whiting, of Birmingham. Ballads, B.M. (1876, e. 2). The "Rambling Sailor," by Disley, circ. 1830; Ballads collected by Crampton, B.M. (11,621, h.), Vol. VIII.

LXXXVIII. **A Single and a Married Life.** Taken down from Henry Bickle, of Bridestowe. This belongs to the class of dialogue Ballads, of which the best known is "The Husbandman and the Serving Man." We have not been able to trace this anywhere so far. But that is no reason why we should not yet light on it somewhere.

LXXXIX. **Midsummer Carol.** Taken down from Will. Aggett, an old crippled labourer, very illiterate, at Changford; melody noted by Mr. Bussell. A very early and curious melody of the same date as that to the "May Day Carol," No. 47; and the words belong to a similar custom. This has not been moralised as has been the "May Day Carol," by the Puritans.

XC. **The Blackbird.** The melody taken down twice by Mr. Sheppard, first from James Parsons, secondly from Roger Hannaford. From Parsons we got but one verse, that with which we begin; but from Hannaford we recovered the entire ballad, that begins thus:—

1. "Three pretty maidens a-milking did go,
Three pretty maids a-milking did go,
When the wind it did blow high,
And the wind it did blow low,
And it tossed their milking pails to and fro.

Then she met with a man that she did know,
O she met with a man that she did know,
And she ask'd have you skill?
And she ask'd have you the will?
To catch me a small bird or two."

Then comes the verse on the blackbird; and two additional verses, not desirable. The same ballad in Lyle's Collection, 1827, "from recollection; air plaintive and pastoral." It is a curious song, as one does not well see what connexion the first verse with the three milkmaids has with the rest, which concerns only one. This is one of the many old English songs which have found their way into Scotland on one side, and into Cornwall on the other. A broadside version of this ballad in nine stanzas, printed by Williamson, of Newcastle. In this, the last verse begins:

"So here's a health to the bird in the bush,
Likewise to the linnet and the thrush," &c.

In order to preserve the charming old air it was necessary to write another ballad, preserving only one verse of the original.

XCI. **The Green Bed.** Taken down from J. Masters, Bradstone, melody noted by Mr. Sheppard. The same melody set to the "Outlandish Knight," sung by Richard Gregory at Two Bridges, Dartmoor; he imported into the air a phrase from the "British Grenadier." The "Green Bed" exists as a broadside in six double verses. Mr. Sheppard has re-written the ballad, as the original was poor, condensing the story into somewhat shorter space. The air somewhat resembles "The girl I left behind me."

XCII. **The Loyal Lover.** Taken down from Mary Sacherley, Huckaby Bridge, and Anne Roberts, Scobbetor, Widdecombe. Mr. Bussell had infinite labour with this air, which we had first from Mary Sacherley, an old illiterate woman, born and bred on the moor, and daughter of a very famous old song-man. She sang it to an interminable ballad, "The Lady and the Apprentice," and never sang two verses alike. Four or five variations were taken from her lips, with much trouble, as she sang quickly, and could not be checked to suit the requirements of the notator. However, we got the same melody afterwards from Mrs. Anne Roberts, now in Widdecome, but formerly of Post Bridge in the heart of the moor; she sang with perfect precision and always the same.

The words exist in part in "Colin and Phœbe's Garland" (B.M., 11,621, c. 5), but this has only two verses.

XCIII. **The Streams of Nantsian.** Taken down from Mathew Baker, a cripple, aged 72, who can neither read nor write, Lew Trenchard. Music noted down by Mr. Sheppard. Again from James Olver, Launceston, and from Matthew Ford, shoemaker, Menheniot, practically the same melody. This song is "The Streams of lovely Nancy," of the broadsides. It was printed about 1830 by Keys of Devonport, with four verses, of which verse three had naught to do with the song. And in many broadside versions the short original, consisting of four verses only, is swelled out with scraps from other ballads, perfectly recognisable, and merely put in by the printer to fill up the available space. The Nancy of the broadsides is Nant—(something or other). Nant or Nan is firstly a falling stream, and then secondly a valley or glen. Nankivell is the Horse-vale, Nanteglos the church-dale, Nanvean is the small vale; there are hundreds of dales and streams with names beginning Nan or Nant, in Cornwall. Devon is Dyfneint, the Deep Vales.

XCIV. **The Drunken Maidens.** Taken down from Edmund Fry, Lydford. Melody noted by Mr. Bussell. This is an old ballad; it is found in "Charming Phillis' Garland," circ. 1710. A Breton version, given by Luzel, "Merc'hed Caudan."

XCV. **Tobacco is an Indian Weed.** This is an old and famous song, originally written, it is conjectured, by George Withers, as Mr. Collier found a copy of it in a MS. of the date of James I. with his initials to it. Previous to this discovery, it was attributed to Ralph Erskine, who died in 1752. It is found in "Merry Drollery Complete," 1670, and on a broadside dated 1672. We give the tune to which it is sung traditionally all round Dartmoor and in Cornwall, and Mr. Sheppard has arranged it in canon form; but it is entirely distinct from that to which it is sung elsewhere, as printed by Chappell, II., 564, which is the air given by D'Urfey in his "Pills to purge Melancholy," 1719.

XCVI. **Fair Susan Slumbered.** Music taken down from George Cole, quarryman, aged 76, Rundlestone, Dartmoor. The music was noted by Mr. Sheppard. The words were too utterly worthless to be given here, and Mr. Sheppard has written a fresh copy of verses to the melody. The original words are found in "The Vocal Library," London, 1822; No. 1,421, "As a fair maid walked."

XCVII. **The False Lover.** Words and music taken down from old Mary Sacherley by Mr. Sheppard. Such, among his broadsides, has two versions of it. The earliest begins "I courted a bonny lass on a rainy day," and is in 7 stanzas. It is No. 49. The other, No. 592, is a modern re-writing of the old theme.

XCVIII. **Barley Straw.** Taken down from the singing of Mr. G. H. Hurell, the blind organist at Chagford, as he heard it sung by a carpenter, William Beare, some fifteen years ago. The words were very vulgar, and consequently Mr. Sheppard has re-written the song. The air is of a robust character, and was better than the words. The air was used by A. S. Rich, without some of the most characteristic passages, for Hunneman's comic "Old King Cole," pub. circ. 1830.

XCIX. **Death and the Lady.** Taken down from Roger Hannaford, South Widdecombe. Melody noted by Mr. Sheppard. The words were also sent by Captain Hale Monro, of Ingesdon House, Newton Abbot, as sung by an old man there. This is quite different from the "Dialogue of Death and the Lady," found in black letter broadsides, and given by Bell in his "Songs of the English Peasantry," p. 32. The tune to this latter is given by Chappell, I., 167. In Carey's "Musical Century," 1738, is given the air of "Death and the Lady," and as "an old tune." But this melody and ours have nothing in common.

C. **Adam and Eve.** This charming old song is a favourite with the peasantry throughout England, and is sung in Yorkshire and in Sussex, in Gloucester and the Midlands, to the same melody. Taken down by Mr. Sheppard from John Rickards, Lamerton. The words are printed in Bell's "Songs of the English Peasantry," p. 231. He says, "We have had considerable trouble in procuring a copy of the old song, which used, in former days, to be very popular with aged people resident in the North of England. It has been long out of print, and handed down traditionally. By the kindness, however, of Mr. S. Swindells, printer, Manchester, we have been favoured with an ancient printed copy." In the original the song consists of 10 verses. The earliest copy of it I know is in "The Lady's Evening Book of Pleasure," printed in Cow Lane, London, about 1740. It will be found in a collection of early Garlands and Ballad Books in the Brit. Mus., made by Mr. J. Bell about 1812, and called by him "The Eleemosynary Emporium." This air is first found in "Vocal Music, or the Songster's Companion," 2nd ed., 1772, to the song, "Farewell, ye green fields and sweet groves," p. 92. Then it was taken into "The Tragedy of Tragedies, or Tom Thumb," as the air to "In hurry post-haste for a license," and was attributed to Dr. Arne. In "Die Familie Mendelsohn," Vol. 2, is a scrap by Felix Mendelsohn, dated Leipzig 16th August, 1840, which is identical with the first four bars of this melody.

CI. **I Rode my Little Horse.** Taken down from Edmund Fry, of Lydford, but the tune was faulty. We afterwards obtained it complete and correct from John Bennett, a labourer, aged 67, at Chagford. This ballad runs on the same lines as "Jolly Roger Twangdillo," by D'Urfey. Can it not be, substantially, the original, which he re-wrote in or about 1700?

CII. **The Saucy Ploughboy.** Melody taken down from Will. Setter, labourer, Two Bridges, Dartmoor. The words he sang to this tune began:—

"As I went down to Salisbury,
'Twas on a market day.
By chance I met a fair pretty maid,
By chance all on the way.
Her business it to market was,
With butter, eggs, and whey.
So we both jog on together, my boys,
With Derry-down weeday."

But, for very sufficient reasons, we could not employ the words.

CIII. **I'll build myself a gallant Ship.** In our first edition we gave the Devonshire form of "The Lowlands of Holland," setting it to a second melody we had taken down for "The Bold Dragoon." But the accent not agreeing satisfactorily with that of the music, I have been compelled to very slightly alter the words so as to agree with the music.

The air was taken down by Mr. Bussell from Richard Cleave, at "The Forest Inn," Huckaby Bridge. Never shall I forget the occasion. Mr. Bussell and I drove across Dartmoor in winter in a furious gale of rain and wind, to Huckaby Bridge, in quest of an old man we had heard of there as a singer. We found the fellow, but he yielded nothing, and our long journey would have been fruitless had we not caught Richard Cleave and obtained from him this air which cost me a bronchitis attack, that held me a prisoner for six weeks.

CIV. **The Everlasting Circle.** A widely-known song in Devon. A version taken down from J. Woodrich, another from Will. Setter, Two Bridges; but the best from "Old Capul," i.e., William Nankivell, an aged quarryman, who for years lived under Roos Tor, on the River Walla above Merrivale Bridge, absolutely illiterate, but with a memory laden with old songs. This same song is sung by the Breton peasants. It is called in Brittany "Ar parc caer" (The fair field). Luzel: "Chans. pop. de la Basse Bretagne," 66. In the variants we have taken down, the latter part differs. That of Nankivell, is:—

"And out of the baby there grew a fine lawyer, &c."
"And then from the lawyer there came a fine parson, &c."
"And out of the parson there sprang a black devil."

Music noted down by Mr. Bussell. A copy of it in broadside. "The Tree in the Wood," printed by Pitts, of Seven Dials, in my possession. This begins:—

"There was a tree grew in a wood,
A dainty curious tree,
For the tree was in the wood,
And the wood was down in the valleys low."

Another Devon version with air in Mason's "Nursery Rhymes and Country Songs," 1877. M. Kidson tells me he has heard the song sung at Oxford to "Le Petit Tambour," with an ending tacked on from "Rule Britannia."

CV. **All in a Garden.** Taken down from Harry Smith, Two Bridges, Dartmoor. Melody noted by Mr. Sheppard. The words follow so closely on "The Broken Token" (No. 44), that we have thought it advisable to give the melody a fresh copy of verses. The original began, "As Polly walked into her garden."

CVI. **Hunting the Hare.** An old country dance, taken down from "Old Capul." The melody noted by Mr. Bussell. Date of the air the begining of the 17th century.

CVII. **Dead Maid's Land.** Taken down from Joseph Paddon, Holcombe Burnell, but he sang the words to the air we have used to No. 108. The first three verses were "I Sowed the Seeds"; then he branched off into what I give. Compare with this the Scottish ballad, "The Gardener," in Child's "English and Scottish Popular Ballads," Pt. VII., No. 219, but the ballad has an entirely different ending. We have set therefore to it an air taken down from Anne Roberts, of Scobbetor, Widdecombe-in-the-Moor. In the major this is a massive hymn-tune.

CVIII. **"Shower and Sunshine."** Air taken down from Joseph Paddon, Holcombe Burnell, N. Devon. New words; the original bear a certain resemblance to "I Sowed the Seeds of Love," and yet differ considerably from it. The melody is the old English air "I Sowed the Seeds of Love," in Chappell, II., 522, and is interesting as a local variant. A Scottish variant is given by Alexander Campbell, in "Albyn's Anthology," 1816, I., p. 40. The Irish in Joyce's "Ancient Irish Music," No. 74.

CIX. **Haymaking Song.** This quaint old carol-like song was taken down first from J. Woodrich. The song was his father's; Woodrich learned it of him about 1850, and he says it was his father's favourite song. We then got it again from J. Parsons. The air belongs to the same date as the May Day Carol. Woodrich could not recall the first stanza, and knew only one or two complete, the rest in fragmentary state. Not till after I had recomposed the fragments did I detect the ballad in "West Country Garlands," cir. 1760 (B.M., 11,621, b. 11), and among the broadsheets of Pitts, about the end of last century. It begins "In the merry month of June." But this is the title of a well-known old English ballad air, different from ours. Moreover, Woodrich's air did not fit the printed words, and I did not like to alter the latter to fit his melody, as the printed ballad went to the air of its initial words. "In the merry month of June" will be found in "The Beggar's Wedding," 1729, air 22.

CX. **Bibberly Town.** Melody taken down from John Bennett, Chagford, labourer, aged 68. Dr. Barrett, to whom I showed the air, believed it to be a variant of "Moll in the Wad," to which, about 1828, Mr. H. Williams set his song of "Sarah Syke," beginning:—

"To me, said Mother, t'other day,
Why Giles you seem to pine away," &c.

Mr. Sheppard and I have compared the tunes, but fail to trace the likeness, as far as we can judge, they are both ¾ time, and there the resemblance begins and ends. The words, as sung, were vulgar, the point being that the tinker kisses all the girls he meets and they pay him with "guineas of gold" for his kisses, and he drinks the guineas away in the tavern. Mr. Sheppard has written fresh words to the ballad. The "Bibberly Town" is, on the broadside copies, "Beverley Town." As we have altered the words, we have thought it well not to take the title, "Beverley Town," that belongs to the original ballad as in print. When we have re-written a ballad, it has been to rescue the melody from being lost. Many an old melody, associated with undesirable words, was saved by Burns, Ramsay, Cunningham, &c., from disappearance by their writing good words to the old tunes. The grossness of the words to which it was associated drove it into the background — drove it out of memory altogether among decent people. We have not had among us such kings and queens of song writing as Burns, Ramsay, Hogg, Tannahill, Baroness Nairne, Lady Anne Barnard, &c., to give the old airs a new spell of life by associating them to imperishable words. We have not re-written words unless there were good cause. Many an old ballad is coarse, and many a broadside ballad is commonplace. Songs that were thought witty in the Elizabethan and Caroline epochs, are no longer sufferable; and broadside ballads are in many cases vulgarised versions of earlier ballads lost in their original forms. Two courses lay open to us. One is that adopted by Dr. Barrett and Mr. Kidson, to print the words exactly as given on the broadsides, with asterisks for the undesirable stanzas. There is a good deal to be said for this course.

On the other hand, there is that adopted by the Scottish and Irish collectors, to re-write and modify where objectionable or commonplace. This has been the course we have adopted. It seemed to me a pity to consign the lovely old melodies to the antiquarian's library, by publishing them with words which were quite fatal to the success of the songs in the drawing-room or the concert-hall. And be it observed some of the best airs were linked to the worst words, not always gross, but utterly commonplace. We resolved, where the old words were good, or tolerable, to retain them intact. When bad, to re-write, adhering as closely as possible to the original. Where the songs were mere broadside ballads we have had no scruple in doing this, for we give reference to the pressmark in the British Museum, where the broadside may be found, or give the number of Mr. Such's series, so that anyone interested may purchase it for a halfpenny. When, however, the ballad or song seemed to be traditional, and not taken from a broadside, then we have printed it as truly as we could, and if we have supplied a hiatus, we frankly say so.

No two singers give the same ballad exactly alike, the variations are sometimes so great that we suspect they are reproductions by local poets of the old themes. A striking instance of this is "The Masterpiece of Love Songs," that was printed about 1670; and has been reproduced by Mr. Ashton, in his "Century of Ballads." I have taken down one form of this, tolerably like the earliest printed form. It exists as a modern broadside in another. Mr. R. N. Worth has sent me another taken down from an old man of 87 quite different, and I have had a fourth also different from another singer.

No topic is more dear to the bucolic mind than that of the young lady who follows her lover to sea, or in the ranks, in male costume. The earliest form of the first of these is perhaps "The Simple Ploughboy," No. 49. The same story has been re-written and re-written again and again, and reappears in a score of forms, the last of which is the fo'castle song of "In Causand Bay Lying."

In conclusion, I may say, in the words of an old song in D'Urfey's "Pills," and in "The Aviary," circ. 1730:—

"Come buy my (old) Ballad
I have in my Wallet.
But 'twill not I fear please every Pallate.
Then mark what ensu'th,
I swear by my youth,
That every Line in my Ballads is Truth:
A Ballad of Wit, a brave Ballad of Worth,
'Tis newly printed, and newly come forth."

S. BARING-GOULD.

LEW TRENCHARD, N. DEVON, *July*, 1891.

ON THE MELODIES OF SONGS OF THE WEST.

By H. FLEETWOOD SHEPPARD.

Of the hundred and ten melodies in this volume, about a dozen are found to have been already published. A few more may yet be identified with tunes known elsewhere, but the bulk can fairly claim to be regarded as traditional tunes of the West of England, and specially of Devonshire.

No account can be given of the origin of folk-songs in England or abroad. It has no history. We know that in Greece the reapers and the sowers, the weavers and herdsmen, the millers and wool-carders, had their distinctive songs; that Britain was a song-loving country before the time of Bede; that in the 13th and 14th centuries the troubadours in France, and the minnesingers in Germany, greatly promoted the spread of song; that Scandinavia has an extensive ballad literature unexplored; that we owe to the Celtic race the preservation of the song-relics of Bards, Scalds, and Minstrels, and that the legitimate successors of these have been the ballad-singers of the last three centuries: all this we know, but of the earliest history of the people's music we know nothing. Only it is certain that, whilst music was being painfully developed as an art, or elaborated as a science, the uneducated of all countries were carolling their songs as freely as the birds; and that their traditional melodies are regarded by authorities, almost without exception, as the productions of untaught composers, singing, as it were, by inspiration.

Why should not this be so? Melody is not a progressive art, nor is any scientific knowledge of music necessary for the production of tunes both striking and touching. We see this in the early hymn-tunes of the Church, which, notwithstanding their strange form, are often full of beauty and expression, and instinct with that devotional feeling which no scientific knowledge can give. Yet these old tunes are no remains of any cultivated musical age: they are simply the inartistic efforts of devout minds to express religious emotions in song.

The same thing happens elsewhere. In many an ancient village church we find attempts at architectural ornament, in which some native genius has striven to embody his idea of the beautiful. Rude though the work may be, it yet reveals the artistic mind. Artistic knowledge may be lacking, but the feeling is there, and asserts itself. So in painting. If the dawning genius of Opie and Reynolds had unhappily been neglected, it would have asserted itself, and served art after its own fashion. Or, in music, if little John Davy, who, at six years old, purloined the friendly smith's horseshoes to make a peal of bells, had never been apprenticed to "Mr. Jackson of Exeter," his gift of melody would not have withered away; he would still have invented charming tunes, picking them out on his horseshoes, or warbling them without premeditation. So it may have been with tunes in this book. I see no reason for doubting that they are, in the main, native productions, or that in other parts of the country may be made similar collections of what are really the true folk-songs of England.

Many no doubt think otherwise. M. Loquin, for instance, maintains that in France there are no such things as folk-songs originating with the people; but that what are so-called are invariably relics of an age of musical culture. It may be so in France. The songs of Adam de la Hale, or de Machault, or Deprés can hardly ever have been popular, but we may seek for inspiration lower down. The Ballard family, who held the sole patent for printing music in France from 1550 to the Revolution, published hundreds of *Chansons pour boire et pour danser*, and these may have leavened the popular music just as Playford's

Dancing Master leavened it in England, as Chappell abundantly shows. But the compositions of our own cultured song-writers had no such influence. You may turn over the pages of scores of collections of songs, printed in the last century, without finding any trace of such tunes as we have brought together in the following pages. These have a strong local flavour and a natural simplicity which are wholly wanting in the printed collections. M. de Coussemaker observes the same thing in the folk-songs of Flanders. He says "Our Flemish melodies are none the less freely original; that is to say, native to the country and the offspring of spontaneous inspiration." Nor can one look into the folk-songs of other countries, Sweden for example, without perceiving that their structure, rudeness, and tonality betray no signs of a cultivated musical origin. What musical culture within reach of the people was there before the thirteenth century? And yet there is a great mass of religious music far older than that. Whence came the earlier Church hymns? Many of them were no doubt spontaneous inspirations, and why should it not have been the same with secular melodies, and in a later age?

In these Songs of the West there are specimens of tunes composed by the men who sang them.* They are not the most original certainly, but what one man does indifferently another with greater but equally untrained gifts may do well. All originality is not equal. To say that ploughmen could not originate melodies is a mere assumption. Ploughmen have produced poetry, why not music? Burns was a ploughman, Clare a farm lad, Bloomfield a shoemaker, Tannahill a weaver; they cultivated their gifts, but the gift was there. People do not postpone using their gifts until they have cultivated them any more than they postpone using their legs until they have learned to walk. I know a sweet singer who composed songs before she had learned a note of music. At seven years old a book of children's poems was put into her hands and she immediately began to sing them, making her own melodies as she went along. I took down one of these tunes, fresh from her childish inspiration, and here it is, as pretty a little child's song as one need wish for.

See, see how the i-ces are melt-ing a-way, The riv-er has burst from its chain; The woods and the hedges with ver-dure look gay, And dai-sies en-am-el the plain!

It is quite conceivable that some of our West Country airs may have had a similar though not so juvenile an origin. But there is no longer the same call for the exercise of the faculty. The article is evolved by machinery, turned out by the thousand, and the world, rural as well as urban, is deluged with songs good, bad and very indifferent. No real folk-songs have been produced in the present century. The popular ditties of the day are imposed upon the people, but do not spring from them. The ballad maker's, no less than the ballad singer's, occupation is gone; and in a very short time the ballads themselves will be gone also.

The dates of these songs can no more be decided than can their origin. They defy chronology. Old tunes are not always quaint, nor graceful ones always new. Here is a tune which we might set down as a dance-tune of the 18th century:

* We met with one Dartmoor minstrel who sang to us a composition of his own, both words and music; unhappily we could make nor head nor tail of either. As a rule authorship is not confessed unless the production be approved.

whereas it is really a hymn - tune of 500 years earlier, extant in a 13th century MS. Assertion, therefore, is hazardous; but we may classify the songs in the different styles to which they apparently belong. We have heard them of all styles. Songs with an archaic ring in them, of the ancient church modes, and as old as the Wars of the Roses, or older (4, 47, 53, 73); common-metre ballad tunes of the 16th century (33, 108); songs of the Elizabethan era, with a quasi-madrigalian flavour about them (28, 78); songs of a didactic turn, of the early Stuart times (89, 107); Puritan songs of the Commonwealth (9); jovial songs of the roystering Restoration days (5, 26, 68); tripping tunes, such as might have come out of Playford's *Dancing Master* (59, 79); hunting and hornpipe tunes of the last century (91, 106); songs of seafaring and shipwreck (38, 48, 52); songs of country life (83, 86, 98); of ploughing and reaping (61, 69); of haytime and harvest (19, 109); of wrestling and bell-ringing (60, 82); of humour, satire, sentiment, drinking, dancing, poaching, and love-making: all sorts and conditions of songs (except religious songs, which did not survive the Reformation) had their place in the memories of our old singers. And so had many more which had no pretence of being traditional: songs of the Hook, Reeve, and Dibdin school; of the Volunteer epoch; of Bishop and Braham's day; of the London streets fifty years ago; mock-rustic and dialect songs, down to songs of the present music-hall and Christy Minstrel type; all were offered as genuine wares for our acceptance, demanding some discretion, lest, instead of preserving local and traditional melodies, we should be merely reproducing music of widely different origin, written to sell, and imported in the way of trade. For no reliance was to be placed on the statements of the singers. The song which an old man of four-score firmly believed that he learned at his mother's knee in his early childhood, proved to be the composition of a well-known London writer thirty years later; and the genuine Devonshire ballad, vouched for as the production of a talented friend forty years ago, was found to be one of Dibdin's, sixty years earlier; and so we came, by degrees, to recognise the professional type, and to learn that songs with too much regularity in the tune, and too much point in the words, were never the genuine ditties of Arcadia.

The Devonshire songs, with all their merits, do not present any strongly-marked melodic peculiarities or features. Less harsh than the northern, less bold than the Welsh tunes, their affinity is rather with those of Ireland; but their character is that of English music, though with a grace and softness which indicates their Celtic vein. Such songs as 31 or 110 should, perhaps, be transferred to Somersetshire; their roughness is foreign to the more western county, whereas such tunes as 39, 70, 84, 93, 96, seem plainly native to it.

As a characteristic song "The Bell Ringing" (82) may be cited. There is an indolent easy grace about this tune which is quite in keeping with the words and charmingly suggestive. The sunny valleys, the breezy downs, the sweet bell-music swelling and sinking on the soft autumn air, the old folk creeping out of their chimney-nooks to listen, and all employment in the little town suspended in the popular excitement at the contest for the hat laced with gold; all this, told in a few words and illustrated by a few notes, quite calls up a picture of Devonshire life, and stamps the song as genuine. The narrator is unhappily slightly intoxicated, but no one thinks the worse of him: stern morality on that or any other score will in vain be looked for in Songs of the West. This very easy morality is perhaps one reason why the younger generation of singers takes no care, nor shows any readiness to hand down the songs which delighted our forefathers. Public opinion will not now tolerate the coarse humour, and coarser sentiment of the 17th and 18th centuries; and, although we may lament the loss of the tunes, the singers who eschew these songs are more to be praised for their good ethical sense than blamed for their bad musical taste.

Gold-laced hats went out of fashion a full hundred years ago. After that date folk-songs cease to be traditional, and lose their interest. The influx of London publications muddied the stream, and to find it pure we must remount higher up. But *very* old songs can hardly be expected to have a local or even national character. Whether we take those of Sweden or Portugal, Flanders or Ireland (before Moore tampered with them) we find them all associated with the Church modes. The ancient scales may be so frequently discovered in the following songs, that it will be as well to point out how they may be recognised. It is easy enough. On the pianoforte, from D to D, *using only the white notes*, is the scale of the Dorian mode; E to E that of the Phrygian; F to F of the Lydian; and G to G of the Mixolydian. Others there are, but these suffice for the purpose. Their peculiarity is, that in each scale the semi-tones occur in different positions, so that no two scales are precisely alike. The Dorian mode may be traced in 47, 73; the Phrygian in 4, 67; the Lydian does not appear, but the Mixolydian is very common, although we have given no example of it. But here is one taken down on Dartmoor. It will be observed that although apparently in the modern key of G, it has ♮F all through.

SONG IN THE MIXOLYDIAN MODE.

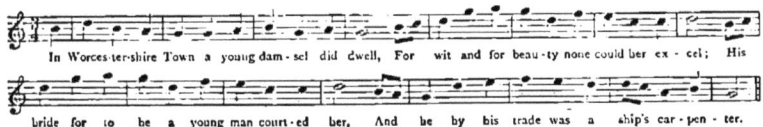

In Worces-ter-shire Town a young dam-sel did dwell, For wit and for beau-ty none could her ex-cel; His bride for to be a young man court-ed her, And he by his trade was a ship's car-pen-ter.

If the last line be played with F♯ instead of F♮, it will at once be evident that the tune does not belong to our key of G major, but that the flat seventh is intentional. So again in the following tune in the same mode:—

I was brought up at Ex-e-ter, The place right well know I— Brought up of hon-est pa-rents, And reared right ten-der-ly, Till I be-came a rov-ing blade, Which proved my des-ti-ny.

This use of the minor seventh, awkward as it may seem to us, finds favour everywhere with rural singers. The late Sir G. Macfarren laid it down* that "the demand of the natural ear is for a semi-tone between the leading note and the tonic, instead of the gross rough major second that lies between the 7th and 8th degrees of some of the Church modes;" and further, "that in melodies preserved by oral tradition, this note is always altered from what we find in early written copies;" *i.e.*, altered from a tone to a semi-tone. With all respect to so great an authority, experience teaches just the opposite: that it is the tendency of untaught singers to change the semitone into a whole tone. I believe that the natural uneducated ear prefers the "gross rough major second." There is an instance of it in the West Riding people. The hymn "Christians Awake" (H. A. M. 61) may almost be called their national hymn. All Christmas-tide it is sung in every church, chapel, or meeting-house, and in every home in every village. It is played by every itinerant band, and sung by every company of carollers or mummers. At line 4, bar 2 of this tune occurs an A♯ leading to the chord of B minor; and wherever this hymn is sung without accompaniment, the gross major second is *always* substituted for the semi-tone. I have noticed it for over thirty years, and the use is becoming traditional. That the effect of this interval is not always disagreeable will be evident to all who sing Molloy's pretty song, "The Clang of the Wooden Shoon."

Other peculiarities connected with the Church modes, such as tunes beginning in one key and ending in another; in major and relative minor (51); or *vice versâ* (99); modulation into unrelated keys (2, 53); endings on the dominant, or 4th or 2nd of the scale (102), are often regarded as mistakes of the singers, whereas they are often marks of antiquity, and found in the folk-songs of all nations. But *variations* of tunes are frequently due to the errors of singers, and possibly to their vanity. There is a curious instance in the well-known song "I sowed the seeds of Love." The

---

* Lectures on Harmony, 1877, p. 40.

Midland county form of the melody is given in Chappell; the Northern form in Northumbrian Minstrelsy; and the Western form in the present volume (108). The three versions are here contrasted: the Devonshire form being reduced to common time for the sake of comparison, and the extension of bar 10 (*vide* song 108) being restricted to the flourish which no doubt it originally was.

The identity of the tune is clear enough, but the variations could hardly be greater. In No. 2, phrase 1 begins in a different key; in No. 3 it ends in a different key. No. 1 repeats phrase 4; No 2 expands it; No. 3 omits it. In No. 1 the leading note is avoided; in No. 2 it appears as an embellishment; in No. 3 it is changed to the gross major second.

Different forms of a tune seldom vary so much as this, but they do vary everywhere. Dr. Petrie states in his "Ancient Irish Airs" that in collecting them he hardly ever found two copies of the same tune precisely alike.

It has not been thought necessary, because these songs were sung by simple folk, to make the accompaniments as simple as possible. Some require to be, and have been so treated; others seem to demand a more elaborate arrangement. When the minstrel of old days sang a ballad like "Chevy Chase" of nearly seventy verses, an occasional chord to sustain the voice was all that was needed. The interest of the hearers lay in the story, not in the music. But when there is no story to tell, or when it has to be told in three verses, and becomes tedious after four, more prominence may well be given to the music. Songs so widely differing as "Brixham Town" (9), "Sweet Nightingale" (15), "The Rout is out" (45), "The Gipsy Countess" (50), "Henry Martyn" (53), "The Blue Flame" (67), "The Rambling Sailor" (87), and "Bibberley Town" (110), surely require very different treatment to bring out the poetical character in the melody, and to impart some interest to the accompaniment. I am sure that this is also the opinion of Mr. Bussell, whose valuable help and great kindness I gratefully acknowledge, and to whose excellent taste and musician-like writing the following pages bear too infrequent testimony. The melodies are preserved as faithfully as lay in our power, and that is the chief thing. They are far too good to be lost, and our desire has been to present them in a form acceptable to the musical public, and in which they may hold their own in the great competition for public favour. Should they fail to do this, they have yet another leg to stand upon; and put in their plea for preservation as being not ephemeral productions (of whatever merit); but melodies which may honestly lay claim to a place in a national collection of the genuine songs of the English people.

H. F. S.

Thurnscoe Rectory, July, 1891.

Nº I. "BY CHANCE IT WAS."

1

By chance it was I met my love,
   It did me much surprise,
Down by a shady myrtle grove,
   Just as the sun did rise.
The birds they sang right gloriously,
   And pleasant was the air;
And there was none, save she and I
   Among the flowers fair.

2

In dewy grass and green we walk'd,
   She timid was and coy.
"How can'st thou choose but pity me,
   My pretty pearl, my joy?
How comes it that thou stroll'st this way?
   Sweet maiden, tell me true,
Before bright Phœbus' glittering ray
   Has supped the morning dew?"

3

"I go to tend the flocks I love
   The ewes and tender lambs,
That pasture by the myrtle grove,
   That gambol by their dams:
There I enjoy a pure content
   At dawning of the day."
Then, hand in hand, we lovers went
   To see the flock at play.

4

And as we wended down the road,
   I said to her, "Sweet Maid,
Three years I in my place abode
   And three more must be stayed.
The three that I am bound so fast,
   O fairest wait for me,
And when the weary years are past,
   Then married we will be!"

5

"Three years are long, three times too long,
   Too lengthy the delay!"
O then I answered in my song,
   "Hope wastes them quick away.
Where love is fervent, fain and fast,
   And knoweth not decay,
There nimbly fleet the seasons past
   Accounted as one day."

No 2. THE HUNTING OF ARSCOTT OF TETCOTT.
(1652)

1
In the month of November, in the year fifty-two,
Three jolly Fox-hunters, all Sons of the Blue,
Came o'er from Penearrow, not fearing a wet coat,
To have some diversion with Arscott of Tetcott;
　Sing, Fol de rol de rol, lol de rol lol
　Sing, Fol de rol de rol, lol de rol lol rol lol.
Came o'er from Penearrow, not fearing a wet coat,
To have some diversion with Arscott of Tetcott.

2
The day-light was dawning, right radiant the morn,
When Arscott of Tetcott he winded his horn;
He blew such a flourish, so loud in the hall,
The rafters resounded, and danced to the call.
　Sing, Fol de rol de rol, &c:

3
In the kitchen the servants, in kennel the hounds,
In the stable the horses were roused by the sounds,
On Black-Cap in saddle sat Arscott, "To day
I will show you good sport, lads, Hark! follow, away!"
　Sing, Fol de rol de rol, &c:

✻ **4**
They tried in the coppice, from Becket to Thorn,
There were Ringwood and Rally, and Princess and Scorn
Then out bounded Reynard, away they all went,
With the wind in their tails, on a beautiful scent.
　Sing, Fol de rol de rol, &c:

✻ **5**
"Hark Vulcan!" said Arscott, "The best of good hounds'
Heigh, Venus!" he shouted, "How nimbly she bounds!
And nothing re-echoes so sweet in the valley,
As the music of Rattler, of Phil-pot, and Rally."
　Sing, Fol de rol de rol, &c:

6
They hunted o'er fallow, o'er field and on moor,
And never a hound, man or horse would give o'er.
Sly Reynard kept distance for many a mile,
And no one dismounted for gate or for stile.
　Sing, Fol de rol de rol, &c:

7
"How far do you make it?" said Simon, the Son
"The day that's declining will shortly be done";fore
"We'll follow till Doom's Day," quoth Arscott.—Be
They hear the Atlantic with menacing roar
　Sing, Fol de rol de rol, &c:

8
Thro' Whitstone and Poundstock, St Gennys they run,
As a fireball, red, in the sea set the sun.
Then out on Penkenner a leap, and they go,
Full five hundred feet to the ocean below.
　Sing, Fol de rol de rol, &c:

9
When the full moon is shining as clear as the day,
John Arscott still hunteth the country, they say;
You may see him on Black-Cap, and hear, in full cry
The pack from Penearrow to Dazard go by.
　Sing, Fol de rol de rol, &c:

10
When the tempest is howling, his horn you may hear,
And the bay of his hounds in their headlong career;
For Arscott of Tetcott loves hunting so well,
That he breaks for the pastime from Heaven — or Hell.
　Sing, Fol de rol de rol, &c:

✻ In singing, these verses may be omitted, for shortness.

Nº 3. UPON A SUNDAY MORNING.

1.

Upon a Sunday morning, when Spring was in its prime,
Along the Church-lane tripping, I heard the Church bells chime,
And there encountered Reuben, astride upon the stile,
He blocked the way, so saucy, upon his lips a smile.

2.

Upon a Sunday morning, there came a rush of bells,
The wind was music-laden, in changeful falls and swells;
He would not let me over, he held, he made me stay,
And promise I would meet him again at close of day.

3.

Upon a Sunday evening, the ringers in the tower,
Were practising their changes, they rang for full an hour;
And Reuben by me walking, would never let me go,
Until a Yes I answered, he would not take a No.

4.

Again a Sunday morning, and Reuben stands by me,
Not now in lane, but chancel, where all the folks may see.
A golden ring he offers, as to his side I cling,
O happy Sunday morning, for us the Church-bells ring.

No. 4. THE TREES THEY ARE SO HIGH.

1
All the trees they are so high,
 The leaves they are so green,
The day is past and gone, sweet-heart.
 That you and I have seen.
  It is cold winter's night,
  You and I must bide alone:
   Whilst my pretty lad is young
    And is growing.

2
In a garden as I walked,
 I heard them laugh and call;
There were four and twenty playing there,
 They played with bat and ball.
  O the rain on the roof,
  Here and I must make my moan:
   Whilst my pretty lad is young
    And is growing.

3
I listened in the garden,
 I looked o'er the wall;
Amidst five and twenty gallants there
 My love exceeded all.
  O the wind on the thatch,
  Here and I alone must weep:
   Whilst my pretty lad is young
    And is growing.

4
O father, father dear,
 Great wrong to me is done,
That I should married be this day,
 Before the set of sun.
  At the baffle of the gale,
  Here I toss and cannot sleep:
   Whilst my pretty lad is young
    And is growing.

5
* My daughter, daughter dear,
 If better be, more fit,
I'll send him to the court awhile,
 To point his pretty wit
  But the snow, snowflakes fall,
  O and I am chill as dead:
   Whilst my pretty lad is young
    And is growing.

6
* To let the lovely ladies know
 They may not touch and taste,
I'll bind a bunch of ribbons red
 About his little waist.
  But the raven hoarsely croaks,
  And I shiver in my bed:
   Whilst my pretty lad is young
    And is growing.

7
I married was, alas,
 A lady high to be,
In court and stall and stately hall,
 And bower of tapestry
  But the bell did only knell,
  And I shuddered as one cold:
   When I wed the pretty lad
    Not done growing

8
At seventeen he wedded was,
 A father at eighteen,
At nineteen his face was white as milk,
 And then his grave was green.
  And the daisies were outspread,
  And buttercups of gold,
   O'er my pretty lad so young
    Now ceased growing

* may be omitted in singing.

PARSON HOGG.

No 5. ♩.=88. Boldly.   H.F.S.

N.º 5. PARSON HOGG.

1

Mess Parson Hogg shall now maintain,
  The burden of my song, Sir.
A single life, perforce he led,
  Of constitution strong, Sir.
      Sing tally-ho! sing, tally-ho!
        Sing, tally-ho! why zounds sir,
        He mounts his mare, to hunt the hare,
        Sing tally-ho! the hounds, Sir.

2

And every day he goes to Mass,
  He first draws on the boot, Sir,
That should the beagles chance to pass,
  He might join in pursuit, Sir!
      Sing, tally-ho! &c.

3

That Parson little loveth prayer,
  And Pater, night and morn, Sir,
For bell and book, hath little care
  But dearly loves the horn, Sir.
      Sing tally-ho! &c.

4

S. Stephen's Day, this holy man
  He went a pair to wed, Sir.
When as the Service he began
  Puss by the Church-yard sped, Sir.
      Sing tally-ho! &c.

5

He shut his book, come on he said,
  I'll pray and bless no more, Sir,
He drew his surplice o'er his head
  And started for the door, Sir
      Sing tally-ho! &c.

6

In pulpit Parson Hogg was strong,
  He preached without a book, Sir,
And to the point, and never long,
  And this the text he took, Sir.
      "O tally-ho! O tally-ho!
        Dearly beloved — zounds, Sir
        I mount my mare to hunt the hare,
        Singing tally-ho! the hounds, Sir!"

Nº 6. "COLD BLOWS THE WIND, SWEET-HEART."

1
"Cold blows the wind of night, sweet-heart,
   Cold are the drops of rain;
The very first love that ever I had,
   In green-wood he was slain.

2
I'll do as much for my true-love
   As any fair maiden may;
I'll sit and mourn upon his grave
   A twelvemonth and a day."

3
A twelvemonth and a day being up,
   The ghost began to speak;
"Why sit you here by my grave-side
   From dusk till dawning break?"

4
"O think upon the garden, love,
   Where you and I did walk.
The fairest flower that blossomed there
   Is withered on its stalk."

5
"What is it that you want of me,
   And will not let me sleep?
Your salten tears they trickle down
   My winding sheet to steep."

6
"Oh I will now redeem the pledge
   The pledge that once I gave,
A kiss from off thy lily white lips
   Is all of you I crave."

7
"Cold are my lips in death, sweet-heart,
   My breath is earthy strong.
If you do touch my clay-cold lips,
   Your time will not be long."

8
Then through the mould he heaved his head,
   And through the herbage green.
There fell a frosted bramble leaf,
   It came their lips between.

9
"Now if you were not true in word,
   As now I know you be,
I'd tear you as the withered leaves,
   Are torn from off the tree.

10
"And well for you that bramble-leaf
   Betwixt our lips was flung.
The living to the living hold,
   Dead to the dead belong."

* * * * *

11
"Now I have mourned upon his grave,
   A twelvemonth and a day,
I'll set my sail before the wind
   To waft me far away."

12
"I'll set my sail before the wind,
   Ere comes the break of day;
I'll seek another lover new,
   And change my roundelay."

FLOWERS AND WEEDS.

№ 7.

H.F.S.

Plaintively ♩.= 106.

In my garden grew plenty of Thyme, It would flourish by night and by day. O'er the wall came a lad, He took all that I had And stole my thyme a-way, And stole my thyme a-way.

Nº 7. FLOWERS AND WEEDS.

1

In my garden grew plenty of Thyme
  It would flourish by night and by day,
O'er the wall came a lad, he took all that I had,
  And stole my thyme away.

2

My garden with heartsease was bright,
  The pansy so pied and so gay;
One slipped through the gate, and alas! cruel fate,
  My heartsease took away.

3

My garden grew self-heal and balm,
  And speedwell that's blue for an hour,
Then blossoms again, O grievous my pain!
  I'm plundered of each flower.

4

There grows in my garden the rue,
  And Love-lies-a-bleeding droops there,
The hyssop and myrrh, the teazle and burr,
  In place of blossoms fair.

5

The willow with branches that weep,
  The thorn and the cypress tree,
O why were the seeds of dolorous weeds,
  Thus scattered there by thee?

Nº 8.   THE ROVING JOURNEY-MAN.

1

Young Jack he was a journeyman
  That roved from town to town,
And when he'd done a job of work,
  He lightly sat him down.
With his kit upon his shoulder, and
  A grafting knife in hand,
He roved the country round about,
  A merry journey-man.

2

And when he came to Exeter
  The maidens leaped for joy;
Said one and all, both short and tall,
  Here comes a gallant boy
The lady dropt her needle, and
  The maid her frying-pan.
Each plainly told her mother that
  She loved the journey-man.

3

He had not been in Exeter.
  The days were barely three,
Before the Mayor, his sweet daughter,
  She loved him desperately;
She bid him to her mother's house,
  She took him by the hand,
Said she,"My dearest mother, see
  I love the journey-man!"

4

Now out on thee, thou silly maid!
  Such folly speak no more:
How can'st thou love a roving man,
  Thou ne'er hast seen before?"
"O mother sweet, I do entreat,
  I love him all I can;
Around the country glad I'll rove
  With this young journey-man.

5

"He need no more to trudge afoot,
  He'll travel coach and pair;
My wealth with me — or poverty
  With him, content I'll share?
Now fill the horn with barleycorn,
  And flowing fill the can;
Here let us toast the Mayor's daughter
  And the roving journeyman.

BRIXHAM TOWN.

№ 9. BRIXHAM TOWN.

1
All ye that love to hear
Music performed in air,
Pray listen, and give ear,
    To what I shall perpend.
Concerning music, who'd, —
—If rightly understood —
—Not find 'twould do him good
    To hearken and attend.

2
In Brixham town so rare
For singing sweet and fair,
Few can with us compare,
    We bear away the bell.
Extolled up and down
By men of high renown,
We go from town to town;
    And none can us excell.

3
There's a man in Brixham town
Of office, and in gown,
Strove to put singing down,
    Which most of men adore.
For House of God unmeet,
The voice and organ sweet!
When pious men do meet,
    To praise their God before.

4
Go question Holy writ,
And you will find in it,
That seemly 'tis and fit,
    To praise and hymn the Lord.
On cymbal and on lute,
On organ and on flute,
With voices sweet, that suit,
    All in a fair concord.

5
In Samuel you may read
How one was troubled,
Was troubled indeed,
    Who crown and sceptre bore;
An evil spirit lay
On his mind both night and day,
That would not go away,
    And vexed him very sore.

6
Then up and uttered one,
Said, "Jesse hath a son,
Of singers next to none;
    David his name they say."
"So send for David, fleet,
To make me music sweet,
That the spirit may retreat,
    And go from me away!"

7
Now when that David, he
King Saul had come to see,
And played merrily,
    Upon his stringéd harp,
The Devil in all speed,
With music ill agreed,
From Saul the King, he fled,
    Impatient to depart

8
So now, my friends, adieu!
I hope that all of you
Will pull most strong and true,
    In strain to serve the Lord.
God prosper us, that we,
Like angels may agree,
In singing merrily
    In tune and in accord.

Broom Green Broom.

Nº 10. GREEN BROOM.

1

There was an old man lived out in the wood,
    His trade was a-cutting of Broom, green Broom;
He had but one son without thrift, without good,
    Who lay in his bed till 'twas noon, bright noon.

2

The old man awoke, one morning and spoke,
    He swore he would fire the room, that room,
If his John would not rise and open his eyes,
    And away to the wood to cut Broom, green Broom.

3

So Johnny arose, and he slipped on his clothes,
    And away to the wood to cut Broom, green Broom,
He sharpened his knives, for once he contrives
    To cut a great bundle of Broom, green Broom.

4

When Johnny passed under a lady's fine house,
    Passed under a lady's fine room, fine room,
She called to her maid, "Go fetch me," she said,
    "Go fetch me the boy that sells Broom, green Broom

5

When Johnny came into the lady's fine house,
    And stood in the lady's fine room, fine room;
"Young Johnny," she said, "Will you give up your trade
    And marry a lady in bloom, full bloom?"

6

Johnny gave his consent, and to church they both went,
    And he wedded the lady in bloom, full bloom
At market and fair, all folks do declare,
    There is none like the Boy that sold Broom, green Broom.

AS JOHNNY WALKED OUT.

No 11.

For 4 Voices.

H.F.S.

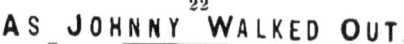

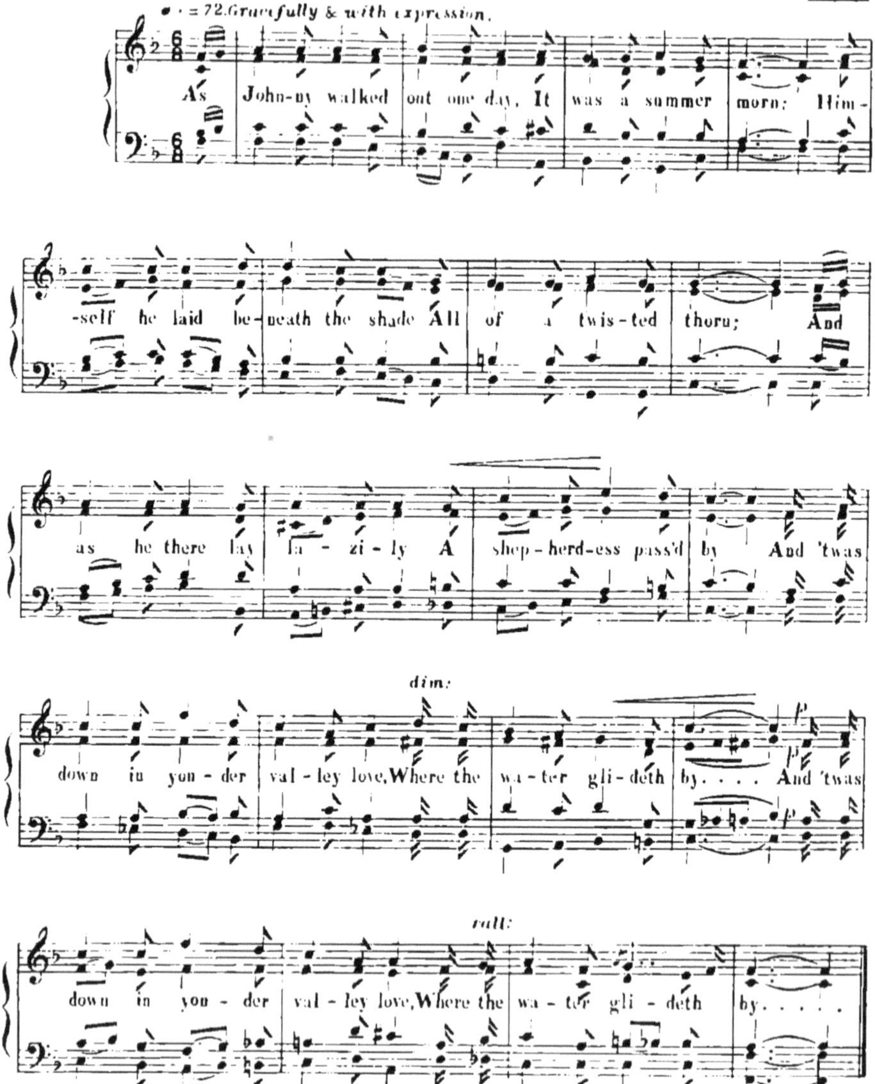

Nº II. AS JOHNNY WALKED OUT.

1

As Johnny walked out one day
 It was a summer morn,
Himself he laid beneath the shade
 All of a twisted thorn,
And as he there lay lazily
 A shepherdess pass'd by
And 'twas down in yonder valley, love,
 Where the water glideth by.

2

'O have you seen a pretty ewe
 That hath a tender lamb,
A strayed from the orchard glade
 That little one and dam?"
"O pretty maid" he answered,
 "They passed as here I lie!"
And 'twas down in yonder valley, love,
 Where the water glideth by.

✻ 3

She wandered o'er the country wide
 The sheep she could not find;
And many times she did upbraid
 Young Johnny in her mind.
She sought in leafy forest green
 She sought them low and high,
And 'twas down in yonder valley, love,
 Where the water glideth by.

4

"Oh silly maid," young Johnny said
 "Alone why did you seek?"
Her heart was full of anger, and
 The flush was in her cheek
"Where one alone availeth not.
 There two your sheep may spie,
And 'tis down in yonder valley, love,
 Where the water glideth by."

5

Then lo! they both forgot their quest
 They found what neither sought,
Two loving hearts long kept apart
 Together now were brought.
He found the words he long had lacked,
 He found and held her eye;
And 'twas down in yonder valley, love,
 Where the water glideth by.

✻ 6

Now married were this loving pair,
 And joined in holy band,
No more they go a seeking sheep,
 Together hand in hand.
Around her feet play children sweet,
 Beneath the summer sky,
And 'tis down in yonder valley, love,
 Where the water glideth by.

✻ These verses may be omitted in singing.

Nº 12. THE MILLER'S LAST WILL.

1

There was a miller, as you shall hear,
Long time he lived in Devonshire.
He was took sick and deadly ill,
And had no time to write his will.
So he call'd up his eldest son,
Said he My glass is almost run.
If I to thee my mill shall give,
Tell me what toll thou'it take to live?"

2

"Father," said he, "My name is Jack.
From every bushel I'll take a peck.
From every grist that I do grind,
That I may thus good living find."
"Thou art a fool," the old man said,
"Thou hast not half acquired thy trade.
My mill to thee I ne'er will give
For by such toll no man can live."

3

Then he call'd up his second son.
Said he, "My glass is almost run.
If I to thee my mill shall make,
Tell me what toll to live thou'lt take?"
"Father you know my name is Ralph,
From every bushel I'll take a half
From every grist that I do grind,
That I may thus a living find."

4

"Thou art a fool," the old man said;
"Thou hast not half acquired thy trade.
My mill to thee I will not give,
For by such toll no man may live"
Then he call'd up his youngest son,
Says he, My glass is almost run
If I to thee my mill shall make
Tell me what toll, to live, thou'lt take?"

5

"Father I am your youngest boy,
In taking toll is all my joy.
Before I would good living lack,
I'd take the whole — forswear the sack."
"Thou art the boy," the old man said,
"For thou hast full acquired the trade.
The mill is thine," the old man cried,
He laugh'd, gave up the ghost, and died.

№ 13. ORMOND THE BRAVE.

1

I am Ormond the brave, did ye never hear of me?
Who lately was driven from my own country.
They tried me, condemned me, they plundered my estate,
For being so loyal to Queen Anne the Great,
  Crying, O! I am Ormond, you know.

2

O to vict'ry I led, and I vanquished every foe,
Some do call me James Butler, I'm Ormond, you know,
I am Queen Anne's darling, and old England's delight,
A friend to the Church, in Presbyterian despite,
  Crying, O! I am Ormond, you know.

3

Then awake Devon dogs, and arise you Cornish cats,
And follow me a chasing the Hanoverian rats,
They shall fly from the country, we'll guard the British throne,
Have no German electors with a king, sirs, of our own.
  Crying, O! I am Ormond, you know.

4

O I wronged not my country as Scottish peers do,
Nor my soldiers defrauded, of that which is their due,
All such deeds I do abhor, by the powers that are above,
I've bequeath'd all my fortune to the country I love.
  Crying, O! I am Ormond, you know.

FATHOM THE BOWL.

N.º 14. FATHOM THE BOWL.

1.
Come all you old minstrels, wherever you be!
With comrades united in sweet harmony.
Whilst the clear crystal fountain thro' England shall roll,
O give me the Punch Ladle — I'll fathom the Bowl.

2.
Let nothing but harmony reign in your breast,
Let comrade with comrade be ever at rest.
We'll toss off our bumper, together will troll,
O give me the Punch Ladle—I'll fathom the Bowl.

3.
From France cometh Brandy, Jamaica gives Rum,
Sweet oranges, lemons from Portugal come.
Of Beer and good Cyder we'll also take toll
O give me the Punch Ladle—I'll fathom the Bowl.

4.
Our brothers lie drowned in the depths of the sea,
Cold stones for their pillows, what matters to me.
We'll drink to their healths, and repose to each soul.
O give me the Punch Ladle—I'll fathom the Bowl.

5.
Our wives they may fluster as much as they please,
Let 'em scold, let 'em grumble, we'll sit at our ease,
In the ends of our pipes we'll apply a hot coal.
O give me the Punch Ladle—I'll fathom the Bowl.

№ 15. SWEET NIGHTINGALE.

1

My sweet heart, come along,
  Don't you hear the fond song
The sweet notes of the Nightingale flow?
  Don't you hear the fond tale,
  Of the sweet nightingale,
As she sings in the valleys below?

2

Pretty Betty, don't fail,
  For I'll carry your pail
Safe home to your cot as we go;
  You shall hear the fond tale
  Of the sweet nightingale,
As she sings in the valleys below.

3

Pray let me alone,
  I have hands of my own,
Along with you Sir, I'll not go.
  To hear the fond tale
  Of the sweet nightingale,
As she sings in the valleys below.

4

Pray sit yourself down
  With me on the ground,
On this bank where the primroses grow.
  You shall hear the fond tale
  Of the sweet nightingale,
As she sings in the valleys below

5

The couple agreed,
  And were married with speed,
And soon to the church they did go:
  No more is she afraid
  For to walk in the shade,
Nor sit in those valleys below.

SWEET NIGHTINGALE.
Arranged as a Song.

N.º 15. SWEET NIGHTINGALE.

1

My sweet heart, come along,
　Don't you hear the fond song
The sweet notes of the Nightingale flow?
　Don't you hear the fond tale,
　Of the sweet nightingale,
As she sings in the valleys below?

2

Pretty Betty, don't fail,
　For I'll carry your pail
Safe home to your cot as we go:
　You shall hear the fond tale
　Of the sweet nightingale,
As she sings in the valleys below.

3

Pray let me alone,
　I have hands of my own,
Along with you Sir, I'll not go.
　To hear the fond tale
　Of the sweet nightingale,
As she sings in the valleys below.

4

Pray sit yourself down
　With me on the ground,
On this bank where the primroses grow.
　You shall hear the fond tale
　Of the sweet nightingale,
As she sings in the valleys below.

5

The couple agreed,
　And were married with speed,
And soon to the church they did go:
　No more is she afraid
　For to walk in the shade,
Nor sit in those valleys below.

WIDDICOMBE FAIR.

№ 16. WIDDICOMBE FAIR.

1

"Tom Pearse, Tom Pearse, lend me your grey mare,
  All along, down along, out along, lee.
For I want for to go to Widdecombe Fair,
  Wi' Bill Brewer, Jan Stewer, Peter Gurney, Peter Davy, Dan'l Whiddon,
  Harry Hawk, old Uncle Tom Cobbleigh and all,"
    CHORUS. Old Uncle Tom Cobbleigh and all.

2

"And when shall I see again my grey mare?"
  All along, &c.
"By Friday soon, or Saturday noon,
  Wi' Bill Brewer, Jan Stewer, &c.

3

Then Friday came, and Saturday noon,
  All along, &c.
But Tom Pearse's old mare hath not trotted home,
  Wi' Bill Brewer, &c.

4

So Tom Pearse he got up to the top o'the hill
  All along, &c.
And he seed his old mare down a making her will
  Wi' Bill Brewer, &c.

5

So Tom Pearse's old mare, her took sick and died.
  All along, &c.
And Tom he sat down on a stone, and he cried
  Wi' Bill Brewer, &c.

6

But this isn't the end o' this shocking affair,
  All along, &c.
Nor, though they be dead, of the horrid career
  Of Bill Brewer, &c.

7

When the wind whistles cold on the moor of a night
  All along, &c.
Tom Pearse's old mare doth appear, gashly white,
  Wi' Bill Brewer, &c.

8

And all the long night be heard skirling and groans,
  All along, &c.
From Tom Pearse's old mare in her rattling bones
  And from Bill Brewer, Jan Stewer, Peter Gurney, Peter Davy, Dan'l Whiddon,
  Harry Hawk, old Uncle Tom Cobbleigh and all.
    CHORUS. Old Uncle Tom Cobbleigh and all

YE MAIDENS PRETTY.

For 4 Voices.

No. 17. H.F.S.

Nº 17 YE MAIDENS PRETTY.

1.

Ye maidens pretty
In town and city,
I pray you pity
 My mournful strain
A maiden weeping,
Her night-watch keeping,
In grief unsleeping
 Makes her complain:
In tower I languish,
In cold and sadness,
Heart full of anguish,
 Eye full of tear.
Whilst glades are ringing
With maidens singing,
Sweet roses bringing
 To crown the year.

2.

Thro' hills and vallies,
Thro' shaded alleys,
And pleached palis —
 A ling or grove;
Among fair bowers,
Midst fragrant flowers,
Pass sunny hours,
 And sing of love.
  In tower I languish, &c

3.

"My cruel father
Gave straitest order,
By watch and warder,
 I barr'd should be.
All in my chamber,
High out of danger,
From eye of ranger,
 In misery.
  In tower I languish, &c

4.

"Enclosed in mortar,
By wall and water,
A luckless daughter
 All white and wan;
Till day is breaking
My bed forsaking,
I all night waking
 Sing like the swan.
  In tower I languish,
  In cold and sadness,
  Heart full of anguish,
   Eye full of tear.
  Whilst glades are ringing
  With maidens singing
  Sweet roses bringing,
   To crown the year."

THE SILLY OLD MAN.

Nº 18. H. F. S.

№ 18. THE SILLY OLD MAN.

1.
Aw! Come now, I'll sing you a song,
  'Tis a song of right merry intent,
Concerning a silly old man,
  Who went for to pay his rent,
    Singing, Too_ra_la_loo_ra_loo.

2.
And as this here silly old man,
  Was riding along the lane,
A Gentleman, thief overtook him,
  Saying "Well over-taken old man".

3.
"What! well over-taken, do'y say?"
  "Yes, well over taken," quoth he.
"No, no," said the silly old man,
  "I don't want thy company."

4.
"I am only a silly old man,
  I farm but a parcel of ground,
And I am going to the landlord to pay,
  My rent which is just forty pound."

5.
"But supposing a highway-man stopped you?
  For the rascals are many, men say,
And take all the money from off you
  As you ride on the king's highway?"

6.
"What! supposing some fellow should stop me?
  Why badly the thief would be sped,
For the money I carry about me
  In the quilt o' my saddle is hid."

7.
And as they were riding along,
  Along and along the green lane,
The Gentleman thief rode afore him
  And summoned the old man to stand.

8.
But the old man was crafty and cunning,
  As, I wot, in the world there be many
Pitched his saddle clean over the hedge,
  Saying, "Fetch'n if thou would'st have any"
    Singing Too_ra_la_loo_ra_loo.

9.
Then the thief being thirsty for gold,
  And eager to get at his bags,
He drawed out his rusty old sword,
  And chopped up the saddle to rags.

10.
The old man slipped off his old mare,
  And mounted the thief's horse astride,
Clapp'd spur, and put him in a gallop,
  Saying "I, without teaching, can ride."

11.
When he to his landlord's had come,
  That old man was almost a-spent,
Says he, "Landlord, provide me a room,
  I be come for to pay up my rent."

12.
He opened the thief, his portmantle
  And there was a sight to behold,
There were five hundred pounds in silver,
  And five hundred pounds in gold.

13.
And as he was on his way home,
  And riding along the same lane,
He seed— his silly old mare,
  Tied up to the hedge by the mane.

14.
He loosed his old mare from the hedge,
  As she of the grass there did crib,
He gi'ed her a whack o' the broad o' the back,
  Saying "Follow me home, old Tib."

15.
Aw! When to his home he were come
  His daughter he dress'd like a duchess,
And his ol' woman kicked and she capered for joy,
  And at Christmas danced jigs on her crutches.
    Singing, Too_ra_la_loo_ra_loo.

THE SEASONS.

N.º 19.   H.F.S.

Andante. In moderate time.

First comes January when the sun lies very low. I see in the farmer's yard,... the cattle feed on straw. The weather being so cold, while the snow lies on the ground, There will be another change of moon Before the year comes round.

Nº 19. THE SEASONS.

1.
First comes January
 When the sun lies very low;
I see in the farmer's yard
 The cattle feed on stro'
The weather being so cold
 The snow lies on the ground.
There will be another change of moon
 Before the year comes round.

2.
Next is February,
 So early in the spring;
The Farmer ploughs the fallows
 The rooks their nests begin.
The little lambs appearing
 Now frisk in pretty play.
I think upon the increase,
 And thank my God, to-day.

3.
March it is the next month.
 So cold and hard and drear.
Prepare we now for harvest,
 By brewing of strong beer.
God grant that we who labour,
 May see the reaping come,
And drink and dance and welcome
 The happy Harvest Home.

4.
Next of Months is April,
 When early in the morn
The cheery farmer soweth
 To right and left the corn.
The gallant team come after,
 A-smoothing of the land.
May Heaven the Farmer prosper
 Whate'er he takes in hand.

5.
In May I go a walking
 To hear the linnets sing.
The blackbird and the throstle
 A-praising God the King.
It cheers the heart to hear them
 To see the leaves unfold,
The meadows scattered over
 With buttercups of gold.

6.
Full early in the morning
 Awakes the summer sun,
The month of June arriving,
 The cold and night are done,
The Cuckoo is a fine bird
 She whistles as she flies,
And as she whistles, Cuckoo,
 The bluer grow the skies.

7.
Six months I now have named,
 The seventh is July,
Come lads and lasses gather
 The scented hay to dry.
All full of mirth and gladness
 To turn it in the sun,
And never cease till daylight sets
 And all the work is done.

8.
August brings the harvest,
 The reapers now advance,
Against their shining sickles
 The field stands little chance.
Well done!—exclaims the farmer,
 This day is all men's friend.
We'll drink and feast in plenty
 When we the harvest end.

9.
By middle of September,
 The rake is laid aside.
The horses wear the breeching
 Rich dressing to provide.
All things to do in season,
 Me-thinks is just and right.
Now summer season's over
 The frosts begin at night.

10.
October leads in winter.
 The leaves begin to fall.
The trees will soon be naked
 No flowers left at all.
The frosts will bite them sharply
 The Elm alone is green,
In orchard piles of apples red
 For cyder press are seen.

11.
The eleventh month, November,
 The nights are cold and long,
By day we're telling timber,
 And spend the night in song.
In cozy chimney corner
 We take our toast and ale,
And kiss and tease the maidens,
 Or tell a merry tale.

12.
Then comes dark December,
 The last of months in turn.
With holly, box, and laurel,
 We house and Church adorn.
So now, to end my story,
 I wish you all good cheer,
A merry, happy Christmas,
 A prosperous New Year.

№ 20. THE CHIMNEY SWEEP.

1

  Oh! sweep chimney, sweep!
  You maidens shake off sleep
 If you my cry can follow.
  I climb the chimney top,
  Without ladder and rope;
Aye and there! aye and there! aye and there you'll hear me halloo!

2

  Arise! maids, arise!
  Unseal and rub your eyes.
Arise and do your duty.
  I summon yet again,
  And do not me disdain,
That my call—that my call—that my calling's poor and sooty.

3

  Behold! here I stand!
  With brush and scrape in hand.
As a soldier that stands on his sentry.
  I work for the better sort,
  And well they pay me for't.
O I work, O I work, O I work for the best of gentry.

4

  Oh! sweep chimney, sweep!
  The hours onward creep.
As the lark I am alert, I
  Clear away, and take
  The smut that others make.
O I clean, O I clean, O I clean what others dirty.

The Saucy Sailor.

Nº 21.   H.F.S.

Sprightly ♩=72.

Come my dear-est Come my fair-est love with me

Come and you shall wed a sail-or from the sea

Faith I want none of your sail-ors She did say.

So be-gone you sau-cy crea-ture So be-gone from me I pray.

№ 21. THE SAUCY SAILOR.

1

"Come my fairest, come my dearest
  Love with me.
Come and you shall wed a sailor
  From the sea."
"Faith I want none of your sailors,"
  She did say.
"So begone you saucy creature,
  So begone from me, I pray.

2

"You are ragged, you are dirty,
  Smell of tar.
Get you gone to foreign countries,
  Hence afar."
"If I'm ragged, if I'm dirty,
  Of tar I smell,
Yet there's silver in my pockets,
  And of gold, a store as well."

3

When she saw the shining silver,
  Saw the gold;
Down she kneeled, and very humbly
  Hands did fold;
Saying "O forgive the folly
  From me fell,
Tarry, dirty, ragged sailors,
  I love more than words can tell."

4

"Do not think, you changeful maiden,
  I am mad.
That I'll take you, when there's other
  To be had.
Not the outside coat and waistcoat
  Make the man.
You have lost the chance that offered,
  Maidens snap — when e'er you can".

BLUE MUSLIN.

No. 22.   H.F.S.

Nº 22. BLUE MUSLIN.

1.

"O will you accept of the mus-e-lin so blue,
 To wear all in the morning, and to dabble in the dew?"
"No, I will not accept of the mus-e-lin so blue,
 To wear all in the morning, and to dabble in the dew,
  Nor I'll walk, nor I'll talk with you."

2.

"O will you accept of the pretty silver pin,
 To pin your golden hair with the fine mus-e-lin?"
"No, I will not accept of the pretty silver pin,
 To pin my golden hair with the fine mus-e-lin,
  Nor I'll walk, nor I'll talk with you."

3.

"O will you accept of a pair of shoes of cork,
 The one is made in London, the other's made in York?"
"No, I will not accept of a pair of shoes of cork,
 The one that's made in London, the other's made in York,
  Nor I'll walk, nor I'll talk with you."

4.

"O will you accept of the keys of Canterbury,
 That all the bells of England may ring, and make us merry?"
"No, I will not accept of the keys of Canterbury,
 That all the bells of England may ring, and make us merry,
  Nor I'll walk, nor I'll talk with you."

5.

"O will you accept of a kiss from loving heart;
 That we may join together and never more may part?"
"Yes, I will accept of a kiss from loving heart,
 That we may join together and never more may part,
  And I'll walk, and I'll talk with you."

"When you might you would not,
 Now you will you shall not.
  So fare you well, my dark eyed Sue."

THE SQUIRE AND THE FAIR MAID.

N.º 23.   H. F. S.

As I was walking out one day Where silver waters glide I saw a squire and gentle maid Down by the river side Thou hast a fair presence she said Thou hast a nimble tongue. I would thou wert my bride fair maid Kind sir I am too young.

1st Chorus.
"The younger you are the better you are, The better you are for me.

Chorus for other Verses.
To all who seek good wives I speak Each forward maid eschew When vow and swear, and do declare I'll marry none save thee! fishes fly as swallows high Such maids as these prove true

№23. THE SQUIRE AND THE FAIR MAID.

1.

As I was walking out one day
  Where silver waters glide,
I saw a Squire and gentle maid,
  Down by the river's side.
"Thou hast a fair presence," she said,
  "Thou hast a nimble tongue!"
"I would thou wert my Bride, fair maid!"
  "Kind Sir — I am too young!"
    CHORUS "The younger you are, the better you are
      The better you are for me.
      I vow and swear, and do declare
      I'll marry none save thee!"

2.

He took her by the lily-white hand,
  Held scarce her fingers press'd,
Ere all around his neck she hung,
  And sank upon his breast.
She kissed him on his cherry lips,
  She kissed his ruddy cheek,
She stroked his flowing flaxen hair,
  No words the Squire might speak.
    CHORUS. To all who seek good wives, I speak; —
      Each forward Maid eschew,
      When fishes fly as swallows high,
      Such maids as these prove true.

3.

Then from her arms himself he loosed
  Her fingers did unbind.
"Fair maid, you may be under age,
  But you are over kind.
If I of marriage spoke a word,
  I bitterly it rue,
Man loveth none so easy won,
  So over-fond as you.
    CHORUS. To all who seek &c.

4.

Go get you where are gardens fair
  Then sit and weep your fill
No man alive, I wot, will wive
  A maid of forward will.
There is a herb in your garden
  I think they call it rue,
And willows weep, o'er waters deep,
  These be the plants for you."
    CHORUS. To all who seek &c.

5.

She went all down to her garden,
  And sitting there did cry,
Was ever found on God's fair ground,
  A maid so used as I?
Whilst some, I ween, dance on the green,
  And others widely roam,
Here I must stay, Alack the day!
  And drink my tears at home."
    CHORUS. To all who seek &c.

№ 24. THE HAL-AN-TOW OR HELSTON FURRY DANCE.

1

Robin Hood and little John
  They both are gone to the fair, O!
And we will go to the merry green wood,
  To see what they do there, O!
      And for to chase, O, to chase the buck and doe!
      With Hal-an-tow, jolly rumble, O,

CHORUS.
    And we were up as soon as the day, O,
    For to fetch the Summer home,
    The Summer, and the May, O!
    Now the Winter is a gone, O.

2

Where are those Spaniards,
  That make so great a boast, O!
Why, they shall eat the grey goose feathers,
  And we will eat the roast, O!
      In every land, O, the land where'er we go,
      With Hal-an-tow, jolly rumble O

Chorus. And we were up, &c:

3

As for that good Knight, S. George,
  S. George he was a Knight, O
Of all the knights in Christendom!
  S. George he is the right, O!
      In every land, O! the land where'er we go,
      With Hal-an-tow, jolly rumble O

Chorus. And we were up, &c:

4

God bless Modryb Maria*
  And all her power and might, O!
And send us peace in merry England,
  Send peace by day and night, O!
      To merry England, O! both now and ever mo'
      With Hal-an-tow, jolly rumble O

Chorus. And we were up, &c.

---

* What is sung actually is Aunt Mary Moses, but this is probably a corrupt alteration from the Cornish Modryb (Aunt). This has been changed to Moses and translated before the name to fill out the line. "Aunt" and "Uncle" are titles of reverence given in Cornwall quite irrespective of relationship.

BLOW AWAY YE MORNING BREEZES.

Nº 25. "BLOW AWAY, YE MORNING BREEZES."

1.

Blow away, ye morning breezes,
Blow, ye winds, Heigh-ho!
Blow away the morning kisses,
Blow, blow, blow.
"O thou shalt rue the very hour,
That e'er thou knew'st the man,
For I will bake the wheaten flour,
And thou shalt bake the bran."
　　CHORUS.
　　　Blow away, ye morning breezes &c.

2.

"O thou shalt sorrow thro' thy soul
Thou stood'st to him so near.
For thou shalt drink the puddle foul,
And I the crystal clear."
　　CHORUS. Blow away ye morning breezes &c.

3.

"O thou shalt rue that e'er thou wo'ld
Behold a love of mine.
For thou shalt sup the water cold,
But I will sup red wine."
　　CHORUS. Blow away ye morning breezes &c.

4.

"Thou shalt lament in grief and doubt.
Thou spake'st with him at all,
For thou shalt wear the sorry clout,
And I the purple pall."

5.

"O thou shalt curse thy day of birth.
And curse thy dam and sire,
For I shall warm me at the hearth,
And thou shalt feed the fire.
　　CHORUS. Blow away ye morning breezes &c.

Note. In the original of the above Ballad each verse is repeated with the variation of "I shall not" for "I shall" &c. Thus after the first verse comes:

　　　I shall *not* rue the very hour
　　　That e'er I knew the man
　　　But *I* will bake the wheaten flour
　　　And *thou* shalt bake the bran.
It seems unnecessary to print these repetitions.

THE HEARTY GOOD-FELLOW.

Nº 26.   Cheerfully ♩=112   H.F.S.

I sad-dled my horse and a-way I did ride Till I came to an ale-house hard by the roadside I call'd for a pot of ale frothing and brown And close by the fireside I sat myself down Singing Tol de rol lol de rol lol de rol dee And I in my pock-et had one pen-ny.

Repeat in Chorus

rall: *Tempo*

№ 26. THE HEARTY GOOD FELLOW.

I saddled my horse, and away I did ride
Till I came to an ale-house hard by the road-side,
I called for a pot of ale-frothing and brown,
And close by the fireside I sat myself down,
   Singing, Tol-de-rol-lol-de-rol-Tol-de-rol dee!
   And I in my pocket had ONE PENNY.
      CHORUS: Singing, Tol-de-rol &c:

2

I saw there two gentlemen playing at dice,
They took me to be some nobleman nice.
With my swagger, and rapier, and countenance bold,
They thought that my pockets were well lined with gold,
   Singing, Tol-de-rol-lol-de-rol-Tol-de-rol dee!
   And I in my pocket had ONE PENNY.
      CHORUS: Singing, Tol-de-rol &c:

3

"A hearty good fellow" they said, "loveth play!"
"That lies with the stakes, pretty sirs, that you lay?"
Then one said "A guinea? but I said "Five Pound,"
The bet it was taken — no money laid down,
   Singing, Tol-de-rol-lol-de-rol-Tol-de-rol dee!
   And I in my pocket had ONE PENNY.
      CHORUS: Singing, Tol-de-rol &c:

4

I took up the dice, and I threw them the main,
It was very good fortune, that evening, to gain;
If they had a won, sirs, there'd been a loud curse
When I threw in naught save a moneyless purse
   Singing Tol-de-rol-lol-de-rol-Tol-de-rol dee!
   And I in my pocket had ONE PENNY.
      CHORUS: Singing, Tol-de-rol &c:

5

Was ever a mortal a quarter as glad,
With the little of money at first that I had!
A hearty good fellow, as most men opine
I am; so my neighbours pray pour out the wine,
   Singing Tol-de-rol-lol-de-rol-Tol-de-rol dee!
   And I in my pocket had FIVE POUNDS, free.
      CHORUS: Singing, Tol-de-rol &c:

6

I tarried all night, and I parted next day,
Thinks I to myself, I'll be jogging away!
I asked of the landlady what was my bill.
"O naught save a kiss of your lips, if you will."
   Singing Tol-de-rol-Tol-de-rol-Tol-de-rol dee!
   And I in my pocket had FIVE POUNDS free.
      CHORUS: Singing, Tol-de-rol-lol-de-rol-Tol-de-rol-dee!
        And I in my pocket had FIVE POUNDS, free.

Nº 27. THE BONNY BUNCH OF ROSES.

1

Beside the rolling ocean
 One morning in the month of June,
The feather'd warbling songsters
 Were sweetly changing note and tune,
  I overheard a damsel fair
  Complain in words of bitter woe,
  With tear on cheek, she thus did speak,
   O for the bonny Bunch of Roses, O!

2

Then up and spake her lover
 And grasped the maiden by the hand,
Have patience, fairest, patience!
 A legion I will soon command.
  I'll raise ten thousand soldiers brave
  Thro' pain and peril I will go
  A branch will break, for thy sweet sake,
   A branch of the bonny Bunch of Roses, O!

3

Then sadly said his mother,
 As tough as truest heart of oak,
That stem that bears the roses,
 And is not easy bent or broke
  Thy father he essayed it first
  And now in France his head lies low;
  For sharpest thorn, is ever borne
   O by the bonny Bunch of Roses, O!

4

He raised a mighty army
 And many nobles joined his throng
With pipe and banner flying
 To pluck the rose, he march'd along;
  The stem he found was far too tough
  And piercing sharp, the thorn, I trow
  No blossom he rent from the tree
   All of the bonny Bunch of Roses, O!

5

'O mother, dearest mother!
 I lie upon my dying bed,
And like my gallant father
 Must hide an uncrowned, humbled head.
  Let none henceforth essay to touch
  That rose so red, or full of woe,
  With bleeding hand he'll fly the Land
   The land of the bonny Bunch of Roses, O!

№. 28. THE OLD SINGING-MAN.

1

I reckon the days is departed,
　When folks ud a listened to me,
And I feels like as one broken-hearted,
　A-thinking o' what used to be.
And I don't know as much be amended,
　Than was in them merry old Times,
When, wi' pipes and good ale, folks attended,
　To me and my purty old rhymes.
　　　　CHORUS: To me and my purty old rhymes.

2

'Tis true, I be cruel asthmatic
　I've lost every tooth i' my head;
And my limbs be that crim'd wi' rheumatic
　D'rsay I were better in bed.
Oh my! all the world be for reading
　Newspapers, and books and what not;
Sure—'tis only conceitedness breeding,
　And the old zinging man is forgot.
　　　　CHORUS: And the old singing man is forgot.

3

I reckon that wi' my brown fiddle
　I'd go from this cottage to that;
All the youngsters 'ud dance in the middle,
　Their pulses and feet, pit-a-pat.
I cu'd zing, if you'd stand me the liquor,
　All the night, and 'ud never give o'er
My voice—I don't deny it getting thicker,
　But never exhausting my store.
　　　　CHORUS: But never exhausting my store.

4

'Tis politics now is the fashion
　As sets folks about by the ear,
And slops makes the poorest of lushing,
　No zinging for me wi'out beer.
I reckon the days be departed
　For such jolly gaffers as I,
Folks never will be so light-hearted
　As they was in the days that's gone by.
　　　　CHORUS: As they was in the days that's gone by.

5

O Lor! what wi' their education,
　And me—neither cypher nor write;
But in zinging the best in the nation
　And give the whole parish delight
I be going, I reckon, full mellow
　To lay in the Churchyard my head;
So say—God be wi' you, old fellow!
　The last o' the Zingers is dead.
　　　　CHORUS: The last o' the Zingers is dead.

N⁰ 29. THE TYTHE-PIG.

1

All you that love a bit of fun, come listen here awhile,
I'll tell you of a droll affair, will cause you all to smile.
    The Parson dress'd, all in his best,
    Cock'd hat and bushy wig,
He went into a farmer's house, to choose a sucking pig
        Good morning said the Parson; good morning, sir, to you!
        I'm come to take a sucking pig, a pig that is my due.

2

Then went the farmer to the stye, amongst the piglings small,
He chose the very weakest pig, the weakest of them all;
    But when the Parson saw the choice,
    How he did stamp and roar!
He snorted loud, he shook his wig, he almost — cursed and swore
    Good morning &c:

3

O then out spake the Farmer, since my offer you refuse
Pray step into the stye yourself, that you may pick and choose.
    So to the stye the Priest did hie,
    And there without ado,
The old sow ran with open mouth, and grunting at him flew.
    Good morning &c:

4

She caught him by the breeches black, that loudly he did cry
O help me! help me from the sow! or surely I shall die.
    The little pigs his waistcoat tore,
    His stockings and his shoes,
The Farmer said, with bow and smile, you're welcome, sir, to choose
    Good morning &c:

5

Away the Parson scamper'd home, as fast as he could run,
His wife was standing at the door, expecting his return,
    But when she saw him in such plight
    She fainted clean away,
Alas! alas! the Parson said, I bitter rue this day.
    Good morning, &c:

6

Go fetch me down a suit of clothes, a sponge and soap, I pray
And bring me, too, my greasy wig, and rub me down with hay
    Another time, I won't be nice,
    When gathering my dues
Another time in sucking pigs, I will not pick and choose.
    Good morning, said the Parson, good morning, sirs, to you,
    I will not pick a sucking pig — I leave the choice to you.

MY LADYE'S COACH.

Nº 30. MY LADYE'S COACH.

1

My Ladye hath a sable coach,
  And horses two and four,
My Ladye hath a gaunt blood-hound,
  That runneth on before.
My Ladye's Coach hath nodding plumes,
  The driver hath no head,
My Ladye is an ashen white,
  As one that long is dead.

2

Now pray step in! my Ladye saith,
  Now pray step in and ride.
I thank thee I had rather walk
  Than gather to thy side.
The wheels go round without a sound
  Of tramp or turn of wheels
As cloud at night, in pale moonlight,
  Along the carriage steals.

3

Now pray step in! my Ladye saith,
  Now prithee come to me.
She takes the baby from the crib,
  She sets it on her knee;
The wheels go round, &c:

4

Now pray step in! my Ladye saith,
  Now pray step in and ride.
Then deadly pale, in waving veil,
  She takes to her the bride;
The wheels go round, &c:

5

Now pray step in! my Ladye saith,
  There's room I wot for you,
She wav'd her hand, the coach did stand,
  The Squire within she drew.
The wheels go round &c:

6

Now pray step in! my Ladye saith,
  Why should'st thou trudge afoot?
She took the gaffer in by her,
  His crutches in the boot.
The wheels go round &c:

7

I'd rather walk a hundred miles
  And run by night and day
Than have that carriage halt for me,
  And hear my Ladye say —
Now pray step in and make no din,
  Step in with me to ride;
There's room I trow, by me for you
  And all the world beside.

JAN'S COURTSHIP.

No. 31.   H.F.S.

With grave humour.
♩=72.

Come hither son Jan since thou art a man I'll gie the best counsel in life Come sit down by me and my sto—ry shall be,— I'll tell how to get thee a wife, Iss I will! man, I will! Zure I will! I'll tell how to get thee a wife, Iss I will!

N⁰ 31. JAN'S COURTSHIP.

1

Come hither, son Jan! since thou art a man,
    I'll gie the best counsel in life,
Come, sit down by me, and my story shall be,
    I'll tell how to get thee a wife.
        Iss, I will! man, I will!
           Zure I will!
      I'll tell how to get thee a wife! Iss, I will!

2

Thy self thou must dress in thy Sunday-go-best;
    They'll at first turn away and be shy,
But boldly, kiss each purty maid that thou seest,
    They'll call thee their Love, by-and-bye.
        Iss, they will! man, they will!
           Zure they will!
      They'll call thee their love by-and-bye! Iss, they will!

3

So a courting Jan goes in his holiday clothes,
    All trim, nothing ragged and torn,
From his hat to his hose, with a sweet yellow rose,
    He looked like a gentleman born.
        Iss he did! man he did!
           Zure he did!
      He looked like a gentleman born! Iss he did!

4

The first pretty lass that Jan did see pass
    A farmer's fat daughter called Grace.
He'd scarce said 'How do!' and a kind word or two,
    Her fetched him a slap in the face.
        Iss, her did! man, her did!
           Zure her did!
      Her fetched him a slap in the face! Iss, her did!

5

As Jan, never fearing o nothing at all,
    Was walking adown by the locks,
He kiss'd the parson's wife, which stirred up a strife,
    And Jan was put into the stocks.
        Iss, he was! man, he was!
           Zure he was!
      And Jan was put into the stocks! Iss, he was!

6

'If this be the way, how to get me a wife
    Quoth Jan, I will never have none
I'd rather live single the whole of my life
    And home to my mammy I'll run.
        Iss, I will! man, I will
           Zure I will!
      And home to my mammy I'll run! Iss, I will.

THE DROWNED LOVER.

N⁰ 32. THE DROWNED LOVER.

1

As I was a-walking down by the sea-shore,
Where the winds whistled high, and the waters did roar,
Where the winds whistled high, and the waves raged around,
I heard a fair maid make a pitiful sound,
    Crying, O! my love is drowned!
      My love must I deplore!
    And I never, O! never
      Shall see my love more!

2

I never a nobler, a truer did see
A lion in courage, but gentle to me
An eye like an eagle, a heart like a dove,
And the song that he sang me was ever of love
    Now I cry, O! my love is drowned!
      My love must I deplore!
    And I never; O! never
      Shall see my love more!

3

He is sunk in the waters, there lies he asleep,
I will plunge there as well, I will kiss his cold feet,
I will kiss the white lips, once coral-like red,
And die at his side, for my true love is dead.
    Now I cry, O! my love is drowned.
      My love must I deplore
    And I never; O! never
      Shall see my love more!

CHILDE THE HUNTER.

No. 33. H.F.S.

No. 33. CHILDE THE HUNTER

1

Come, listen all, both great and small,
    To you a tale I'll tell,
What on this bleak and barren moor,
    In ancient days befell.

2

It so befell, as I've heard tell,
    There came the hunter Childe,
All day he chased on heath and waste,
    On Dart-a-moor so wild.

3

The winds did blow, then fell the snow,
    He chased on Fox-tor mires
He lost his way, and saw the day,
    And winter's sun expire.

4

Cold blew the blast, the snow fell fast,
    And darker grew the night;
He wandered high, he wandered low,
    And nowhere saw a light.

5

In darkness blind, he could not find
    Where he escape might gain,
Long time he tried, no track espied,
    His labours all in vain.

6

His knife he drew, his horse he slew,
    As on the ground it lay;
He cut full deep, therein to creep,
    And tarry till the day.

7

The winds did blow, fast fell the snow,
    And darker grew the night,
Then well he wot, he hope might not
    Again to see the light.

8

So with his finger dipp'd in blood,
    He scrabbled on the stones,—
"This is my will, God it fulfil,
    And buried be my bones.

9

"Whoe'er he be that findeth me
    And brings to a grave,
The lands that now to me belong,
    In Plymstock he shall have."

10

There was a cross erected then,
    In memory of his name;
And there it stands, in wild waste lands,
    To testify the same.

The Cottage Thatched With Straw.

N⁰ 34. THE COTTAGE THATCHED WITH STRAW.

In the days of yore, there sat at his door,
An old farmer, and thus sang he,
'With my pipe and my glass, I wish every class
On the earth were as well as me!'
For he envied not any man his lot,
The richest, the proudest, he saw,
For he had home brew'd — brown bread,
And a cottage well thatch'd with straw,
       A cottage well thatch'd with straw,
       A cottage well thatch'd with straw;
       For he had home-brew'd, brown bread,
       And a cottage well thatch'd with straw.

2

My dear old dad this snug cottage had,
And he got it, I'll tell you how.
He won it, I wot, with the best coin got.
With the sweat of an honest brow.
Then says my old dad, 'Be careful lad
To keep out of the lawyer's claw,
So you'll have home-brew'd — brown bread,
And a cottage well thatch'd with straw.
       A cottage well thatch'd with straw, &c:

3

The ragged, the torn, from my door I don't turn,
But I give them a crust of brown;
And a drop of good ale, my lad, without fail,
For to wash the brown crust down.
Tho' rich I may be, it may chance to me,
That misfortune should spoil my store,
So — I'd lack home-brew'd — brown bread,
And a cottage well thatch'd with straw.
       A cottage well thatch'd with straw, &c:

4

Then in frost and snow to the Church I go,
No matter the weather how,
And the service and prayer that I put up there,
Is to Him who speeds the plough.
Sunday saints, i'feck, who cheat all the week,
With a ranting and a canting jaw,
Not for them is my home-brew'd — brown bread,
And my cottage well thatch'd with straw.
       My cottage well thatch'd with straw,
       My cottage well thatch'd with straw,
       Not for them is my home-brew'd — brown bread,
       And my cottage well thatch'd with straw.

N⁰ 35. CICELY SWEET.

1
HE.

Cicely sweet, the morn is fair,
Wilt thou drive me to despair!
  Oft have I sued in vain
  And now I'm come again,
Wilt thou be mine, or Yes or No!
Wilt thou be mine, or No!

3

Cicely sweet, if thou'lt love me,
Mother'll do a deal for thee,
  Her'd rather sell her cow,
  Than I should die for thou,
Wilt thou be mine, or Yes, or No!
Wilt thou be mine, or No!

5

Cicely sweet, you do me wrong,
My legs be straight, my arms be strong
  I'll carry thee about,
  Thou'lt go no more afoot,
Wilt thou be mine, &c:

2
SHE.

Prithee, Simon quit thy suit,
All thy pains will yield no fruit;
  Go booby, get a sack.
  To stop thy ceaseless clack.
Go for a booby, go, go, go!
Go for a booby, go!

4

Mother thine had best by half,
Keep her cow and sell her calf;
  No, never for a crown;
  Will I marry with a clown;
Go for a booby, go, go, go!
Go for a booby go!

6

Keep thy arms to fight in fray,
Keep thy legs to run away;
  Ne'er will I — as I'm a lass,
  Care to ride upon an ass
Go for a booby &c:

A Sweet Pretty Maiden.

Nº 36. H.F.S.

No 36. A SWEET PRETTY MAIDEN.

1

A sweet pretty maiden sat under a tree,
She sighed and said, Would that I married might be!
My mammy is so crabb'd, and my daddy is so cross
That a husband for certain could never be worse.

2

I'll drudge in the kitchen, I'll bake and I'll brew,
A cradle be rocking the weary night through.
A husband, he may scold, he is welcome, I agree,
If that only a husband be granted to me.

3

My husband may beat me, I little will mind,
If only a husband to beat me I find,
My fingers I will work, I will work them to the bone,
If I get but a husband and home of my own.

4

A husband they tell me will make me his slave;
So be it if only a husband I have.
A sweet pretty maiden sat under a tree,
Singing, O come and marry, O, come! marry me!

No 37. THE GREEN COCKADE.

1

Alas! my love's enlisted,
    He wears a green cockade.
He is as gay a gallant
    As any roving blade.
He's gone the king a serving,
    The green cockade to wear,
Whilst my poor heart is breaking,
    For the love to him I bear.

2

"Leave off your grief and sorrow,
    And quit this doleful strain.
The green cockade adorns me
    Whilst marching o'er the plain.
When I return I'll marry,
    By this cockade I swear.
Your heart from grief must rally,
    And my departure bear."

3

"Fair maid, I bring bad tidings,"
    So did the Sergeant say;
"Your love was slain in battle,
    He sends you this to-day.
The green cockade he flourished
    Now dabbled in his gore.
With his last kiss he sends it,
    The green cockade he wore!"

4

She spoke no word — her tears.
    They fell a salten flood;
And from the draggled ribbons
    Washed out the stains of blood.
"O mother I am dying!
    And when in grave I'm laid,
Upon my bosom mother!
    Then pin the green cockade."

No. 38. THE SAILORS' FAREWELL.

1

Farewell! farewell, my Polly dear!
   A thousand times adieu!
'Tis sad to part; but never fear,
   Your sailor will be true.
And must I go, and leave you so, —
   While thund'ring billows roar?
I am afraid, my own sweet maid,
   Your face I'll see no more.

2

The weavers and the tailors
   Are snoring fast asleep,
While we poor 'jolly sailors'
   Are tossing on the deep:
Are tossing on the deep, dear girl,
   In tempest, rage and foam;
When seas run high, and dark the sky,
   We think on those at home.

3

When Jack's ashore, safe home once more,
   We lead a merry life;
With pipe and glass, and buxom lass,
   A sweetheart or a wife;
We call for liquor merrily,
   We spend our money free,
And when our money's spent and gone,
   Again we go to sea.

4

You'll not know where I am, dear girl,
   But when I'm on the sea,
My secret thoughts I will unfurl
   In letters home to thee.
The secrets, aye! of heart, I say,
   And best of my good will,
My body may lay just where it may
   My heart is with you still.

N.º 38. THE SAILOR'S FAREWELL.
2nd VERSION AS DUET AND CHORUS.

1

Tenor. Farewell! farewell, my Polly dear!
A thousand times adieu!
'Tis sad to part, but never fear,
Your sailor will be true.
Sopr. And must you go and leave us so,
While thund'ring billows roar,
I am afraid that I, sweet man,
Will see your face no more.
Chorus. Farewell! farewell ye (sailors / maidens) dear!
A thousand times adieu!
'Tis sad to part, but never fear,
Your (maidens / sailors) will be true.

2

Sopr. The weavers and the tailors
Are snoring fast asleep,
Whilst you poor sailor boys
Are tossing on the deep.
Ten. Are tossing on the deep, dear girls,
In tempest, rage and foam;
When seas run high, and dash to sky,
We think of those at home.
Chorus. Farewell! farewell! &c.

3

Ten. When Jack's ashore, safe home once more,
We lead a merry life.
With pipe and glass, and box and lass,
A sweetheart or a wife.
Sopr. You call for liquor merrily,
You spend your money free,
And when your money's spent and gone,
Again you go to sea.
Chorus. Farewell! farewell! &c.

THE FORSAKEN MAIDEN.

№ 39. THE FORSAKEN MAIDEN.

1
A maiden sat a weeping
    Down by the sea shore,
What ails my pretty mistress?
What ails my pretty mistress?
    And makes her heart sore!

2
Because I am a-weary,
    A weary in mind,
No comfort, and no pleasure, love,
No comfort, and no pleasure, love
    Henceforth can I find.

3
I'll spread my sail of silver,
    I'll loose my rope of silk,
My mast is of the cypress-tree,
My mast is of the cypress-tree,
    My track is as milk.

4
I'll spread my sail of silver
    I'll steer toward the sun
And thou, false love wilt weep for me,
And thou, false love wilt weep for me,
    For me — when I am gone.

THE BLUE KERCHIEF.

Nº 10.   F. W. B.

Cheerfully.

I saw a sweet maiden trip o-ver the lea, Her eyes were as load-stones at-tract-ing of me. Her cheeks were the ro-ses that Cu-pid lurks in, With a bon-ny blue ker-chief tied un-der her chin.

№ 40. THE BLUE KERCHIEF.

1

I saw a sweet maiden trip over the lea,
Her eyes were as loadstones attracting of me,
Her cheeks were the roses, that Cupid lurks in,
With a bonny blue kerchief tied under her chin.

2

O where are you going, my fair pretty maid !
O whither so swift through the dew drops? I said,
I go to my mother, kind sir, for to spin,
O the bonny blue kerchief tied under her chin.

* 3

Why wear you that kerchief tied over your head ?
'Tis the country girls'fashion, kind sir, then she said,
And the fashion young maidens will always be in
So I wear a blue kerchief tied under my chin.

4

To kiss her sweet lips then I sought to begin,
O nay Sir ! she said, 'ere a kiss you would win,
Pray show me a ring, tho' of gold the most thin,
O slyest blue kerchief tied under the chin !

5

Why wear a *blue* kerchief, sweet maiden, I said,
Because the blue colour is one not to fade,
As a sailor's blue jacket who fights for the king,
So's my bonny blue kerchief tied under the chin.

6

The love that I value is certain to last,
Not fading and changing, but ever set fast,
That only the colour, my love sir to win,
So goodbye from the kerchief tied under the chin.

* May be omitted in singing.

An Evening So Clear.

No. 41.

F. W. B.

Simply & not too fast.

An ev'n-ing so clear, O I would that I were; To kiss thy soft cheek With the faint-est of air The star that is twink-ling so bright-ly a-bove I would that I might be, To en-light-en my love.

No 41. AN EVENING SO CLEAR.

1

An evening so clear,
O I would that I were,
To kiss thy soft cheek
With the faintest of air.
The star that is twinkling
So brightly above,
I would that I might be,
To en-lighten my love!

2

If I were the seas
That about the world run,
I'd give thee my pearls
Not retaining of one.
If I were the Summer,
With flowers and green,
I'd garnish thy temples
And would crown thee my queen!

3

If I were a kiln
All in fervour and flame
I'd catch thee, and thou'd be
Consumed in the same.
But because I am nothing
Save love totafd* Bill,
Pray take of me, make
Of me just what you will.

* *Totated* is foolish, crazed.

THE WARSON HUNT.

No. 42. THE WARSON HUNT.

1

Come all you jolly hunters bold,
   I'll sing you something new,
'Twas in the springing of the year
   In eighteen hundred two.
A pack of hounds from Kelly came,
   And cobs from far and nigh,
The huntsman swore of oaths a score,
   This day a Hare shall die.

2

The Squire was on his silver tail
   The Parson on his bay,
And Surgeon Stone bestrode a roan,
   The huntsman rode a grey;
And some on horses from the plough,
   And such as coaches drew,
But some were there on shinks's mare,
   And one on crutches too.

3

They tried the down by Warson town,
   At last they start the hare,
And full in view the hounds pursue,
   With tirl and taff, and tare.
The MASTER said, "I stake my head,
   A golden guinea lay,
We'll kill that hare, by George, I swear
   Before the turn of day."

4

Long time they toil'd, with sweat were soiled,
   That Puss was not overtook,
Away she wore to Sandry moor
   She leap'd full many a brook.
The Squire he rode with whip and spur
   His gallant silver tail;
And they on foot were hard put to't,
   And some began to fail.

5

Then said the hunters drawing rein
   That Puss us all has beat,
A mighty run, and we well done
   Acknowledge our defeat,
And some went east, and some went west
   And some returned south,
But not a few went into Lew
   To fill the hungry mouth.

6

The Squire he opened wide his door
   The hunt to entertain,
With beef and beer and such good cheer
   As hunters ne'er disdain.
Then it is said, he who staked his head,
   That he would kill, that day,
He lost his head, all night as dead,
   Beneath the table lay.

7

Then, Hey! down derry! let's be merry!
   And drink a hunter's toast
And never swear to kill a hare,
   Lest we should rue the boast.
Yet — should we fail; — on flowing ale
   And punch, a royal brew,
We do not care — let's miss our hare,
   And lose our heads—at Lew!

THE GREEN BUSHES.

№ 43. THE GREEN BUSHES.

1

As I was a walking one morning in May,
To hear the birds whistle, see lambkins at play,
I spied a fair damsel, O sweetly sang she —
'Down by the green bushes he thinks to meet me.'

2

'O where are you going, my sweet pretty maid?'
'My lover I'm seeking, kind sir,' she said
'Shall I be your lover, and will you agree,
To forsake the old love, and forgather with me?

3

'I'll buy you fine beavers, a gay silken gown,
With fur belowed petticoats flounced to the ground,
If you'll leave your old love, and following me,
Forsake the green bushes, where he waits for thee?'

4

'Quick, let us be moving, from under the trees,
Quick, let us be moving, kind sir, if you please;
For yonder my true love is coming, I see,
Down by the green bushes He thinks to meet me'.

5

The old love arrived, the maiden was gone
He sighed very deeply, he sighed all alone,
'She is on with another, before off with me,
So, adieu, ye green bushes for ever!' said he.

6

'I'll be as a schoolboy, I'll frolic and play,
No false hearted maiden shall trouble my day,
Untroubled at night, I will slumber and snore
So, adieu, ye green bushes! I'll fool it no more.

THE BROKEN TOKEN.

N.º 44.   H.F.S.

One summer ev'n_ing, a mai_den fair Was walking forth in the balmy air; She met a sai_lor up_on the way, "Maiden stay" he whisper'd "Maiden stay" he whis_per'd, O pret_ty mai_den stay!

№44. THE BROKEN TOKEN.

1

One summer evening, a maiden fair
Was walking forth in the balmy air,
She met a sailor upon the way;
    'Maiden stay' he whispered,
    'Maiden stay' he whispered
        'O pretty maiden, stay!'

2

Why art thou walking abroad alone?
The stars are shining, the day is done',
O then her tears they began to flow
    For a dark eyed sailor,
    For a dark eyed sailor
        Had filled her heart with woe.

3

'Three years are pass'd since he left this land,
A ring of gold he took off my hand,
He broke the token, a half to keep,
    Half he bade me treasure,
    Half he bade me treasure,
        Then cross'd the briny deep'.

4

'O drive him damsel from out your mind,
For men are changeful as is the wind,
And love inconstant will quickly grow
    Cold as winter morning
    Cold is winter morning
        When lands are white with snow'.

5

'Above the snow is the holly seen,
In bitter blast it abideth green,
And blood red drops it as berries bears
    So my aching bosom,
    So my aching bosom,
        Its truth and sorrow wears'.

6

Then half the ring did the sailor show,
Away with weeping and sorrow now!
In bands of marriage united we
    Like the broken Token
    Like the broken Token
        In one shall welded be.

Nº 45. THE ROUT IS OUT.

A midsummer morning fresh and bright,
 And all the world is gay,
The Rout it is out, we must all turn out,
 The lads they march away.
The pretty maids are left in town,
 They look from the windows high,
They stand in the street, they crowd in the door,
 With many a tear and sigh,
  Singing, Adieu, my boys, Adieu! my boys!
   Adieu, my boys, adieu!
   Alack the day, they be going away!
   Pray girls what shall we do!

2

O bind them posies of pleasant flowers,
 Of Marjoram, mint, and rue.
And blow them kisses, to take away,
 As favours to wear — of you.
And wave the kerchiefs from off your necks,
 And ribbons about them bind;
And bid them never, O never forget
 The pretty maids left behind
  Singing, Adieu &c:

3

My Johnny, a bonnet, he swore would buy
 The bravest in all the town,
But now my Johnny must march away,
 I know not whither bound.
He'd dress me, he said, in velvet red,
 He'd wrangle my hair in blue,
And now he is gone from me along
 I doubt it he will prove true
  Singing, Adieu &c:

4

O, why are you looking so sad, my child!
 O why does your colour change!
I'm thinking of Johnny, who's march'd away
 I know not where to range.
My lover he was a gallant blade,
 He warbled a merry lay,
And now am I sad, for my pretty lad
 So far, O! so far away!
  Singing, Adieu &c:

DRINKING SONG.

Nº 46. F.W.B.

N⁰ 46. WHY SHOULD WE BE DULLARDS SAD.

Why should we be dullards sad,
　Whilst on earth we moulder?
See the gay the good the glad,
　Every day grow older.
Fill the flask sweet music bring,
　Joy shall quickly find us,
We will shout and laugh and sing,
　And cast dull care behind us.
　　　　　Chorus: Fill the flask, &c

2

Hail good comrades every one,
　Round the polished table,
Pass the bottle with the sun,
　Drink, sirs, whilst yo're able.
Life is but a little span,
　Full of painful thinking,
Let us live as fits a man,
　All good liquors drinking.
　　　　　Chorus: Fill the flask, &c.

3

When at [Uncle Tom's]* we meet,
　A glass to take together,
Hand in hand, in union sweet,
　Friendship we'll keep ever.
We're no moles throughout the night
　Blind in darkness groping,
But are crickets, sons of light
　Singing, chirping, toping!
　　　　　Chorus: Fill the flask, &c

4

[Uncle] brim the flowing bowl,
　Here's to each good liver
Harmony pervade the soul,
　Discord enter never!
Fill the flask, sweet music bring
　Joy shall quickly find us,
We will shout and laugh, and sing,
　And cast dull care behind us.
　　　　　Chorus: Fill the flask, &c

* Name of host or of place given here

MAY-DAY CAROL.

No. 47. H.F.S.

No. 47. MAY-DAY CAROL.

1

Awake, ye pretty maids, awake,
    Refreshed from drowsy dream,
And haste to dairy house, and take
    For us a dish of cream.

2

If not a dish of yellow cream,
    Then give us kisses three.
The woodland bower is white with flower,
    And green is every tree.

3

A branch of May we bear about
    Before the door it stands;
There's not a sprout unbudded out,
    The work of God's own hands.

4

Awake, awake ye pretty maids,
    And take the May-bush in,
Or 'twill be gone ere tomorrow morn,
    And you'll have none within.

5

Through-out the night, before the light,
    There fell the dew or rain.
It twinkles bright on May bush white,
    It sparkles on the plain.

6

The heavenly gates are open wide
    To let escape the dew,
And heavenly grace falls on each place
    It drops on us and you.

7

The life of man is but a span,
    He blossoms as a flower,
He makes no stay, is here to-day,
    And vanished in an hour. *

8

My song is done, I must be gone,
    Nor make a longer stay.
God bless you all, both great and small,
    And send you gladsome May.

---

* Verses 6 & 7, and there have been others of like moralising nature were added when the character of the May-Day visit was altered from one of lovers to their sweethearts into one of children seeking May-Gifts. Then the "Kisses three" were changed to "Pennies one or three."

N.º 48. NANCY.

1

My own pretty Nancy
  My love and delight;
This is the kind letter
  To you I indite.
It is to inform you,
  Wherever I go,
In tempest, in battle
  I'm faithful to you.

2

When blust'ring and roaring
  We're tossed about
Five hundred bright sailors,
  All sturdy and stout,
One moment deep plunged,
  Then high in the air,
To see my sweet Nancy
  I almost despair.

3

We fought with a Spaniard,
  A galleon of pride,
With cutlass and pike, love,
  We climbed up her side
We fought as sea lions,
  The deck ran with blood
But soon all was over,
  And victors we stood.

4

Storm, battle, all ended,
  If God spares our lives,
We'll come to our sweethearts,
  Our children and wives.
A health to sweet Nancy!
  I drink on the main,
God send me to Nancy,
  And England again.

LULLABY.
1st Version.

N⁰ 49. (1.)　　　　　　　　　　　　　　　　　　　　　　　H. F. S.

No. 49. LULLABYE.

1

Sleep baby sleep!
  Dad is not nigh,
Tossed on the deep,
  Lul-lul-a-by!
Moon shining bright,
  Dropping of dew,
Owls hoot all night
  To-whit! to-whoo!

2

Sleep, baby, sleep!
  Dad is away,
Tossed on the deep,
  Looking for day.
In the hedge row
  Glow-worms alight,
Rivulets flow,
  All through the night.

3

Sleep baby sleep!
  Dad is afar,
Tossed on the deep,
  Watching a star.
Clock going tick,
  Tack,—in the dark,
On the hearth-click!—
  Dies the last spark.

4

Sleep, baby, sleep!
  What! not a wink!
Dad on the deep,
  What will he think?
Baby dear, soon
  Daddy will come,
Bringing red shoon
  For baby at home.

LULLABY.
2nd Version with Violin.

№49. LULLABYE.

1

Sleep baby sleep!
　Dad is not nigh,
Tossed on the deep,
　Lul-lul-a-by!
Moon shining bright,
　Dropping of dew.
Owls hoot all night
　To-whit! to-whoo!

2

Sleep, baby, sleep!
　Dad is away,
Tossed on the deep,
　Looking for day.
In the hedge row
　Glow-worms alight,
Rivulets flow,
　All through the night.

3

Sleep baby sleep!
　Dad is afar,
Tossed on the deep,
　Watching a star.
Clock going-tick,
　Tack,-in the dark.
On the hearth - click! -
　Dies the last spark.

4

Sleep, baby, sleep!
　What! not a wink!
Dad on-the deep,
　What will he think?
Baby dear, soon
　Daddy will come,
Bringing red shoon
　For baby at home.

THE GIPSY COUNTESS.
Part I.

N° 50.   F. W. B.

There came an Earl a-riding by, A gipsy maid espied he, "O out-brown maid, from greenwood glade, O prithee come along with me." "In greenwood glade, fair sir!" she said, "I am so blythe, as bird so gay, In thy castle tall, in bow'r and hall, I fear for grief I'd pine away."

N⁰ 50. THE GIPSY COUNTESS.

PART. I.

1.

There came an Earl a riding by,
   A gipsy maid espyed he;
"O nut-brown maid, from green wood glade,
   O prithee come along with me!"
"In greenwood glade, fair Sir!" she said,
   I am so blythe, as bird so gay.
In thy castle tall, in bower and hall,
   I fear for grief I'd pine away."

2

"Thou shalt no more be set in stocks,
   And tramp about from town to town,
But thou shalt ride in pomp and pride
   In velvet red and broidered gown."
"My brothers three no more I'd see,
   If that I went with thee, I trow.
They sing me to sleep, with songs so sweet,
   They sing as on our way we go."

3

"Thou shalt not be torn by thistle and thorn,
   With thy bare feet all in the dew.
But shoes shall wear of Spanish leather
   And silken stockings all of blue."
" I will not go to thy castle high,
   For thou wilt weary soon, I know,
Of the gipsy maid, from green-wood glade,
   And drive her forth in rain and snow."

4

"All night you lie 'neath the starry sky
   In rain and snow you trudge all day,
But thy brown head, in a feather bed,
   When left the gipsies, thou shalt lay."
"I love to lie 'neath the starry sky,
   I do not heed the snow and rain,
But fickle is wind, I fear to find
   The man who now my heart would gain."

5

"I will thee wed, sweet maid," he said,
   "I will thee wed with a golden ring,
"Thy days shall be spent in merriment;
   For us the marriage bells shall swing."
The dog did howl, and screech'd the owl,
   The raven croaked, the night-wind sighed;
The wedding bell from the steeple fell,
   As home the Earl did bear his bride.

THE GIPSY COUNTESS.
Part II.

Nº 50. THE GIPSY COUNTESS.
PART 2.

Three Gipsies stood at the Castle gate,
  They sang so high, they sang so low.
The lady sate in her chamber late,
  Her heart it melted away as snow,
     Away as snow,
     Her heart it melted away as snow.
       2

They sang so sweet, they sang so shrill,
  That fast her tears began to flow.
And she laid down her silken gown,
  Her golden rings, and all her show,
     All her show, &c:
       3

She plucked off her high-heeled shoes,
  A-made of Spanish leather, O.
She would in the street, with her bare, bare feet,
  All out in the wind and weather, O.
     Weather, O! &c:
       4

She took in hand but a one posie,
  The wildest flowers that lo grow.
And down the stair went the lady fair,
  To go away with the gipsies, O!
     The gipsies O! &c:
       5

At past midnight her lord came home,
  And where his lady was would know;
The servants replied on every side,
  She's gone away with the gipsies, O!
     The gipsies, O! &c:
       6

Then he rode high, and he rode low,
  And over hill and vale, I trow.
Until he espied his fair young bride,
  Who'd gone away with the gipsies, O!
     The gipsies, O! &c:
       7

O will you leave your house and lands,
  Your golden treasures for to go,
Away from your lord that weareth a sword,
  To follow along with the gipsies, O!
     The gipsies O! &c:
       8

O I will leave my house and lands,
  My golden treasures for to go,
I love not my lord that weareth a sword,
  I'll follow along with the gipsies, O!
     The gipsies O! &c:
       9

'Nay, thou shalt not!' then he drew, I wot,
  The sword that hung at his saddle bow,
And once he smote on her lily-white throat,
  And there her red blood down did flow,
     Down did flow, &c:
       10

Then dipp'd in blood was the posie good,
  That was of the wildest flowers that blow.
She sank on her side, and so she died,
  For she would away with the gipsies O!
     The gipsies O!
     For she would away with the gipsies O!

THE GREY MARE.

N⁰ 51. THE GREY MARE.

1

Young Roger, the Miller, went courting of late
A farmer's sweet daughter called Beautiful Kate;
Now Kitty was buxom, and bonny and fair,
Had plenty of humour, of frolic a share,
And her father possessed an uncommon grey mare,
           A grey mare, a grey mare
           An uncommon grey mare.

2

So Roger he dressed himself up as a beau,
He comb'd down his locks, and in collars of snow,
He went to the farmer, and said, "How d'y do!
I love pretty Kitty to her I'll prove true;
Will you give me the grey mare and Katherine too,
           The grey mare, the grey mare &c:

3

"She's a very nice maiden, a-courting I'm come,
Lawks! how I would like the grey mare to ride home!
I love your sweet daughter so much I declare,
I'm ready my mill — and my stable — to share,
With Kitty the charming, and with the grey mare.
           The grey mare, the grey mare &c:

4

"You're welcome to her, to her hand and her heart,
But from the grey mare, man, I never will part!"
So said the old farmer, — then Roger, "I swear,
It is up with my courting, for Kate I don't care,
Unless I be given as well the grey mare.
           The grey mare, the grey mare &c:

5

The years had pass'd swiftly, when withered and grey,
Old Roger, the Miller, met Katherine one day,
Said he, "I remember you, buxom and fair,
As roses your cheeks and as broom was your hair,
And I came a courting! — Ah, Kate! the grey mare,
           The grey mare, the grey mare &c.

6

"I remember your coming to court the grey mare
Very well, M! Roger, when golden my hair,
And cheeks were as roses that bloom on the wall.
But, lawks! M! Roger, — I can not recall
That e'er you came sweet-hearting me, man, at all,
           But the mare, the grey mare
           That uncommon grey mare."

A Wreck off the Scilly.

№ 52. THE WRECK OFF SCILLY.

1

Come all you brisk young sailors bold
  That plough the raging main,
A tragedy I will untold
  In story sad and plain.
From my true love 'twas pressed was I
  The gallant ship to steer
To Indies west, — each heart beat high
  With confidence and cheer.

2

A year was gone, and home at last,
  We came with swelling sail,
When — 'ere the Scilly over-passed
  There broke on us a gale.
The boatswain up aloft did go,
  He went aloft so high,
More angry did the ocean grow,
  More menacing the sky.

3

To make the strips in vain, we tried
  The Scilly rocks to clear,
The thunder of the furious tide
  Was filling every ear.
There came a sharp and sudden shock, —
  Each thought of wife and home!
The gallant ship was on a rock,
  And swept with wave and foam.

4

Of eighty seamen 'prised the crew,
  But one did reach the shore,
The gallant vessel, good and true,
  Was shattered aft and tore.
The news to Plymouth swift did fly,
  That our good ship was gone;
And wet with tears was many an eye,
  And many a widow lone.

5

And when I came to Plymouth sound
  Alive, of eighty dead,
My pretty love, then false I found
  And to a landsman wed.
O gentles all that live on land
  Be-think the boys at sea,
Lo! here I stand with cap in hand,
  And crave your charity.

HENRY MARTYN.

N⁰ 53. HENRY MARTYN.

1
In merry Scotland, in merry Scotland,
  There lived brothers three,
They all did cast lots which of them should go,
  A robbing upon the salt sea.

2
The lot it fell upon Henry Martyn,
  The youngest of the three,
That he should go rob on the salt, salt sea,
  To maintain his brothers and he.

3
He had not a sailed a long winter's night,
  No yet a short winter's day,
Before he espied the King's gallant ship,
  Come sailing along that way.

4
How far, how far, cried Henry Martyn,
  How far are you going? said he
For I am a robber upon the salt seas,
  To maintain my brothers and me.

5
Stand off, stand off! the Captain he cried,
  The lifeguards they are aboard.
My cannons are loaden with powder and shot,
  And every man hath a sword.

6
For three long hours they merrily fought,
  For hours they fought full three.
And many a blow it dealt many a wound,
  As they fought on the salt, salt sea.

7
Twas broadside against a broadside then,
  And at it, the which should win,
A shot in the gallant ship bored a hole,
  And then did the water rush in.

8
Bad news! bad news, for old England
  Bad news has come to the town,
The king his vessel is wrecked and lost,
  And all his brave soldiers drown.

9
Bad news! bad news through the London street!
  Bad news has come to the King.
The lives of his guards they be all a lost,
  O the tidings be sad that I bring.

10
O had I a twisted rope of hemp,
  A bowstring strong though thin;
I'd soon hang him up to his middle yard arm,
  And have done with Henry Martyn.

P. & W. 1506.

N.º 54. PLYMOUTH SOUND.

1

O the fair town of Plymouth is by the sea-side,
The Sound is so blue, and so still and so wide,
Encircled with hills and with forests all green,
As a crown of fresh leaves on the head of a queen.
    O dear Plymouth town, and O blue Plymouth Sound!
    O where is your equal on Earth to be found.

2

O the maidens of Plymouth are comely and sweet,
So mirthful of eye and so nimble of feet,
I love all the lasses of Plymouth so well,
That the which I love best not a prophet can tell.
    O dear Plymouth town, & c.

3

O the bells of old Plymouth float over the bay,
My heart it does melt, as I'm sailing away.
O be they a ringing when I do return,
With thoughts matrimonial my bosom will burn.
    O dear Plymouth town, & c.

4

For the maidens of Plymouth my love is so hot,
With a bushel of rings I would marry the lot.
But as I can't marry them all well-a-day!
Perhaps it's as well that I'm sailing away.
    O dear Plymouth town, & c.

P. & W. 1506.

FAREWELL TO KINGSBRIDGE.

Nº 55.

N.º 55. FAREWELL TO KINGSBRIDGE.

1

Of the ninth day of November, at the dawning in the sky,
Ere we sailed away to New York, we at anchor here did lie,
O'er the meadows fair of Kingsbridge, then the mist was lying grey;
We were bound against the rebels, in the North America.

2

O so mournful was the parting of the soldiers and their wives,
For that none could say for certain, they'd return home with their lives.
Then the women they were weeping, and they curs'd the cruel day,
That we sailed against the rebels, in the North America.

3

O the little babes were stretching out their arms with saddest cries,
And the bitter tears were falling, from their pretty simple eyes,
That their scarlet coated daddies, must be hurrying away,
For to fight against the rebels, in the North America.

4

Now with God preserve our Monarch, I will finish up my strain,
Be his subjects ever loyal, and his honour all maintain.
May the Lord our voyage prosper, and our arms across the sea
And put down the wicked rebels in the North America.

P. & W. 1506.

FURZE BLOOM.

N.º 56. FURZE BLOOM.

1
There's not a cloud a sailing by,
  That does not hold a shower;
There's not a furze-bush on the moor,
  That doth not put forth flower.
About the roots we need not delve,
  The branches need not prune,
The yellow furze will ever flower,
  And ever love's in tune!
    Golden furze in bloom!
    O Golden furze in bloom!
    When the furze is out of flower,
    Then love is out of tune.

2
There's not a season of the year,
  Nor weather hot nor cold,
In windy spring, in watery fall,
  But furze is clad in gold.
It blossoms in the falling snow,
  It blazes bright in June,
And love, like it, is always here,
  And ever opportune.
    O golden furze & c.

3
*There's not a saucy lad I wot,
  With light and roguish eye,
That doth not love a pretty lass,
  And kiss her on the sly,
There's not a maiden in the shire
  From Hartland Point to Brent,
In velvet, or in cotton gown,
  That will his love resent.
    O golden furze & c.

4
Beside the fire with toasted crabs,
  We sit and love is there,
In merry spring, with apple flowers,
  It flutters in the air.
At harvest when we toss the sheaves,
  Then Love with them is toss't.
At fall when nipp'd and sere the leaves,
  Unnippt is Love by frost.
    O golden furze, & c.

*May be omitted in singing.

THE OXEN PLOUGHING.

N⁰ 57. THE OXEN PLOUGHING.

1

Prithee lend your jocund voices,
   For to listen we're agreed;
Come sing of songs the choicest,
   Of the life the plough-boys lead.
There are none that live so merry
   As the ploughboy does in Spring
When he hears the sweet birds whistle
   And the nightingales to sing.
      With my Hump-a-long! Jump-a-long!
      Here drives my lad along!
      Pretty, Sparkle, Berry
      Good-luck, Speedwell, Cherry!
      We are the lads that can follow the plough.

2

For it's, O my little ploughboy
   Come awaken in the morn,
When the cock upon the dunghill
   Is a-blowing of his horn.
Soon the sun above Brown Willy,*
   With his golden face will show;
Therefore hasten to the linney
   Yoke the oxen to the plough.
      With my Hump-a-long! &c.

3

In the heat of the daytime
   It's but little we can do,
We will lie beside our oxen
   For an hour, or for two.
On the banks of sweet violets,
   I'll take my noontide rest,
And it's I can kiss a pretty girl
   As hearty as the best.
      With my Hump-a-long! &c.

4

When the sun at eve is setting
   And the shadows fill the vale,
Then our throttles we'll be wetting,
   With the farmer's humming ale.
And the oxen home returning
   We will send into the stall.
Where the logs and turf are burning,
   We'll be merry ploughboys all.
      With my Hump-a-long! &c.

5

O the farmer must have seed, sirs
   Or I swear he cannot sow.
And the miller with his mill wheel
   Is an idle man also.
And the huntsman gives up hunting,
   And the tradesman stands aside,
And the poor man bread is wanting,
   So 'tis we for all provide.
      With my Hump-a-long! &c.

*Or any other suitable hill.

SOMETHING LACKING.

N.º 58.

F. W. B.

N.º 58. SOMETHING LACKING.

1

I chanced to rise at the dawning of day,
To walk in the sweet summer air.
I buckled my belt, donned my ribbons so gay,
To travel to Hatherleigh fair.
Then as I went over the road I espied
Some blackberries hanging all in the hedge side,
So pleasant, inviting to taste by their look,
But I could not get at them for lack of a crook.

2

As I was a-taking my way to the town,
Before that bright Phœbus did rise,
I saw some red roses, their heads hanging down,
Red roses to gladden girls' eyes.
I said, Pretty roses, I'll pluck you, I swear,
That's one for my hat, and two others to spare.
But, gloveless, alack! with my hands in the thorn,
No roses I got, though I got my hands torn.

3 *

As I was awalking along by the stream,
I saw a blue kingfisher dart.
Your plumage I'll wear pretty bird, I declare,
No lad at the fair'll be as smart.
With feathers arrayed, in my beaver displayed,
Admired I shall be, in request by each maid,
But, alack! without trap, without sling, without bow,
Ungarnished with feathers I was forced to go.

4

I went to the fair, and I heard the bells ring,
The maidens were many and gay.
I said, with the lasses I'll frolic and fling,
But every one laughed and said Nay!
They'd have a bright ribbon, a kerchief, a toy,
And none would say aught to a penniless boy,
So, having no money, my journey in vain,
Alone, lacking sweetheart, I trudged home again.

* May be omitted in singing.

The Ploughboy.

N.º 59. H. F. S.

N.° 59. THE PLOUGHBOY.

1
O the Ploughboy was a ploughing
With his horses on the plain,
    And was singing of a song as on went he.
"Since that I have fall'n in love,
If the parents disapprove,
    'Tis the first thing that will send me to the sea!"

2
When the parents came to know
That their daughter loved him so,
    Then they sent a gang, and pressed him for the sea.
And they made of him a tar,
To be slain in cruel war;
    Of the simple Ploughboy singing on the lea.

3
The maiden sore did grieve,
And without a word of leave,
    From her father's house she fled secretly,
In male attire dress'd,
With a star upon her breast,
    All to seek her simple Ploughboy on the sea.

4
Then she went o'er hill and plain,
And she walked in wind and rain,
    Till she came to the brink of the blue sea.
Saying, "I am forced to rove,
For the loss of my true love,
    Who is but a simple Ploughboy from the lea."

* 5
Now the first she did behold,
O it was a sailor bold,
    "Have you seen my simple ploughboy?" then said she.
"They have press'd him to the fleet,
Sent him tossing on the deep,
    Who is but a simple Ploughboy from the lea."

6
Then she went to the Captain,
And to him she made complain,
    "O a silly Ploughboy's run away from me!"
Then the Captain smiled and said,
"Why Sir! surely you're a maid!
    So the Ploughboy I will render up to thee."

7
Then she pulled out a store,
Of five hundred crowns and more,
    And she strewed them on the deck, did she,
Then she took him by the hand,
And she rowed him to the land,
    Where she wed the simple Ploughboy back from sea.

* May be omitted in singing.

THE WRESTLING MATCH.

N.º 60. THE WRESTLING MATCH.

1

I sing of champions bold,
That wrestled not for gold.
    And all the cry was Will Tretry!
That he should win the day.
So, Will Tretry Huzzah!
The ladies clap their hands and cry
    Tretry! Tretry! Huzzah!

2

Then up sprang little Jan,
A lad scarce grown a man,
    He said, Tretry! I wot, I'll try
A hitch with thee this day.
So, little Jan, Huzzah!
The ladies clap their hands and cry,
    O little Jan, Huzzah!

3

They wrestled on the ground
His match Tretry had found
    And back he bore, in struggle sore,
He felt his force give way.
So little Jan, Huzzah!
So some did say — but others, Nay,
    Tretry! Tretry! Huzzah!

4

Then with a desperate toss.
Will showed the flying hoss.
    And little Jan fell on the tan.
And never more he spake.
O little Jan! alack!
The ladies say, O woe's the day,
    O little Jan, — alack!

5

Now little Jan, I ween,
That day had married been;
    Had he not died, a gentle bride,
That day he home had led.
The ladies sigh, the ladies cry
    O little Jan is dead!

P. & W. 1506.

THE PAINFUL PLOUGH.

Nº 61. THE PAINFUL PLOUGH.

1
O Adam was a ploughboy, when ploughing first begun,
The next that did succeed him was Cain, his eldest son;
Some of the generation the calling still pursue,
That bread may not be wanting, they labour at the plough.

2
Samson was the strongest man, and Solomon was wise,
And Alexander conquering, he made the world his prize,
King David was a valiant man, and many thousands slew,
Yet none of all these heroes bold could live without the plough.

3
Behold the wealthy merchant, that trades on foreign seas,
And brings home gold and treasure, for such as live at ease,
With spices and with cinnamon, and oranges also,
They're brought us from the Indies, by virtue of the plough.

4
I hope there's none offended at me for singing this,
For never I intended to sing you ought amiss.
And if you well consider, you'll find the saying true,
That all mankind dependeth upon the painful plough.

Broadbury Gibbet.

No. 62.

H. F. S.

N.º 62. BROADBURY GIBBET.

1

On Broadbury down the ravens croak,
    The breezes shriek and groan,
Now low, now high, the white owls fly,
    As snowflakes in the moon.
The cotton-grass grows under me,
    In tufts of silver white,
I swing and sway throughout the day,
    I sway and swing all night.

2

On Broadbury down my gibbet stands,
    Just where the highways cross,
It tells the moments, marks the hours,
    With shadow on the moss.
And I am as a pendulum,
    That swing and never stay,
The Death Clock of a bad old world
    That cankereth away.

P. & W. 1506.

THE ORCHESTRA.

Nº 63.

F. W. B.

N.º 63. THE ORCHESTRA.

1
I went unto my true love's house
At eight o'clock at night,
And in her chamber-window high
There burnt a taper's light.
Of windows had that maiden four,
They looked every way,
And from each window, in the night,
Shone forth an equal ray.
 There was I with my flageolet,
 There was also fiddling Bill.
 There was lanky Tom, with his big trombone,
 With a tooth-comb, Humphry Hill.

2
Each lover deemed himself alone
Her chosen swain to prove,
And she looked out on every one
With equal words of love.
So I began on my flageolet,
And Bill his Violin.
And Tom—Bimbom!—on his Trombone,
And Hill his tooth-comb thin.
 There was I, &c.

3
*Why what a marvel! then said I,
Such echoes be most rare!
And round the corner ran to spy,
And found the fiddler there.
The fiddler round the corner ran,
On lanky Tom he hit;
And Tom he hushed his bom bom bom,
And next on Humphry hit.
 There was I, &c.

* May be omitted in singing.
P. & W. 1506.

4
My pipe I split on Willy's head
His violin broke Will,
And Tom struck home with his Trombone,
Upon the head of Hill.
And Humphry round the corner ran,
And when he did me spy;
He up with his tooth-comb like a man,
And hit me in the eye.
 There was I, &c.

5
Now Brothers, peace! I said, Be calm,
Tom Humphry and Willie,
Let's walk away, all arm in arm,
And leave her solitary.
Our broken instruments we'll let
Upon her doorstep lie.
We'll love abjure, we'll court no more,
Not Hill, Tom, Bill, nor I.
 There was I, &c.

THE GOLDEN VANITY.

Nº 64. THE GOLDEN VANITY.

1
A ship I have got in the North Country
And she goes by the name of the Golden Vanity,
O I fear she'll be taken by a Spanish Ga_la_lie,
　　As she sails by the Low-lands low.

2
To the Captain then upspake the little Cabin-boy,
　He said, What is my fee, if the galley I destroy?
The Spanish Ga_la_lie, if no more it shall annoy,
　　As you sail by the Low-lands low.

3
Of silver and of gold I will give to you a store;
And my pretty little daughter that dwelleth on the shore,
Of treasure and of fee as well, I'll give to thee galore,
　　As we sail by the Low-lands low.

4
Then the boy bared his breast, and straightway leaped in,
And he held all in his hand, an augur sharp and thin,
And he swam until he came to the Spanish galleon,
　　As she lay by the Low-lands low.

5
He bored with the augur, he bored once and twice,
And some were playing cards, and some were playing dice,
When the water flowed in it dazzled their eyes,
　　And she sank by the Low-lands low.

6
* So the Cabin-boy did swim all to the larboardside,
Saying Captain! take me in, I am drifting with the tide!
I will shoot you! I will kill you! the cruel Captain cried,
　　You may sink by the Low-lands low.

7
Then the Cabin-boy did swim all to the starboard side
Saying, Messmates take me in, I am drifting with the tide!
Then they laid him on the deck, and he closed his eyes and died,
　　As they sailed by the Low-lands low.

8
* They sewed his body up, all in an old cow's hide,
And they cast the gallant cabin-boy, over the ship's side,
And left him without more ado adrifting with the tide,
　　And to sink by the Low-lands low.

* May be omitted in singing
P & W. 1506.

THE BOLD DRAGOON.

Nº 65. H. F. S.

A bold dragoon from out of the North, To a la_dy's house came ri_ding, Bring
With clank of steel and spur at his heel His con_sequence no_ways hi_ding.

forth good cheer, Tap claret and beer, For here I think of a_bi_ding; A_

_bi_ding, A_bi_ding, Bring forth good cheer Tap claret and beer, For

Nº 65. THE BOLD DRAGOON.

1

A bold dragoon from out of the North,
To a lady's house came riding;
With clank of steel, and spur at his heel,
His consequence noways hiding.
"Bring forth good cheer, tap claret and beer,
For here I think of abiding.
Abiding, Abiding.

2

The chamber best with arras be dress'd
I intend to be comfortable.
Such troopers as we always make ourselves free,
Heigh!— lead my horse to the stable!
Give him corn and hay, but for me Tockay,
We'll eat and drink whilst able,
Able, aye! Able.

3

The daintiest meat upon silver plate,
And wine that sparkles and fizzes.
Wax candles light, make the chamber bright,
And— as soldiers love sweet Misses,
My moustache I curl with an extra twirl,
The better to give you kisses,
Kisses, aye! Kisses.

4

"There's cake and wine," said the lady fine,
There's oats for the horse, and litter.
There's silver plate, there are servants to wait,
And drinks, sweet, spark'ling, bitter.
Tho. bacon and pease, aye! and mouldy cheese,
For such as you were fit'er,
Fitter aye! Fitter.

5

"Your distance keep, I esteem you cheap
Tho' your wishes I've granted, partly.
But no kisses for me from a Chimpanzee,"
The lady responded tartly.
"Why! a rude dragoon is a mere Baboon."
And she boxed his ears full smartly,
Smartly, aye! smartly.

P. & W. 1506.

TRINITY SUNDAY.

Nº 66.

With Simplicity and cheerfulness.

H. F. S.

N⁰ 66. TRINITY SUNDAY.

1
When bites the frost and winds are a blowing,
   I do not heed I do not care;
If Johnny's by me, what if it be snowing.
   'Tis summer time with me all the year.
The icicles they may hang on the fountain,
   And frozen over the farm yard pool.
The bleak wind whistle across the mountain,
   No wintry blast our love can cool.

2
O what to me the wind and the weather?
   O what to me the wind and the rain?
My Johnny loves me, and being together,
   Why let it bluster — it blows in vain.
I never tire, I never am weary,
   I drudge and think it is only play;
As Johnny loves me, and I am his deary,
   Why all the year it is holiday.

3
I shall be wed upon Trinity Sunday,
   And then adieu to my holiday.
Come frost and frown the following Monday,
   Why then beginneth my workaday.
If drudge and smudge begins on the Monday,
   If scold and grumble — I do not care,
My winter follow Trinity Sunday.
   I can't have summertime all the year.

THE BLUE FLAME.

Nº 67.   H. F. S.

N⁰ 67. THE BLUE FLAME.

1

All under the stars, and beneath the green tree,
All over the sward, and along the cold lea,
    A little blue flame
    A flattering came,
It came from the churchyard for you or for me.

2

I sit by the cradle, my baby's asleep,
And rocking the cradle, I wonder and weep.
    O little blue light,
    In the dead of the night,
O prithee, O prithee no nearer to creep.

3

Why follow the church path, why steal you this way?
Why halt in your journey, on threshold why stay?
    With flicker and flare,
    Why dance up my stair?
O I would, O I would, it were dawning of day.

4

All under the stars, and along the green lane,
Unslaked by the dew, and unquenched by the rain,
    Of little flames blue
    To the churchyard steal two,
The soul of my baby! now from me is ta'en.

P. & W. 1506.

STRAWBERRY FAIR.

N⁰ 68. STRAWBERRY FAIR.

1
As I was going to Strawberry Fair,
   Singing, singing, Butter-cups and Daisies
I met a maiden taking her ware,
   Fol-de-dee!
Her eyes were blue and golden her hair,
As she went on to Strawberry Fair,
   Ri-fol, Ri-tol, Tol-de-rid-dle-li-do,
   Ri-fol, Ri-tol, Tol-de-rid-dle-dee.

2
Kind Sir, pray pick of my basket! she said
   Singing, &c.
"My cherries ripe, or my roses red,
   Fol-de-dee!
My strawberries sweet, I can of them spare,
As I go on to Strawberry Fair."
   Ri-fol &c.

3
Your cherries soon will be wasted away,
   Singing, &c.
Your roses wither and never stay,
   Tol-de-de.
'Tis not to seek such perishing ware,
That I am tramping to Strawberry Fair
   Ri-fol &c.

4
I want to purchase a generous heart,
   Singing, &c.
A tongue that neither is nimble nor tart
   Tol-de-dee!
An honest mind, but such trifles are rare
I doubt if they're found at Strawberry Fair:
   Ri-fol &c.

5
The price I offer, my sweet pretty maid
   Singing, &c.
A ring of gold on your finger displayed,
   Tol-de-dee!
So come make over to me your ware,
In church to-day at Strawberry Fair.
   Ri-fol &c.

P. & W. 1506.

№ 69. FARMER'S SON.

1
I would not be a monarch great;
  With crown upon my head,
And Earls to wait upon my state,
  In broidered robes of red.
For he must bear full many a care,
  His toil is never done,
'Tis better I trow behind the plough,
  A Country Farmer's Son.

2
* I would not be the Pope of Rome,
  And sit in Peter's chair;
With priests to bow and kiss my toe,
  No wife my throne to share.
And never know what 'tis to go,
  With beagles for a run;
'Tis better for me at liberty
  A Country Farmer's Son.

3
I would not be a merchant rich,
  And eat off silver plate.
And ever dread, when laid abed
  Some freakish turn of fate.
One day on high, then ruin nigh,
  Now wealthy, now undone,
'Tis better for me at ease to be
  A Country Farmer's Son.

4
I trudge about the farm, all day,
  To know that all things thrive
A maid I see that pleaseth me,
  Why then I'm fain to wive.
Not over rich, I do not itch,
  For wealth, but what is won,
By honest toil, from out the soil,
  A Country Farmer's Son.

* May be omitted in singing.

THE HOSTESS' DAUGHTER.

№ 70. THE HOSTESS' DAUGHTER.

1

The Hostess of the Ring of Bells
   A daughter hath with auburn hair;
Go where I will, o'er plain and hill,
   I do not find a maid more fair;
She welcomes me with dimpled smiles,
   And e'en a kiss will not deny.
O! would for us the bells did ring!
   And we were wed — that maid and I!

2

But as I travelled down the road,
   There went by me a packer-train:
'Twas Roger Rawle, and Sandy Paul,
   And Hunchback Joe, and Philip Mayne.
Says Roger, I have had a kiss,
   From that sly maiden at the Bell,
And I, said Joe, and Paul said so,
   And so did Philip Mayne as well.

3

Till weather-beaten as the sign
   That doth before the tavern swing,
That maid will stay, and none essay,
   To make her his with bell and ring.
Methinks I'll take another road,
   Where hap some modest maiden dwells,
No sumey miss, with ready kiss,
   And then for us shall ring the Bells.

P & W. 1506.

The Jolly Goss-Hawk.

№ 71. THE JOLLY GOSS-HAWK.

1
I sat on a bank in trifle and play,
  With my jolly goss-hawk, and her wings were grey;
She flew to my breast, And she there built her nest,
  I am sure pretty bird you with me will stay.

2
She builded within, and she builded without,
  My jolly goss-hawk and her wings were grey;
She fluttered her wings, And she jingled her rings,
  So merry was she, and so fond of play.

3
I got me a bell, to tie to her foot,
  My jolly goss-hawk, and her wings were grey;
She mounted in flight, And she flew out of sight,
  My bell and my rings she carried away.

4
I ran up the street, with nimblest feet,
  My jolly goss-hawk, and her wings were grey;
I whooped and hallo'd, But never she shewed,
  And I lost my pretty goss-hawk that day.

5
In a meadow so green, the hedges between,
  My jolly goss-hawk and her wings were grey;
Upon a man's hand, She perch'd did stand,
  In sport, and trifle, and full array.

6
Who's got her may keep her as best he can,
  My jolly goss-hawk and her wings were grey;
To every man she is frolic and free,
  I'll cast her off if she come my way.

P. & W. 1506.

N° 72. "FAIR GIRL, MIND THIS!"

1

A woman that hath a bad husband, I find,
  By scolding won't make him the better.
So let her be easy, contented in mind,
  Nor suffer his foibles to fret her.
Let every good woman her husband adore,
Then happy her lot, though't be humble and poor,
We live like two turtles, no sorrows we know,
  And, fair girl! Mind this when you marry!
    Fair girl! Mind this when you marry!

2

My wife has been wedded full many a year,
  And blesses the day she was married,
She never fell out in her life with her dear,
  Tho' he at the ale-house has tarried.
She kindles the candle, and goes to her bed,
  No word of contention and chiding is said,
We live like two Turtles, &c.

3

At morning full early my wife's on the trot,
  Is laying and lighting the fire;
She gets me a pot of brown coffee, and hot;
  Or anything else I desire.
She's under subjection, is dapper and fair,
She greeteth me always with Darling, and Dear!
We live like two Turtles, &c.

4

Should Saturday come and the money run short,
  Why then — there is less for the Sunday.
She says she's contented, — no angry retort;
  Only — work all the harder on Monday!
She gives me a kiss, and away I do go,
She never says, Husband, why worry me so?
We live like two Turtles, &c.

P & W. 1506.

ON A MAY MORNING SO EARLY.

№ 73.

H.F.S.

№ 73. ON A MAY MORNING SO EARLY.

1
As I walked out one May morning,
  One May morning so early;
I there espied a fair pretty maid,
    All in the dew so pearly.
      O! 'twas sweet, sweet spring,
        Merry birds did sing,
          All in the morning early.

2
Stay, fair one, stay! Thus did I say,
  On a May morning so early;
My tale of love, your heart will move,
    All in the dew so pearly.
      O! 'tis sweet, sweet spring, Merry birds do sing,
        All in the morning early.

3
No tales for me, Kind sir, said she
  On a May morning so early;
My swain is true, I dont want two
    All in the dew so pearly.
      O! twas sweet sweet spring, Merry birds did sing,
        All in the morning early.

4
With lightsome tread, Away she sped,
  This May morning so early;
To meet her lad, And left me sad,
    All in the dew so pearly.
      O! 'twas sweet, sweet spring, Merry birds did sing,
        All in the morning early.

P & W. 1506.

THE SPOTTED COW.

Nº 74. H.F.S.

One morn-ing so gay, In the glad month of May, When I from my cot-tage strayed;..... As broke the ray of a-wake-ning day, I met a pret-ty maid..... A

neat lit-tle lass on the twink-ling grass, To see, my foot I stayed.

Nº 74. THE SPOTTED COW.

1
One morning so gay, in the glad month of May,
    When I from my cottage strayed;
As broke the ray of awakening day,
    I met a pretty maid.
A neat little lass on the twink'ling grass,
    To see, my foot I stayed.

2
"My fair pretty maid, why wander?" I said
    "So early, tell me now?"
The maid replied, "Pretty Sir!" and sighed,
    "I've lost my Spotted Cow.
She's stolen," she said, many tears she shed,
    "Or lost, I can't tell how."

3
No further complain in dolorous strain,
    I've tidings will you cheer.
I know she's strayed, in yonder green glade,
    Come, love! I'll shew you where.
So dry up your tears and banish fears,
    And bid begone despair."

4
"I truly confess in my bitter distress,
    You are most good," said she
"With help so kind, I am certain to find,
    My cow, so I'll with thee.
Four eyes, it is true are better than two,
    And friend, four eyes have we."

5
Through meadow and grove, we together did rove,
    We crossed the flow'ry dale,
Both morn and noon, we strayed till the moon
    Above our heads did sail.
The old Spotted Cow, clean forgotten was now,
    For love was all our tale.

6
Now never a day, do I go my way,
    To handle flail or plough.
She comes again, and whispers, "Sweet swain
    I've lost my Spotted Cow."
I pretend not to hear, she shouts "My dear,
    I've lost my Spotted Cow!"

CUPID THE PLOUGH BOY.

Nº 75.　　　　　　　　　　　　　　　　　　　　H.F.S.

As I one day walked out in May, When may was white in bloom, I bent my path across the swath And breath'd the sweet perfume. I wandered near a tillage field And leaning on a stile, I saw go by a ploughing boy With lips and eye a-smile.

P & W.1506.

№ 75. CUPID THE PLOUGH-BOY.

1

As I one day walked out in May,
    When May was white in bloom,
I bent my path across the swath,
    And breathed the sweet perfume.
I wandered near a tillage field,
    And leaning on a stile
I saw go by a ploughing boy,
    With lips and eye asmile.

2

O Cupid was that saucy boy
    Who furrows deeply drew,
He broke soil, destroyed the spoil
    Of wild thyme wet with dew.
Before his feet the field was sweet
    With flowers and grasses green,
Behind turn'd down, and bare and brown,
    By Cupid's coulter keen.

3

O cruel, cruel ploughing boy!
    With sharp and cutting share!
O why thy plough turn on me now,
    And leave me rent and bare?
I would, I wot, that I had not,
    A wended down this way,
Naught did I gain save rack and pain
    And dolour night and day.

4

"Thy heart I trow full deep I plough,
    My seed therein to sow,
A crop will soon upspring and bloom,
    And make a pretty show.
There'll come this way a gallant, gay,
    He'll view this flowery field,
Then straight to him, unquestioning,
    The crop of Love you'll yield."

P & W. 1506.

COME MY LADS, LET US BE JOLLY.

No 76. F.W.B.

Come my lads, let us be jol-ly! Drive a-way dull mel-an-cho-ly
For to grieve it is a fol-ly, When we've met to - ge-ther!
Come, let's live and well a - gree, Al - ways shun bad com - pan - y.
Why should we not merry, merry be, When we're met to - ge - ther.

P. & W. 1506.

N°76. COME MY LADS, LET US BE JOLLY.

1
Come my lads let us be jolly!
Drive away dull melancholy
For to grieve it is a folly,
    When we're met together.
Come, let's live and well agree,
Always shun bad company,
Why should we not merry merry be,
    When we're met together?
    Chorus. Come my lads let us be jolly &c.

2
Here's the bottle, as it passes,
Do not fail to fill your glasses,
Water-drinkers are dull asses,
    When they're met together.
Milk is meet for infancy,
Ladies like to sip Bohea,
Not such stuff for you and me
    When we're met together.
    Chorus. Come my lads, let us be jolly, &c.

3
Solomon a wise man hoary
Told us quite another story.
In our drink we'll chirp and glory,
    When we're met together.
Come my lads let's sing in chorus,
Merrily, but yet decorous,
Praising all good drinks before us,
    When we're met together.
    Chorus. Come my lads, let us be jolly &c.

P & W. 1506.

POOR OLD HORSE.

Nº 77. H.F.S.

N⁰ 77. POOR OLD HORSE.

1

O once I lay in stable, a hunter, well and warm,
I had the best of shelter, from cold and rain and harm;
But now in open meadow, a hedge I'm glad to find,
To shield my sides from tempest, from driving sleet and wind.
          Poor old horse, let him die!

2

My shoulders once were sturdy, were glossy, smooth and round,
But now, alas! they're rotten, I'm not accounted sound.
As I have grown so aged, my teeth gone to decay,
My master frowns upon me; I often hear him say,
          Poor old horse, let him die!

*__3__

A groom upon me waited, on straw I snugly lay,
When fields were full of flowers, the air was sweet with hay;
But now there's no good feeding prepared for me at all,
I'm forced to munch the nettles upon the kennel wall.
          Poor old horse, let him die!

4

My shoes and skin, the huntsman, that covets them shall have,
My flesh and bones the hounds, Sir! I very freely give,
I've followed them full often, aye! many a score of miles,
O'er hedges, walls and ditches, nor blinked at gates and stiles.
          Poor old horse, let him die!

5

Ye gentlemen of England, ye sportsmen good and bold,
All you that love a hunter, remember him when old,
O put him in your stable, and make the old boy warm,
And visit him and pat him, and keep him out of harm.
          Poor old horse, till he die!

* May be omitted in singing.

№ 78. THE DILLY SONG.

1

Come, and I will sing you.
        What will you sing me?
I will sing you One O!
        What is your One O?
One of them is all all alone, and ever will remain so.

2

Come, and I will sing you.
        What will you sing me?
I will sing you Two, O!
        What is your Two, O?
Two of them are lily-white babes, and dress'd all in green, O.

3

Come, &c.
I will sing you Three, O!
        What is your Three, O?
Three of them are strangers, o'er the wide world they are rangers.

4

Come, &c.
I will sing you Four, O
        What is your Four, O?
Four it is the Dilly Hour, when blooms the gilly flower.

5

Come, &c.
I will sing you Five, O!
        What is your Five, O?
Five it is the Dilly Bird, that's never seen, but heard, O!

6

Come, &c.
I will sing you Six, O!
        What is your Six, O?
Six the Ferryman in the Boat, that doth on the river float, O!

7

Come, &c.
I will sing you Seven, O!
        What is your Seven, O?
Seven it is the crown of Heaven, the shining stars be seven, O!

8

Come, &c.
I will sing you Eight, O!
        What is your Eight, O?
Eight it is the morning break, when all the world's awake, O!

9

Come, &c.
I will sing you Nine, O!
        What is your Nine, O?
Nine it is the pale moonshine, the pale moonlight is nine. O!

10

Come, &c.
I will sing you Ten, O!
        What is your Ten, O?
Ten forbids all kind of sin, and ten again begin, O!

THE MALLARD.

No. 79.   H.F.S.

P & W 1506.

Nº 79. THE MALLARD.

(A COUNTRY DANCE)

1

She: When lambkins skip, and apples are growing,
　　　Grass is green, and roses ablow,
He: When pigeons coo, and cattle are lowing,
　　　Mist lies white in vallies below,
Together: Why should we be all the day toiling?
　　　Lads and lasses, along with me!
　　　Done with drudgery, dust and moiling
　　　Haste away to the greenwood tree
She: The cows are milked, the team's in the stable,
　　　Work is over, and play begun,
He: Ye farmer lads all lusty and able
　　　Ere the moon rises, we'll have our fun,
Chorus: Why should we, &c.

*2

She: The glow-worm lights, as day is afailing,
　　　Dew is falling over the field,
He: The meadow-sweet its scent is exhaling,
　　　Honeysuckles their fragrance yield.
Together: Why should we, &c.
She: There's Jack o'lantern lustily dancing
　　　In the marsh with flickering flame,
He: And Daddy-long-legs, spinning and prancing,
　　　Moth and midge are doing the same,
Chorus: Why should we, &c.

3

She: So Bet and Prue, and Dolly and Celie,
　　　With milking pail 'tis time to have done.
He: And Ralph and Phil, and Robin and Willie,
　　　The threshing flail must sleep with the sun.
Together: Why should we, &c.
She: Upon the green beginneth our pleasure,
　　　Whilst we dance we merrily sing.
He: A country dance, a jig, and a measure,
　　　Hand in hand we go in a ring.
Chorus: Why should we, &c.

4

She: O sweet it is to foot on the clover,
　　　Ended work and revel begun.
He: Aloft the planets never give over,
　　　Dancing, circling round of the sun.
Together: Why should we, &c.
She: So Ralph and Phil, and Robin and Willie,
　　　Take your partners each of you now.
He: And Bet and Prue, and Dolly and Celie,
　　　Make a curtsey; lads! make a bow.
Chorus: Why should we.

*May be omitted in singing.

CONSTANT JOHNNY.

THE DUKE'S HUNT.

No. 81. THE DUKE'S HUNT.

1

'Twas on a bright and shining morn
I heard the merry hunting horn,
    At earliest hour of the morning.
There rode the Duke of Buckingham,
And many a squire and yeoman came,
    Dull sleep and phantom shadows scorning
        There was Dido, Spendigo
        Gentry too, and Hero,
        And Traveller that never looks behind him
        Countess and Towler,
        Bonny-lass and Jowler,
        These were some of the hounds that did find him.

2

Old Jack he courses o'er the plain,
Unwearied tries it back again,
    His horse and his hounds fail never.
Our hearty huntsman he will say,
For ever and for ee'r a day,
    Hark! Forward! gallant hounds together.
        There was Dido, &c.

3

The fox we followed, being young,
Our sport today is scarce begun,
    Ere out of the cover breaking,
Away he runs o'er hill and dale,
Away we followed without fail
    Hark! Forward! sleeping echoes awaking!
        There was Dido, &c.

4

Shy Reynard being well nigh spent,
His way he to the water bent,
    And speedily crossed the river.
To save his life he sought to swim,
But Dido sharp went after him,
    Heigh! Traveller destroyed his life for ever.
        There was Dido, &c.

5

So, whoo-too-hoo! we did proclaim
God bless the Duke of Buckingham,
    Our hounds they have gained great glory.
This maketh now the twentieth fox,
We've killed in river, dale and rocks,
    So here's an end to my story.
        There was Dido, &c.

THE BELL RINGING.

Nº 82.   F. W. B.

One day in October, being neither drunken nor sober, O'er Broadbury Down I was wending my way; When I heard of some ringing, some dancing and singing, I ought to remember that Jubilee day. 'Twas in Ashwater town The bells they did sound; They rang for a belt and a hat laced with gold. But the men of North Lew, Rang so steady and true That never were better in Devon I hold.

№82. THE BELL RINGING.

1.

One day in October,
Neither drunken nor sober,
O'er Broadbury Down I was wending my way.
When I heard of some ringing,
Some dancing and singing,
I ought to remember that Jubilee Day.

REFRAIN.

'Twas in Ashwater Town,
The bells they did soun'
They rang for a belt and a hat laced with gold.
But the men of North Lew
Rang so steady and true,
That never were better in Devon, I hold.

2.

'Twas misunderstood,
For the men of Broadwood,
Gave a blow to the tenor should never have been.
But the men of North Lew,
Rang so faultlessly true,
A difficult matter to beat them I ween
    'Twas in Ashwater Town &c:

3.

They of Broadwood being naughty
Then said to our party,
We'll ring you a challenge again in a round.
We'll give you the chance,
At St Stephen's or Launce-
-ston the prize to the winners a note of five pound.
    'Twas in Callington Town
    The bells next did soun'
    They rang,&c:

P&W. 1506.

4.

When the match it came on,
At good Callington,
The bells they rang out o'er the valleys below.
Then old and young people,
The halt and the feeble,
They came out to hear the sweet bell music flow.
    'Twas at Callington town
    The bells then did soun'
    They rang,&c:

5.

Those of Broadwood once more,
Were obliged to give o'er,
They were beaten completely and done in a round.
For the men of North Lew
Pull so steady and true,
That no better then they in the West can be found.
    'Twas at Ashwater town
    Then at Callington town
    They rang,&c:

THE BELL RINGING.

H.F.S.

N⁰ 83. A NUTTING WE WILL GO.

1.
'Tis of a jolly ploughingman,
Was ploughing of his land,
He call-d, Ho! he call-d, Wo!
And bade his horses stand.
Upon his plough he sat, I trow,
And loud began to sing,
His voice rang out, so clear and stout,
It made the horse bells ring.
    For a nutting we will go my boys,
      A nutting we will go,
    From hazel bush, loud sings the thrush,
      A nutting we will go!

2.
A maiden sly was passing by
With basket on her arm,
She stood to hear his singing clear,
To listen was no harm.
The ploughboy stayed that pretty maid,
And clasped her middle small,
He kissed her twice, he kissed her thrice
Ere she could cry or call.
      For a nutting &c:

3.
Now all you pretty maidens that
Go nutting o'er the grass
Attend my rede, and give good heed,
Of ploughboys that you pass.
When lions roar, on Afric's shore,
No mortal ventures near,
When hoots the owl, and bears do growl,
The heart is full of fear.
      For a nutting &c:

4.
And yet,'tis said, to pretty maid,
There is a graver thing,
In any clime, at any time,
- A ploughboy that doth sing.
So all you maidens, young and fair
Take lesson from my lay,
When you do hear a ploughman sing,
Then lightly run away.
      For a nutting &c:

DOWN BY A RIVER-SIDE.

N.º 84. DOWN BY A RIVER SIDE.

1.
Down by a River-side,
A fair maid I espied,
Lamenting for her own true love;
Lamenting, crying, sighing, dying;
Dying for her own true love.

THE BARLEY RAKING.

Nº 85. THE BARLEY RAKING.

1.
'Twas in the prime of summer time,
When hay it was a making;
And harvest tide was coming on,
And barley wanted raking;
Two woeful lovers met one day,
With sighs their sad farewell to say,
For John to place must go away,
And Betty's heart was breaking.
    Lovers oft have proved untrue;
    'las! what can poor maidens do!

2.
But hardly was her sweetheart gone,
With vows of ne'er forsaking;
The foolish wench did so take on,
To ease her bosom's aching—
She sent a letter to her love,
Invoking all the powers above,
If he should e'er inconstant prove,
To her and the Barley raking.
    Lovers oft have proved untrue;
    'las! what can poor maidens do!

3.
Now when this letter reached the youth,
It put him in a taking;
Sure of each other's love and truth,
Why such a fuss be making!
But being a tender hearted swain,
From hasty words he did refrain,
And wrote to her in gentle strain,
To bid her cease from quaking.
    Lovers oft have proved untrue;
    'las! what can poor maidens do!

4.
"I've got as good a pair of shoes
As e'er were made of leather;
I'll pull my beaver o'er my nose,
And face all wind and weather;
And when the year has run its race,
I'll seek a new and nearer place;
And hope to see your bonnie face
At time of the Barley raking."
    Lovers oft have proved untrue;
    'las! what can poor maidens do!

5.
So when the year was past and gone,
And hay once more was making;
Back to his love came faithful John,
To find a rude awaking:
For Betty thought it long to wait,
So she had ta'en another mate,
And left her first love to his fate,
In spite of the Barley raking.
    Lovers oft have proved untrue;
    'las! what can poor maidens do!

DEEP IN LOVE.

N⁰ 86. DEEP IN LOVE.

1.
A ship came sailing over the sea
As deeply laden as she could be;
My sorrows fill me to the brim,
I care not if I sink or swim.

⁎2.
Ten thousand ladies in the room,
But my true love's the fairest bloom,
Of stars she is my brightest sun,
I said I would have her or none.

3.
I leaned my back against an oak,
But first it bent and then it broke;
Untrusty as I found that tree,
So did my love prove false to me.

4.
Down in a mead the other day,
As carelessly I went my way,
And plucked flowers red and blue,
I little thought what love could do.

5.
I saw a Rose with ruddy blush,
And thrust my hand into the bush,
I pricked my fingers to the bone,
I would I'd left that rose alone!

6.
I wish! I wish! but 'tis in vain,
I wish I had my heart again!
With silver chain and diamond locks,
I'd fasten it in a golden box.

⁎ May be omitted in singing.

THE RAMBLING SAILOR.

No 87. THE RAMBLING SAILOR.

1.

I toss my cap up into the air,
  And away whilst all are sleeping,
The host may swear, and the hostess stare,
  And the pretty maids be weeping:
There is never a place that I do grace,
  Which a second time shall see my face;
For I travel the world from place to place,
  And still am a Rambling Sailor.

2.

O when I come to London town,
  Or enter any city,
I settle down at the Bell or Crown,
  And court each lass that's pretty.
And I say, "My dear, be of good cheer,
  I'll never depart, you need not fear!"
But I travel the county far and near
  And still am a Rambling Sailor.

3.

And if that you would know my name,
  I've any that you fancy,
'Tis never the same, as I change my flame.
  From Bet, to Joan, or Nancy.
I court maids all, marry none at all,
  My heart is round, and rolls as a ball,
And I travel the land from Spring to Fall,
  And still am a Rambling Sailor.

A Single and a Married Life.

№ 88. A SINGLE AND A MARRIED LIFE.

A DIALOGUE.

1. THE MARRIED MAN SAITH:—

Come all you young men bold,
And use your best endeavour,
As a woman's heart is gold,
To win and truly wear her.
For a man that is alone
Doth lack the richest treasure,
Makes a solitary moan,
Nor knows the highest pleasure.
  And some the seas have cross't
  For wealth on foreign coast,
  And so their lives have lost,
  Yet treasure best lies nearest.
  It e'er shall be my boast
  That a married life is fairest!

2. THE SINGLE MAN SAITH:—

I trust fond woman-kind
No further than I prove her,
She's fickle as the wind,
And is a faithless rover.
When first you her embrace,
She sootheth all your sorrow,
Yet speedy shifts her face,
And curst* is on the morrow.
  You have her love to-day;
  To-morrow she saith, Nay!
  Nor constant e'er doth stay.
  When skies are at their clearest,
  I'll leave, and fare away,
  For a single life is rarest.

3. THE MARRIED MAN SAITH:—

My contention is not done,
Man's half a man unmated.
"Man is not well alone!"
Said He who man created,
The wife life's loads doth bear,
Relieves the burdened shoulder;
Shares youthful joy and care,
And comforts thee, grown older.
  In spring she is thy flower,
  In drought a quickening shower,
  She's warmth in wintry hour,
  And food when thou goest sparest.
  God's blessing is her dower
  So a married life is fairest!

4. THE SINGLE MAN SAITH:—

Don't marry one that's young,
Mayhap her love will wander,
Nor marry one that's old,
There's no one may command her,
Nor marry one that's bold,
She'll seem to be above you,
Nor marry one that's cold,
She'll never truly love you.
  For the old ones they grow stale,
  And the scolding rant and rail,
  And pride must have a fall,
  And death doth end the fairest.
  So I'll have none at all
  Faith! a single life's the rarest.

5. THE MARRIED MAN SAITH:—

In marrying a wife
I hold in vindication,
A man completes his life,
It is the true vocation,
A wife's a golden crown
For brow of man intended,
With children rising round
His life is never ended.
  A married man doth sing,
  As proud as any king,
  New days new pleasures bring,
  Though a single life be rarest,
  Yet a wife's the choicest thing,
  So a married life is fairest.

* cross, crusty.

MIDSUMMER CAROL.

Nº 89. MIDSUMMER CAROL.

1.

'Twas early I walked on a midsummer morning
  The fields and the meadows were decked and gay,
The small birds were singing, the woodland is a-ringing,
  It was early in the morning, at breaking of day,
I will play on my pipes, I will sing thee my lay!
It is early in the morning, at breaking of day.

2.

O hark! oh! O hark! to the nightingales wooing,
  The lark is aloft piping shrill in the air.
In every green bower the turtle-doves cooing,
  The sun is just gleaming, arise up my fair!
Arise, love, arise! none fairer I spie
Arise, love, arise! O why should I die!

3.

Arise, love, arise! go and get your love posies,
  The fairest of flowers in garden that grows,
Go gather me lilies, carnations and roses
  I'll wear them with thoughts of the maiden I chose
I stand at thy door, pretty love, full of care,
O why should I languish so long in despair!

✽ 4.

O why love, O why, should I banished be from thee!
  O why should I see my own chosen no more!
O why look your parents so slightingly on me!
  It is all for the rough ragged garments I wore,
But dress me with flowers, I'm gay as a king,
I'm glad as a bird, when my carol I sing.

5.

Arise, love, arise! in song and in story,
  To rival thy beauty was never a may,
I will play thee a tune on my pipes of ivory,
  It is early in the morning, at breaking of day,
I will play on my pipes, I will sing thee my lay!
It is early in the morning, at breaking of day.

✽ be omitted in singing.

THE BLACKBIRD.

N⁰ 90. THE BLACKBIRD.

1
Here's a health to the Blackbird in the bush!
Likewise to the bonny Wood-dove (dove)!
If you'll go along with me,
Unto yonder flow'ring tree,
I will catch you a small bird or two.

* 2
O the breath of the May is sweet as hay,
And pleasant where ever it pass.
And the butterfly's light wing,
Is a-flutter all the spring,
And the golden-cups gleam in the grass.

3
All the birds of the air consort in pair,
And nest in each pretty green tree,
Then my merry little maid,
Be not coy, be not afraid,
I've a cottage well fitted for thee.

4
On the roof there is thatch; O, lift the latch,
Come in, take your place there as bride.
You will find the hearth-stone clean,
Find a throne set for my Queen,
'Tis the settle the chimney beside.

5
Well, I reckon, 'tis so ruled by Fate,
That I should be married this May.
Then so long as you're inclined,
Why — I wont go far to find,
Clap your hand, Miss! in mine with a Yea!

* May be omitted in singing.

THE GREEN BED.

No. 91.   H.F.S.

N⁰ 91. THE GREEN BED.

1

Young Sailor Dick, as he stepped on shore,
    To his quarters of old return'd
The hostess glad, cries "Dick my lad!
    What prize-money have you earn'd!"
"Poor luck! poor luck! yet Molly, my duck,
    Your daughter I've come to see:
Get ready some supper, with pipes and grog,
    And the best Green Bed for me."

2

"My daughter, she's gone out for a walk;
    My beds are all bespoken;
My larder's bare, like the rum-keg there,
    And my baccy pipes all are broken."
Says Dick, "I'll steer for another berth,
    I fear I have made too bold:
But I'll pay for the beer that I've just drunk here,
    And he pulled out a hand-ful of gold."

3

"Come down Molly, quick! here's your sweetheart Dick
    Has just come back from sea:
He wants his supper, his grog, and a bed,
    The best Green Bed it must be."
"No bed," cries Dick "no supper, no grog,
    No sweetheart for me I swear!
You shewed me the door when you thought me poor,
    So I'll carry my gold elsewhere."

THE LOYAL LOVER.

N.º 92. THE LOYAL LOVER.

1

I'll weave my love a garland,
   It shall be dressed so fine;
I'll set it round with roses,
   With lilies, pinks and thyme.
And I'll present to my love
   When he comes back from sea,
For I love my love, and I love my love,
   Because my love loves me.
      Ri-fol-di-rol fol-di-rol
      Ri-fol-riddle-li-do.

2

I wish I were an arrow,
   That sped into the air;
To seek him as a sparrow,
   And if he was not there,
Then quickly I'd become a fish
   To search the raging sea,
For I love my love, and I love my love,
   Because my love loves me.
      Ri-fol &c.

3

I would I were a reaper,
   I'd seek him in the corn,
I would I were a keeper,
   I'd hunt him with my horn.
I'd blow a blast, when found at last,
   Beneath the greenwood tree,
For I love my love, and I love my love,
   Because my love loves me.
      Ri-fol &c.

THE STREAMS OF NANTSIAN.

N⁰ 93. THE STREAMS OF NANTSIAN.

1
O the Streams of Nant-si-an
   In two parts divide,
Where the young men in dancing
   Meet sweetheart and bride.
They will take no denial,
   We must frolic and sing,
And the sound of the viol
   O it makes my heart ring.

2
On the rocky cliff yonder
   A castle up-stands;
To the seamen a wonder
   Above the black sands.
'Tis of ivory builded
   With diamonds glazed bright,
And with gold it is gilded,
   To shine in the night.

3
Over yonder high mountain
   The wild fowl do fly;
And in ocean's deep fountain,
   The fairest pearls lie.
On eagle's wings soaring,
   I'll speed as the wind;
Ocean's fountain exploring,
   My true love I'll find.

4
O the streams of Nant-si-an
   Divide in two parts
And rejoin as in dancing
   Do lads their sweethearts.
So the streams, bright and shining
   Tho' parted in twain
Re-unite, intertwining,
   One thenceforth remain.

The Drunken Maidens.

No. 94.   F. W. B.

No 94. THE DRUNKEN MAIDENS.

1

There were three drunken maidens,
  Came from the Isle of Wight.
They drank from Monday morning,
  Nor stayed till Saturday night.
When Saturday night did come, Sirs!
  They would not then go out;
Not the three drunken maidens,
  As they pushed the jug about.

2

Then came in Bouncing Sally,
  With cheeks as red as bloom.
"Make space my jolly sisters,
  Now make for Sally room.
For that I will be your equal,
  Before that I go out."
So now four drunken maidens,
  They pushed the jug about.

3

It was woodcock and pheasant,
  And partriges and hare,
It was all kinds of dainties,
  No scarcity was there.
It was four quarts of Malaga,
  Each fairly did drink out,
So the four drunken maidens,
  They pushed the jug about.

4

Then down came the landlord,
  And asked for his pay.
O! a forty-pound bill, Sirs!
  The damsels drew that day.
It was ten pounds apiece, Sirs!
  But yet, they would not out.
So the four drunken maidens,
  They pushed the jug about.

5

"O where be your spencers!
  Your mantles rich and fine!"
"They all be a swallowed
  In tankards of good wine."
"O where be your characters
  Ye maidens brisk and gay!"
"O they be a swallowed!
  We've drunk them clean away."

TOBACCO IS AN INDIAN WEED.

DUET.

No. 95. H.F.S.

N⁰ 95. TOBACCO IS AN INDIAN WEED.

1

Tobacco is an Indian weed,
Grows green at morn, cut down at eve;
    It shows our decay;
    We fade as hay.
    Think on this,—when you smoke tobacco.

2

The pipe that is so lily-white,
Wherein so many take delight,
    Gone with a touch;
    Man's life is such,
    Think on this,—when you smoke tobacco.

3

The pipe that is so foul within,
Shows how the soul is stained with sin;
    It doth require
    The purging fire.
    Think on this,—when you smoke tobacco.

4

The ashes that are left behind,
Do serve to put us all in mind,
    That unto dust,
    Return we must,
    Think on this,—when you smoke tobacco.

5

The smoke that doth so high ascend,
Shows that our life must have an end;
    The vapours' gone,
    Man's life is done.
    Think on this,—when you smoke tobacco.

FAIR SUSAN.

No. 96.

H.F.S.

pass - ing by

№ 96. FAIR SUSAN.

1

Fair Susan slumbered in shady bower,
    Safe hid, she thought, from every eye;
Nor dreamed she in that tranquil hour
    Her own true love was passing by.

2

He gazed in rapture upon her beauty,
    Sleep did her charms but more reveal;
He deemed it sure a lover's duty
    From those sweet lips a kiss to steal.

3

In shame and anger poor Susan started,
    With eyes aflame she bade him go;
"Return no more! — for ever parted;
    Cruel and base to use me so!"

4

"By too much love I have offended,
    Forgive me if I cause you pain;
But if indeed our love be ended,
    Pray give me back my kiss again."

THE FALSE LOVER.

Nº 97.   H.F.S.

I courted a lass that was buxom and gay, Unheeding what people against her did say; I thought her as constant and true as the day; But now she is going to be married! But now she is going to be married!

№ 97. THE FALSE LOVER.

1

I courted a maiden both buxom and gay,
Unheeding what people against her did say,
I thought her as constant and true as the day
    But now she is going to be married.

2

O when to the church I my fair love saw go,
I followed her up with a heart full of woe,
And eyes that with tears of grief did o'erflow,
    To see how my suit had miscarried.

3

O when in the chancel I saw my love stan',
With ring on her finger, and true love in han',
I thought that for certain 'twas not the right man,
    Although 'twas the man she was taking.

4

O when I my fair love saw sit in her seat
I sat myself by her, but nothing could eat;
Her company, thought I, was better than meat,
    Although my heart sorely was aching.

5

O woe be the day that I courted the maid,
That ever I trusted a word that she said,
That with her I wander'd along the green glade,
    Accurs'd be the day that I met her.

6

O make me a grave that is long, wide and deep,
And cover me over with flowers so sweet,
That there I may lie, and may take my last sleep;
    For that is the way to forget her.

THE BARLEY STRAW.

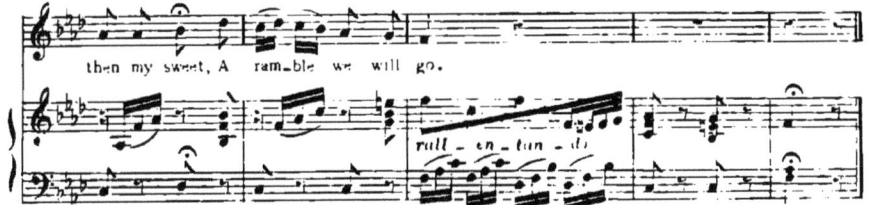

Nº 98. THE BARLEY STRAW.

1

As Jan was hurrying down the glade,
    He met his sweetheart Kit;
"O whither so fast?" the maiden ask'd,
    "Let's bide and talk a bit."
"I'm going to the barn, and if you'll come,
    And help me thresh the stro',
That task complete, why then my sweet,
    A ramble we will go."

2

She gave consent, to work they went,
    As if 'twere only play;
The flail he plied, whilst Kit untied,
    The sheaves, and cleared away.
O willing hands made labour light,
    And ere the sun was low,
With arms entwined, these lovers kind,
    Did down the vallies go.

3

Said Jan, "thou art a helpful lass,
    Wilt thou be mine for life?"
"For sure!" she said. To church they sped,
    And soon were man and wife.
A lesson then, for all young men
    Who would a courting go,
Your sweetheart ask to share your task,
    And thresh the Barley Stro'.

4

Now many a year, this couple dear,
    They lived in harmony;
And children had, both lass and lad,
    I think 'twas thirty three.
The sons so hale did wield the flail,
    And like their father grow;
The maidens sweet, like mother were neat;
    And clean as the Barley Stro'.

DEATH AND THE LADY.

Nº 99. DEATH AND THE LADY.

1
As I walked out one day, one day,
All in the merry month of May,
When lambs did skip and thrushes sing,
And ev'ry bush with buds did spring.

2
I met an old man by the way,
His head was bald, his beard was grey,
His coat was of the Myrtle-green,
But underneath his ribs were seen.

3
He in his hand a glass did hold,
He shook as one that shakes with cold.
I asked of him what was his name,
And what strange place from which he came.

4
"My name is Death, fair maiden, see
Lords, Dukes and Squires bow down to me;
For of the Branchy Tree* am I
And you, fair maid, with me must hie."

5
"I'll give you gold, if me you'll spare,
I'll give you costly robes to wear!"
"O no, sweet maid, make no delay
Your sand is run, you must away!"

6
Alas! alack! the fair maid died,
And these the last sad words she cried: —
"Here lies a poor, distressed maid,
By Death — and Death alone betrayed."

*What is meant by the "Branchy Tree" I do not know, but so the words run in all versions.

ADAM AND EVE.

№ 100. ADAM AND EVE.

1

Both sexes give ear to my fancy,
　In praise of sweet woman I sing
Confined not to Doll, Sue, or Nancy,
　The mate of the beggar or king.
When Adam was first a-created,
　And lord of the universe crown'd,
His happiness was not completed,
　Until that a helpmate was found.

2

A garden was planted by Nature,
　Man could not produce in his life.
But no rest had he till his Creator
　Discovered he wanted a wife
He had horses and foxes for hunting
　Which most men love dearly as life
No relishsome food was a wanting
　But still — he was short of a wife.

3

As Adam was resting in slumber,
　He lost a small rib from his side,
And when he awoke — twas in wonder,
　To see a most beautiful bride.
In transport he gazed upon her,
　His happiness now was complete
He prais'd the bountiful Donor.
　Who to him had given a mate.

4

She was not taken out of his head, sir,
　To rule and to triumph in man.
Nor was she took out of his foot, sir,
　By him to be trampled upon.
But she was took out of his side, sir,
　His equal co-partner to be;
So, united is man with his bride, sir,
　Yet man is the top of the tree.

5

Then let not the fair be despised
　By man, as she's part of himself.
Let woman by man be a-prized
　As more than the world full of wealth.
A man without woman's a beggar,
　That by him the world we're possess'd
But a beggar that's got a good woman
　With more than the world is he blessd.

I RODE MY LITTLE HORSE.

No. 101. F.W.B.

№ 101. I RODE MY LITTLE HORSE.

1

I rode my little horse, from London town I came,
I rode into the country, to seek myself a dame.
And if I meet a pretty maid, be sure I'll kiss her then;
And swear that I will marry her — but will not tell her *when!*

2

I found a buxom widow, with many tons of gold,
I lived upon her fortune, as long as it would hold.
Of pounds I took five hundred, bestrode my horse, and then,
I promised I would marry her — but never told her *when!*

3

A vintner had a daughter, the Golden Sun his sign.
I tarried at his tavern, I drank his choicest wine;
I drank out all his cellar, bestrode my horse, and then,
I said the maid I'd marry, — but never told him *when!*

4

The guineas are expended, the wine is also spent;
The widow and the maiden, they languish and lament.
And if they come to seek me, I'll pack them back again,
With promises of marriage, — but never tell them *when.*

5

My little horse I mounted, the world that I might see,
I found a pretty maiden — as poor as poor could be.
My little horse neglected, to London ran away.
I asked if she would marry, and bade her name the day.

THE SAUCY PLOUGHBOY.

N° 102. H.F.S.

№ 102. THE SAUCY PLOUGHBOY.

1

Come all you pretty maidens,
  And listen unto me.
Be sure and wed a plough-boy,
  None hath a heart more true.
The plough-boy is so saucy,
  Yet never doth annoy,
O who in all the world, maids,
  Is like a ploughing-boy!

2

He riseth in the morning,
  Awaking with the sun.
And as a dew-drop flashing,
  So gleams his eye with fun.
When all the birds are singing,
  He singeth too for joy.
O who in all the world, maids,
  Is like the ploughing-boy!

3

When coming from the milking,
  And carrying my pail,
The saucy plough-boy leaveth
  To help me, hook and flail.
And when the hay is making,
  I cannot well be coy;
For who in all the world, maids,
  Is like the ploughing-boy!

4

At even-tide he waiteth
  Beneath the green-wood tree
And will not dance with others,
  He'll only dance with me.
No pleasures of the country
  His honest heart can cloy,
O who in all the world, maids,
  Is like the ploughing-boy!

5

I swear to you young maidens,
  A plough-boy I will wed,
I will not have a soldier
  For all his jacket red,
No sailor, no, nor footman,
  Shall e'er my thoughts employ
The lad to win my heart, maids,
  Shall be a ploughing-boy.

I'll Build Myself a Gallant Ship.

(SOLO or QUARTETTE.)

№ 103. F.W.B.

N.º 103. I'LL BUILD MYSELF A GALLANT SHIP.

1

I'll build myself a gallant ship,
    A ship of noble fame;
And four and twenty mariners,
    Shall box and man the same;
And I will stand, with helm in hand,
    To urge them o'er the main.

2

No scarf shall o'er my shoulders go,
    I will not comb my hair;
The pale moonlight, the candle bright
    Shall neither tell I'm fair.
Beside the mast I stand so fast,
    Unresting in despair.

3

The rain may beat, and round my feet
    The waters wash and foam,
O thou North wind lag not behind
    But bear me far from home!
My hands I wring, and sobbing sing
    As over seas I roam.

4

The moon so pale shall light my sail,
    As o'er the sea I fly,
To where afar the Eastern star
    Is twinkling in the sky.
I would I were with my love fair,
    Ere ever my love die!

THE EVERLASTING CIRCLE.

№ 104. THE EVERLASTING CIRCLE.

All in a wood there grew a fine tree,
The finest tree that ever you did see.
    And the green grass grew around, around, around,
    And the green grass grew around.

2

And on this tree there grew a fine bough
The finest bough that ever you did see.
    And the bough on the tree, and the tree in the wood,
    And the green leaves flourished thereon, thereon, thereon,
    And the green leaves flourished thereon.

3

And on this bough there grew a fine twig
The finest twig that ever you did see,
    And the twig on the bough, and the bough on the tree, and the tree in the wood,
    And the green leaves flourished thereon &c.

4

And on this twig there stood a fine nest,
The finest nest that ever you did see,
    And the nest on the twig, and the twig on the bough, &c.

5

And in this nest there sat a fine bird,
The finest bird, &c.

6

And on this bird there grew a fine feather
The finest feather, &c.

7

And of this feather was made a fine bed
The finest bed, &c.

8

And on this bed was laid a fine mother,
The finest mother &c.

9

In the arms of this mother was laid a fine babe
The finest babe, &c.

10

And the babe he grew up and became a fine boy
The finest boy, &c.

11

And boy put an acorn all into the earth
The finest acorn &c.

12

And out of this acorn there grew a fine tree
The finest tree &c.

WITHIN A GARDEN.

N.º 105. WITHIN A GARDEN.

1

Within a garden a maiden lingered,
   When soft the shades of evening fell
   Expecting, fearing,
   A footstep hearing,
   Her love appearing,
      To say farewell.

2

With sighs and sorrow their vows they plighted
   One more embrace, one last adieu;
   Tho' seas divide, love,
   In this confide, love,
   Whate'er betide, love
      To thee I'm true.

3

Long years are over, and still the maiden
   Seeks oft at eve the trysting tree;
   Her promise keeping,
   And, faithful, weeping
   Her lost love sleeping
      Across the sea.

THE HUNTING OF THE HARE.

A COUNTRY DANCE.

F. W. B.

Nº 106. THE HUNTING OF THE HARE.

1

I hunted my Merry all into the hay,
The Hare was before and the hounds "ware away!"
  With my Hickerly, Tout, ticklesome Tout,
  Hipperly, tipperly, eversheen, nipperly,
  Up the middle, van jigo-van
'Twas up the hill, down the form,
Here a step, there a turn,
  Turn and sing merrily,
    Hunt hounds, away!

2

I hunted my Merry all into the barley,
And there the poor puss was pursued by hound Snarley.
  With my Hickerly tout, &c.

3

I hunted my Merry all into the wheat,
And there the sly puss did attempt us to cheat.
  With my Hickerly tout, &c.

4

I hunted my Merry all into the rye,
And there the poor hare was constrained to die.
  With my Hickerly tout, &c.

5

I hunted my Merry all into the oats
And there I cut off both his paws and his scut.
  With my Hickerly tout, &c.

DEAD MAID'S LAND.

№ 107.   H.F.S.

No. 107. DEAD MAID'S LAND.

1
There stood a gardener at the gate
And in each hand a flower;
"O pretty maid, come in," he said,
And view my beauteous bower.

2
The lily it shall be thy smock,
The jonquil shoe thy feet;
Thy gown shall be the ten-week stock,
To make thee fair and sweet.

* 3
The gilly-flower shall deck thy head,
Thy way with herbs I'll strew,
Thy stockings shall be marigold,
Thy gloves the violet blue."

* 4
"I will not have the gilly flower
Nor herbs my path to strew,
Nor stockings of the marigold,
Nor gloves of violet blue.

5
I will not have the ten-week stock,
Nor jonquils to my shoon;
But I will have the red, red rose,
That flow'reth sweet in June."

* 6
"The red, red rose it hath a thorn
That pierceth to the bone."
"I little heed thy idle rede;
I will have that or none."

7
"The red, red rose it hath a thorn,
That pierceth to the heart"
"The red, red rose, O I will have,
I little heed the smart."

8
She stooped down unto the ground,
To pluck the rose so red.
The thorn it pierced her to the heart,
And this fair maid was dead.

9
There stood a gardener at the gate,
With cypress in his hand,
And he did say, "let no fair may,
Come into Dead Maid's Land."

* May be omitted in singing.

SHOWER AND SUNSHINE.

№ 108. SHOWER AND SUNSHINE.

1

There went a wind over the sea,
  And borne on its wings was rain.
A wond'rous breath passed over me,
  And steeped all my soul in pain.
  I wept, but I wept in vain.

2

Along with the wind went a sigh,
  And shadows fell deep around;
In darkness I lay, with desolate cry,
  Despairing I toss'd on the ground;
  In anguish and fear profound.

3

The sun in the sky shines clear;
  And glittering after rain,
The flowers in brighter tints appear,
  A rainbow o'er arches the plain.
  I wept—but I wept not in vain.

4

Thou love art the mightiest gale,
  To shatter to wither and rive.
Thou makest all nature grow fresh and hale,
  Thou dost the whole world revive.
  I was dead; and am now alive.

HAYMAKING SONG.

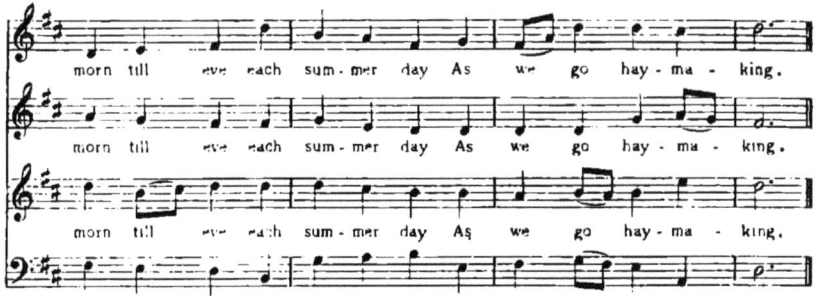

№ 109. HAYMAKING SONG.

1

The golden sun is shining bright,
    The dew is off the field;
To us it is our main delight,
    The fork and rake to wield.
The pipe and tabor both shall play,
    The viols loudly ring,
From morn till eve each summer day,
    As we go hay-making.
Chorus: The pipe and tabor, &c.

2

As we my boys haymaking go,
    All in the month of June.
Both Tom and Bet, and Jess and Joe
    Their happy hearts in tune.
O up come lusty Jack and Will,
    With pitchfork and with rake,
And up come dainty Doll and Jill,
    The sweet, sweet hay to make.
Chorus: The pipe and tabor, &c.

3

O when the haysel all is done,
    Then in the arish grass,
The lads shall have their fill of fun,
    Each dancing with his lass.
The good old farmer and his wife,
    Shall bring the best of cheer,
I would it were, aye, odds my life!
    Hay-making all the year.
Chorus: The pipe and tabor, &o.

IN BIBBERLEY TOWN.

Nº 110. H.F.S.

N⁰ 110. IN BIBBERLEY TOWN.

1

In Bibberley town a maid did dwell,
A buxom lass, as I've heard tell;
As straight as a wand, just twenty two,
And many a bachelor had her in view.
      Ri fal de ral diddle, ri fal de ral dee,
      What ups and downs in the world there be!

2

This maid so beautiful fair and free,
Was sought by a squire of high degree;
He courted her honestly for his wife,
But she could'nt venture so high in life.
      Ri fal de ral &c.

3

A tinker there came to mend the kettle,
She fell in love with the man of metal;
His songs and his jokes won her heart and her hand,
And she promised with him in the church to stand.
      Ri fal de ral &c.

4

They wed, and this jovial mender of pots
Proved only a brute and the prince of sots;
He beat her, he starved her, she gave him the slip,
And back to Bibberley town did trip.
      Ri fal de ral &c.

5

She found that the Squire her former flame
Had wooed and married a wealthy dame,
But a vacant place in the house she took,
And, instead of his wife, she became his cook.
      Ri fal de ral diddle, ri fal de ral dee;
      What ups and downs in the world there be!

ALPHABETICAL INDEX.

Name of Song.	Words.	Name of Tune.	No. of Song.
Adam and Eve	O.W.	Traditional	100
All in a Garden	N.W.	As Polly Walked Out	105
A Maiden sat a Weeping	O.W.	Traditional	39
An Evening so Clear	N.W.	,,	41
A Nutting we will Go	Altered	,,	83
Arscott of Tetcott	Altered	,,	2
As Johnny Walked Out	O.W.	,,	11
A Sweet Pretty Maiden	N.W.	A Maiden sweet in May	36
A Ship came Sailing	O.W.	Traditional	86
Barley Raking, The	Altered	,,	85
Barley Straw, The	Altered	,,	98
Bell-ringing, The	O.W.	,,	82
Bibberley Town	N.W.	,,	110
Blackbird in the Bush	N.W.	Three Pretty Maidens a Milking did Go	90
Blow Away, ye Morning Breezes	O.W.	Traditional	25
Blue Flame, The	N.W.	Rosemary Lane	67
Blue Muslin	O.W.	Traditional	22
Bold Dragoon, The	Altered	,,	65
Bonny Blue Kerchief, The	O.W.	,,	40
Bonny Bunch of Roses, The	O.W.	,,	27
Brixham Town	O.W.	,,	9
Broadbury Gibbet	N.W.	A 2nd to "My Lady's Coach"	62
Broken Token, The	Altered	Traditional	44
By Chance it was	O.W.	,,	1
Childe the Hunter	O.W.	2nd to "Cold blows the Wind"	33
Chimney Sweep, The	O.W.	Traditional	20
Cicely Sweet	O.W.	,,	35
Cold Blows the Wind	O.W.	,,	6
Come, my Lads	O.W.	,,	76
Constant Johnny	O.W.	,,	80
Cottage Thatched with Straw	O.W.	,,	34
Country Farmer's Son	N.W.	,,	69
Cupid the Ploughboy	Altered	,,	75
Deadmaid's Land	O.W.	3rd tune to "Cold blows the Wind"	107
Death and the Lady	O.W.	Traditional	99
Deep in Love	O.W.	,,	86
Dilly Song, The	O.W.	,,	78
Down by a River Side	O.W.	,,	84
Drowned Lover	O.W.	,,	32
Drunken Maidens	O.W.	,,	94
Duke's Hunt, The	O.W.	,,	81
Everlasting Circle	O.W.	,,	104
Fair Girl, mind this	O.W.	,,	72
Fair Susan Slumbered	N.W.	In Yonder Grove	96
False Lover, The	O.W.	Traditional	97
Farewell to Kingsbridge	O.W.	,,	55
Farmer's Son, The	N.W.	,,	69
Fathom the Bowl	O.W.	,,	14

Name of Song.	Words.	Name of Tune.	No. of Song.
Flowers and Weeds	{ pt. old { pt. new	Traditional	7
Gipsy Countess	O.W.	,, ...	50
Golden Furze in Bloom	N.W.	Gosport Beach	56
Golden Vanity, The	O.W.	Traditional	64
Green Bed, The	Altered	,, ...	91
Green Broom	O.W.	,, ...	10
Green Bushes, The	O.W.	,, ...	43
Green Cockade, The	Altered	,, ...	37
Grey Mare, The	{ pt. old { pt. new	,, ...	51
Hal-an-Tow	O.W.	,, ...	24
Haymaking Song	{ pt. old { pt. new	,, ...	109
Hearty Good Fellow, The	O.W.	,, ...	26
Henry Martyn	O.W.	,, ...	53
Hostess' Daughter, The	N.W.	{ To London Town when { first I came ...	70
Hunting the Hare	O.W.	Traditional	106
I'll build myself a gallant Ship ...	Altered	,, ...	103
I rode my little Horse	O.W.	,, ...	101
Jan's Courtship	O.W.	,, ...	31
Jolly Gosshawk, The	O.W.	,, ...	71
Last of the Singers, The	N.W.	Little Girl down the Lane ...	28
Loyal Lover	O.W.	Lady and Apprentice ...	92
Lullaby	{ pt. old { pt. new	Traditional	49
May-day Carol	O.W.	,, ...	47
Mallard, The	N.W.	,, ...	79
Midsummer Carol	O.W.	,, ...	80
Miller's last Will	O.W.	,, ...	12
My Garden grew plenty of Thyme ...	{ pt. old { pt. new	,, ...	7
My Lady's Coach	O.W.	,, ...	30
Nancy	O.W.	,, ...	48
On a May Morning	N.W.	Seventeen on Sunday ...	73
Ormond the Brave	O.W.	Traditional	13
Orchestra, The	N.W.	Cruel Miller	63
Oxen Ploughing, The	O.W.	Traditional	57
Painful Plough, The	O.W.	,, ...	61
Parson Hogg	O.W.	,, ...	5
Ploughboy, The	O.W.	,, ...	59
Plymouth Sound	N.W.	,, ...	54
Poor Old Horse	O.W.	,, ...	77
Punch Ladle, The	O.W.	,, ...	14
Rambling Sailor, The	Altered	,, ...	87
Rout is out, The	O.W.	,, ...	45
Roving Jack	O.W.	,, ...	8
Sailor's Farewell	O.W.	,, ...	38
Saucy Ploughboy, The	N.W.	Salisbury Plain	102
Saucy Sailor, The	O.W.	Traditional	21
Seasons, The	O.W.	,, ...	19
Silly old Man, The	O.W.	,, ...	18
Single and Married Life	O.W.	,, ...	83

Name of Song.			Words.	Name of Tune.			No. of Song.
Something Lacking	...	...	O.W.	Traditional	...	...	58
Spotted Cow, The	...	...	Altered	,,	...	...	74
Squire and Fair Maid, The	...	...	O.W.	,,	...	...	23
Strawberry Fair	...	...	Altered	,,	...	...	68
Streams of Nantsian, The	...	...	(slightly altered)	,,	...	...	93
Sunshine and Shadow	...	...	N.W.	I sowed the seeds of Love		...	95
Sweet Nightingale	...	...	O.W.	Traditional	...	...	15
There went a Wind	...	...	N.W.	I sowed the seeds of Love		...	95
Tobacco is an Indian Weed	...	...	O.W.	Traditional	...	...	95
Trees they are so High, The	...	...	O.W.	,,	...	...	4
Trinity Sunday	...	...	N.W.	("As I walked out one beautiful morning")			66
'Twas on a Sunday Morning	...	...	N.W.	(Traditional Alteration (?) from Mori)			3
Tythe Pig, The	...	...	O.W.	Traditional	...	...	29
Warson Hunt, The	...	...	O.W.	,,		...	42
Why should we be Dullards Sad		...	O.W.	,,		...	46
Widdecombe Fair	...	...	O.W.	,,		...	16
Wreck off Scilly, The	...	...	O.W.	,,		...	52
Wrestling Match, The	...	...	O.W.	,,		...	60
Ye Maidens Pretty	...	...	O.W.	,,	...	...	17

Tunes have been unaltered except where mentioned in Introduction. O.W. for Old Words N.W. for New Words.

www.ingramcontent.com/pod-product-compliance
Ingram Content Group UK Ltd.
Pitfield, Milton Keynes, MK11 3LW, UK
UKHW040433091225
9449UKWH00047B/404